RAGE

NETTA NEWBOUND

Junction Publishing

Junctionpublishing@outlook.com

www.junction-publishing.com

Rage/Netta Newbound -- 1st ed.

To Gary and Lynda
- brainstormers extraordinaire...

PROLOGUE

"You can't section him. He's a national treasure!" Miriam barked at the perspiring specialist, Cecil Bain.

"We have no choice, Ms Maidley. He's a danger to society as well as to himself."

"But he has money. He's a millionaire—I'm sure you're aware of that already," she said matter-of-factly, folding her arms across her ample bosom.

"It's nothing to do with money, and you know it," Imran Singh, the hospital's CEO cut in. "Your brother's psychosis is out of control, Ms Maidley. We can't chance another attack."

"But he's been calm since you admitted him last week," Miriam argued. Her voice had taken on an annoying whine which irritated her.

"Yes, that's correct, but only because of the medication," Cecil said. "The high doses he's on have wiped him out—we cannot prescribe those doses to an out-patient. There would be nobody to administer the medication for a start."

"So, you choose to section him instead? How will that look for your hospital?" she asked Singh. "My brother has funded this place for the past ten years almost single-handedly and this is how you treat him?"

"What choice do we have, Miriam?" Singh said. "You know we wouldn't do this if there was any other way."

"Well, you can kiss goodbye to his money. A scandal like this will ruin him if it gets out. He's a living legend and an incredibly private man." Her brother's football career was all Singh cared about. Seven years as a top-class player had paved the way for Charlie to take over as manager—turning the team around and putting them on the map.

"We have a responsibility to the community, Ms Maidley," Singh asserted. "We can't allow him to hurt anyone else. You're lucky that girl's family were money hungry and didn't press charges."

"She was asking for it—did you see the way she was dressed?"

Cecil coughed and shuffled his feet, clearly uncomfortable.

"The way she was dressed isn't an invitation for abuse," Singh growled.

"Maybe not, but that combined with the brain tumour—he can't help it. Can't we get someone to care for him at home? Administer the medication?"

The two men looked at each other and Cecil gave a slight nod.

"If you employ a full-time nurse, we could perhaps overlook the reports, considering there have been no charges laid," Singh said. "But I must warn you, if anything else happens we will have no choice but to contact the authorities ourselves."

"I understand."

"His tumour is growing at a remarkable rate," Cecil said. "I don't think it will be long before he's unable to get out of bed, regardless of the medication. But promise me, he will remain sedated for the rest of his life."

"Miss Miriam has an ambulance outside her house. Do you think she's gonna die?" six-year-old Catherine asked, her huge blue eyes like saucers.

Ben, her fourteen-year-old brother, got to his feet and peered from the window at their neighbour's house. "No. She's walking beside a stretcher. The ambulance crew are taking someone in —not out."

"So she's not gonna die then?"

Ben shook his head. "No, squirt, not today anyway." The last ambulance that had been on their street had taken away their mother. She never came home. He stroked his sister's blonde curls. "I don't know why you're so bothered. You don't like her anyway."

Catherine shrugged. "She's okay. I like Thomas, and she lets me pet him sometimes."

"Well, I don't like her. She's a bitch."

"Dad will ground you if he hears you say that naughty word."

Ben blew a raspberry. "Dad doesn't care about anything we do these days."

"Yes, he does. He's just busy, that's all."

He smiled at her. "Since when did you get so grown up?"

Catherine shrugged. "I *am* six!" she said, hands on her hips.

CHAPTER ONE

I put down the paperback and closed my eyes. After such a hectic work schedule over the past thirteen years, I felt guilty doing nothing *and* getting paid handsomely to boot.

I'd recognized the patient—who wouldn't? His face had been plastered on the front cover of every newspaper and women's magazine for as far back as I could remember. But I hadn't heard about his illness. It didn't take a rocket scientist to realise if news got out, we would be bombarded with paparazzi. The quaint little village would be transformed overnight. There had been a scandal a few months ago when his fiancée, the model, Laura Sanders, had vanished without a trace. Of course, there were hundreds of theories if you looked online, but Charlie had never been charged with anything as far as I knew.

I jumped up at the sound of tyres crunching on the driveway. It was my boss, the lady of the house, Miriam Maidley.

Thomas, the resident pug, flew off the sofa and began yapping at the front door.

In the week since I'd arrived, this was only the second time Miriam had returned home, and, for some reason, I suddenly felt jumpy.

Rushing from the room, I crossed the hall into one of the two downstairs bedrooms to check on my patient, who was still sleeping. He'd been out of it all week, apart from two days ago when I'd fallen asleep and forgotten to administer his medication. But that was just a blip. I began plumping up his pillows and straightening his bedding—anything to make myself appear busy.

"Ah, Miss Yates, there you are," Miriam said, suddenly appearing in the doorway. "How is he?"

"No different, to be honest." I smiled awkwardly, unsure how to behave around her.

"Good. You must be bored rigid stuck in this place twenty-four-seven."

"I won't deny it's nice to see another person. I was starting to go a little stir crazy." I grinned.

Miriam nodded without returning the smile. "I'll be here for the rest of the evening and then I'm off to Atlanta for a conference. I'll be away for a couple of weeks."

"Really?" I wasn't sure how I felt about that. One week alone had been bad enough.

"Has he had his meds?" Miriam nodded at her brother.

"Yes. He's all up-to-date."

"Then I suggest you take yourself off for a couple of hours. You won't get another chance for a while."

I didn't need telling twice and ran to my bedroom to grab my handbag and jacket.

"Miss Yates?"

My heart dropped. Had she changed her mind? "Yes?" I met her in the hallway.

"Here. Take my car." She rummaged in her bag and handed me the keys.

"Really?" It hadn't occurred to me that I didn't have a car in my haste to escape the place. "Thanks so much. Oh, and please, call me Lizzi."

Miriam turned and headed back into her brother's room without saying another word.

––––––––

Stepping from the house, I took several deep breaths. Freedom, even if it was only for a short while, felt good. I'd wanted for nothing inside the house. There was a fully stocked kitchen, a library of books, including a bookshelf filled with Blu-ray movies —there was nothing at all I could possibly need apart from human contact. When Charlie had woken up, he'd been charming and much nicer than I'd imagined he'd be. We chatted for half-an-hour until his medication kicked in, and I'd been sorry when he drifted off again.

"Hey, lady. Do you live here?" a little voice came from the other side of the hedge.

I grinned and walked over to the voice. "Hello. I can hear you, but I can't see you? Are you a talking bush?"

Tinkling laughter followed. "No, silly. I'm a girl."

I stepped closer to the hedge and peered through. "Oh, so you are." A pair of huge blue eyes and a mass of blonde curls came into view. "What's your name?"

"Catherine, but my friends call me Kate."

"Hi, Kate. My name's Elizabeth, but my friends call me Lizzi."

"Am I your friend?" she asked, sounding unsure.

"I think so. Don't you?"

Kate nodded. "Hi, Lizzi." She shoved her teeny hand through the hedge.

I shook it warmly.

"So, *do* you?" Kate asked.

"Do I what?"

"Do you live here?"

"I guess I do, for the time being."

"Good. Maybe you can let me pet Thomas. I miss him."

"Thomas has been my best friend this week. Maybe I'll call you tomorrow when I take him out the back for his run."

"Yay! Daddy won't let me have a doggy."

"Catherine?" A deep male voice startled me.

"I'm here, Daddy. Come and meet Elizabeth. She lives next door."

The sound of footsteps approached and the voice was much closer. "Nice to meet you, Elizabeth."

Tilting my head from side to side, I could see an unshaven chin and beautiful brown eyes. "Hi. Same to you."

"I can call her Lizzi because *I'm* her friend," Kate said.

"Is that right?" Her dad chuckled. "My name's Phil."

"Lizzi said I can go over and pet Thomas tomorrow, Daddy."

"Don't be bothering Elizabeth, Catherine. She's probably very busy."

"Honestly—I don't mind," I cut in. "In fact, I'd be glad of the company."

"Well, if you're sure."

The front door opened and Miriam appeared on the doorstep. "Oh, I thought you'd gone."

I gasped. "I'm just leaving. I was chatting to your neighbour."

Miriam scowled. "Not a good idea."

"Sorry. I'll get going then." I smiled an apology towards the hedge and then climbed into the sleek black Audi feeling self-conscious with the car's owner watching. I slowly backed out of the drive.

Pulling away, I felt a pang of anger. *How rude! She might pay my wages, but she has no say in who I can and who I can't fucking talk to.*

CHAPTER TWO

Phil pulled the pizza out of the oven and placed it beside the tray of oven chips in the middle of the dining table. "Tea's ready," he shouted.

The clatter of feet confirmed they'd heard him.

"Wash your hands first!" he added.

A few minutes later, the kids appeared in the kitchen. His heart swelled as he listened to them chattering away—he loved them more than life itself, but it hadn't been the easiest few months. Sam had been their world, and she'd left a gargantuan hole when she'd died. Ben had struggled the most—being a teenager was difficult enough without anything else, but the last few days Phil felt like he was finally coming right.

"My friend, Lizzi, said I can go over there tomorrow," Catherine prattled on to Ben as they made their way to the table.

"That's nice. She's not really your friend though."

"Yes! Dad, tell him. Isn't she my friend?"

"Yes, sweetheart, she's your friend." He gave his son a warning look. The last thing they needed was one of Catherine's melt-downs. "Come on, tuck in before it goes cold." Just as Phil sat down, there was a knock at the front door. Groaning, he got to his feet again.

"Who is it, Daddy?" Catherine said.

"My x-ray vision seems to be on the blink, sweetheart, or else I'd be able to tell you."

"Gutted!" Ben laughed at his sister, his blue eyes twinkling with amusement.

"Less of that and eat your dinner. I'll be back in a tick."

Catherine poked her tongue out at Ben. He knew he should've told her off too, but he often ignored her bad behaviour—she had him wrapped around her little finger.

He opened the door and was surprised to see two women he'd seen hanging around at the school gates. Both were attractive—one tall with long blonde hair, the other short and mousy.

"Hello, Catherine's dad," the blonde one said.

Hi," he said, taken aback.

"We're looking for the missing teacher and wondered if you'd seen her at all?"

"The missing teacher? Sorry, this is the first I've heard of it. Who's missing?"

"Erin, the young German girl." She handed him a flyer with the photo of a young, dark-haired woman with laughing eyes.

He looked at the image and his stomach muscles clenched. It took all his self-control to keep his breathing and voice steady. "Nah, sorry. I don't think I've *ever* seen her, to be honest."

"She's only been in the country for a few weeks. She went missing two nights ago."

His pulse quickened and he gulped. "How awful. If there's anything I can do, please let me know."

The short woman winked at him, blatantly flirting. He was used to women doing this. Since Sam died, they must think him fair game, but he wasn't interested.

He watched as they strolled up the drive and back out onto the street to several other people gathered on the corner.

"Who was it?" Ben asked when he returned to the table.

"Some people looking for a missing teacher. Have you heard about it?"

"Yeah, they were talking about her today at school. She was a primary teacher."

"Miss Lieber. She talks funny," Catherine said.

"She's German, that's why. Hopefully they'll find she's just gone home again." He ruffled his daughter's hair. "But until we know she's safe, promise me you won't talk to any strangers."

"We promise," Catherine said.

"Benjamin?"

"Yes, Dad. I promise," his son said in an impatient tone.

After dinner, the three of them shared the washing up. Phil washed, Ben wiped, and Catherine put away—something they did every evening.

"Can Kev come over for a couple of hours, Dad? It *is* the weekend."

Phil shrugged. "I guess so, but maybe his parents won't want him wandering the streets until that woman's found."

"Nah! His olds don't care what he does."

"I'm sure that's not true, Ben. And what's all this tough talk all of a sudden? They're his parents, not his olds."

"It's not tough talk. It's just the way kids speak these days."

"Well, I don't like it. Please try not to speak like that around me."

"Yes, Dad. Is it okay to ring Kev then?"

Phil nodded. He knew he was always on his son's case, but he couldn't help it. He figured if he let up on him, he might get in with the wrong crowd. Without Sam's input in the child-raising stakes he felt like a fish out of water, but he was doing his best.

"What are we doing this weekend, Daddy?" Catherine asked once they were alone.

He bent and kissed the tip of her nose. "What would you like to do?"

"Go to the park? And visit my new friend too."

"Well, don't be disappointed if that doesn't happen. Miriam can be difficult at the best of times, and you saw how she reacted with Elizabeth just talking to us earlier."

Catherine's bottom lip stuck out, and he feared she may start crying.

"But you never know. If not. I'll take you to the pet shop in town—see if they have any puppies."

"I can buy a puppy?"

He laughed. "No, sweetie, but you can pet them if they have any."

That seemed to cheer her up, for now.

"Can I stay up late, Daddy?"

"We'll see. Let's run you a bath and get you into your pjs then we can curl up on the sofa."

"Can I choose the movie?"

He rolled his eyes. "Not if it's *Frozen* again."

"Aw, why not, Daddy?"

"Because I know it word for word already."

She giggled.

On their way up the stairs, someone knocked on the door again.

"Bloody hell, it's like Grand Central Station around here." He trotted back down the stairs and swung open the door to find his son's best mate standing there. He was tall for his age, lanky, with a face full of acne and a mop of greasy dark blond hair.

"Hi, Mr Mathews," Kevin said.

"Hi. Come on in. Ben's upstairs."

Kevin turned and waved to the car backing out of the driveway. "Mum's worried about the missing teacher. She didn't want me to walk here alone."

"Very wise, Kevin."

"Ben?" Catherine yelled. "Your friend's here."

Ben popped his head over the balustrade. "Come up, Kev. You got here fast."

"His mum didn't want him walking because of the missing teacher." Phil wiggled his eyebrows in jest. Hoping to prove a point—he wasn't the only paranoid parent in the village.

CHAPTER THREE

Unfamiliar with the local area of Kenby, a village on the outskirts of Greater Manchester, I didn't know what to do. My family and friends lived over half an hour's drive away in Manchester, and I didn't think it very polite to drive all that way in someone else's car. So, I followed the signposts in the direction of the town centre and, after strolling up and down the high-street, ducked into the cinema—Belinda-no-mates.

I wasn't a movie buff by any means and looked forward to catching a chick flick or tantalising thriller, but it was classic movie night, and the only thing on offer was *Meet Me in St. Louis,* a musical starring Judy Garland. I surprised myself by knowing some of the songs and even hummed along to one or two.

Afterwards, I headed back to the house. There was nothing else to do in the village, unless you counted a clapped-out looking pub or the leisure centre.

"Oh, it's you," a sour-faced Miriam said as I let myself in.

"Yeah. Hi. I'll just check on your brother, and then I'll go to my room."

"No need. He's fine. Why don't you come through to the kitchen, and I'll pour you a coffee?"

Taken aback at the change in her attitude, I nodded. "Okay." I hung my handbag and jacket over the newel post and followed her into the kitchen. It felt strange. I'd lived there for a week and was more than familiar with the place, but now Miriam was there, I felt like an intruder.

"Take a seat." Miriam indicated the bar stool, the merest hint of a smile on her lips.

"Thanks."

"Milk? Sugar?"

"A drop of milk, ta."

She handed me a mug and sat beside me. "I'm sorry if I sounded a little blunt earlier."

I shrugged. "That's okay." I wanted to stand up to the older woman and say how much she'd embarrassed me in front of the neighbours, but of course I didn't.

"It's just... I'm worried someone will find out Charlie is here, and the shit will hit the fan."

"I won't tell anyone. I signed a non-disclosure agreement, remember? It's more than my job's worth."

"I know. And I'm so sorry. I wanted to bite off my tongue as soon as the words had left my mouth."

"Don't worry about it. It's forgotten." I smiled.

"I've lived here for eleven years and I've managed to keep Charlie a secret all that time. This is the first time I've let anybody know we're related. We're a private family."

"Honestly, nobody will find out from me. But I'm amazed you've been able to keep it quiet for so long. Charlie Maidley is a household name. Has he never been to visit you before?"

"He's been lots of times, but he drives straight into the garage usually and wears a disguise if he goes out. If he didn't have this place to escape to, he'd never get a break from the media."

"I can't imagine being that famous. I don't think I'd like it, though."

"I hate it. I told him right from the start that if it ever got out I was his sister, I'd disown him. He chose his career and to live in the spotlight. I didn't."

I thought it was a little extreme to threaten to disown her own brother, but I didn't say anything. Instead I just nodded and changed the subject. "What time is your flight?"

"I have to leave here no later than 5am." She nodded at the suitcase in the hall. "I'm all packed, though."

"Will I be able to contact you in an emergency?"

"Certainly. I'll leave the details of the hotel and I'll still be available via email. Are you sure you'll be okay on your own?"

"I should be fine. I made a little friend next door if I need human interaction. She wants to come over and pet Thomas. Where is he anyway?"

"In the garage. He was getting under my feet while I was packing. I'll take him out to do his business before I go to bed. Catherine is sweet. The only person I have any time for around here."

"Really? Why? What's wrong with your neighbours?"

She made a face. "Just not my cup of tea. Although Catherine's dad is okay. I feel a little sorry for him, actually. His wife died last year—breast cancer."

"That's terrible, and with a lovely little girl like that. Tragic."

"Yes. He has an older boy too. Polite boy really, as youngsters go."

"So you like the entire family then?"

"Like is a little strong." She smiled back at me. "But yes. If you need... how did you put it? ...human interaction, you won't go far wrong with them. So long as..." Her fingers made a zipping and locking motion on her lips.

"Don't worry. I won't tell a soul."

"I know you won't. Right, I'd best get a few hours shuteye. I'll try not to wake you in the morning."

CHAPTER FOUR

I woke at the sound of a car engine outside my room and glanced at the clock—just after 5am. I'd enjoyed chatting with Miriam last night. My boss had turned out to be a lot nicer than I first gave her credit for. But now I was alone again, and for how long was anybody's guess. Miriam had said two weeks but then mentioned it could be a while longer.

I dragged myself out of bed and, after using the bathroom, popped into the room next door to check on Charlie. A vase of flowers sat on the side table next to the patient, which surprised me all the more. Clearly Miriam thought more of her brother than she let on.

I studied his face for a while. There was no denying he was a handsome man. Not my cup of tea as he was slight and had a wiry build, but handsome all the same. It was no secret that he was a womaniser. Every single one of his affairs had been highly publicised, and there were the masses of kiss and tell stories each of the scorned women couldn't wait to sell to the highest bidder. Then there was the scandal of Laura Sanders going missing, and he'd even been suspected of foul play initially, but, as far as I could remember, they hadn't been able to pin anything on him.

I stroked his hair deciding he could do with a good wash.

He was such a mystery to me. I'd been told he had a brain tumour, but I didn't know why he would need to be so highly sedated. I'd presumed it was because of the immense pain he must be in, but when I woke up the other morning and found him wide awake, I'd been surprised how *with it* he'd seemed, and there had been no mention of any pain.

Of course, I'd panicked. I woke to the sound of the toilet flushing and, after jumping out of bed, screamed when I came face-to-face with my patient wandering about stark naked. He'd pulled out his nasogastric tube and his catheter. He had blood all over his hands and penis, and I'd been horrified.

I'd turned on the shower and cleaned him up. Once I'd urged him back into bed, I wasted no time in administering his medication. Within thirty minutes, he was out of it once again. I hurriedly replaced his NG tube and catheter hoping Miriam wouldn't return and catch me out. I had no doubt I'd be given my marching orders and maybe even prosecuted if anyone discovered what I'd done.

How could I have been so stupid? I'd fallen asleep on the sofa and, upon waking, had staggered to bed forgetting to give him his last medication for the day. So, getting myself further and further in the shit, I filled out the medication sheet as though he'd had every dose and prayed no-one would ever discover my neglect.

I should've asked Miriam last night why he had to be so drugged up all the time, but I couldn't say I knew he wasn't in pain or that would catch me out. It was a strange situation—I'd never known anything like it in my almost fourteen years of nursing.

Thomas was whimpering in his cage in the garage, so I let him out and picked up the cute little dog. I never understood why people, like Miriam, had pets if they weren't welcome to live in the house. The small square cage was cold and unwelcoming, in my opinion. But he wasn't my dog, and I had to be seen to follow my boss's house rules when she was home at least.

I opened the back door and the little dog's legs went ten to the dozen to get out there to relieve himself. Back indoors, I made myself a coffee, donned my coat over my nightie, and then followed him outside.

"Thomas? Where did you go?" I called.

"Hi, Lizzi." Once again, Kate's voice came from behind the hedge.

"Hello, my friend. You're up early. You haven't seen Thomas, have you?"

"No. Would you like me to help you look for him?"

"Sure, come on over, but maybe you should go and tell your dad first?"

"Okay." The sound of Kate's retreating footsteps followed.

I walked to the bottom of the garden. "Thomas?" I said, gruffly. He'd never run away before. He usually just did his business and headed straight back indoors.

"I'm here!"

I whirled around, startled, and there was Kate in the flesh. "You don't look like a bush."

She chuckled, a delightful tinkling sound. "Because I'm a people."

"That explains it then. I don't know where that pesky dog has gone, though. Maybe you can help me call him?"

"Thomas, come here, boy!" she shouted.

The sound of movement beyond the hedge gave me hope that I hadn't lost the dog after all. Suddenly, Thomas launched himself through a gap and straight at Kate. They were indeed good friends.

Kate dropped to her knees and began rolling all over the grass with the excitable little pooch.

I laughed at them both.

When Kate returned to her feet, we walked back towards the house and sat on the garden bench beside the back door.

"I've never been over here before," Kate said.

"Really? I thought the two of you were old mates?"

"We are. Miriam lets me walk with him when she's in a good mood. She once let me go to the park with them too."

"Ah, I see. Well, while I'm in charge, you're welcome to pop by whenever you like. Do you fancy an orange juice?"

"Oh, yes, please."

"Give me a few minutes while I check on my patient and I'll be right back."

Kate nodded. "I'll look after Thomas."

"Thanks. His ball is in that garden bed over there." I pointed to the side of the garden.

Kate jumped to her feet and went to retrieve it.

The sound of delighted laughter followed me back indoors where I quickly prepared Charlie's meal replacement and medication. I daren't leave it too long for fear of him waking up again. Although I didn't really mind him waking up, at least he would be a bit of company for me. It was the damage he'd done to himself tearing out his catheter that had bothered me the most.

Once complete, I threw on my leggings and a baggy T-shirt before pouring two glasses of juice and returning to Kate and Thomas who were having a wonderful time.

The three of us played for around an hour until Phil called Kate in though the hedge.

"Aw, but Dad, we're having fun."

"I know you are, sweetheart, but Elizabeth has work to do."

I walked over to the hedge and, from where he was standing, got a better view of him than I had last night, and I wasn't disappointed. He was tall, around six feet and stocky, with messy brown hair and lovely deep brown eyes. His lips were delectable.

"She's really no bother. She's been keeping me company. And please, call me Lizzi."

"Thank you for entertaining my daughter, but she's got to get ready now. We're going out."

"Five more minutes, Daddy. Please?"

I looked up at him and smiled. "Fancy a cuppa?"

He hesitated then shook his head. "No. Thanks, anyway."

"Oh, well. Maybe another time?" I smiled. "I'll see you again, Kate. Come over anytime, even if I'm busy. Thomas will always be pleased to see you."

"Catherine. Come now!" Phil barked and then stomped away.

I stared at the vacant space in the hedge, shocked. Had I said something to offend him? Surely not. I replayed the conversation in my mind, but nothing seemed off to me at all. "Best do as he says, Kate." I stroked the girl's lovely tumble of curls. "You can come back again when Daddy says it's okay."

Phil stormed back into the house and slammed the kitchen door. Why had he behaved like that? The way she casually called his daughter Kate had irritated him. Nobody called her that. It had been Sam's name for their daughter and hearing it like that made his heart skip a beat.

He peered from the window and tried to see through the hedge, but it was too dense from where he stood. He'd have to apologise later. Rushing off like that was rude and unforgiveable. He would give the children a telling off if they'd behaved in that manner. But he didn't feel like himself today.

The image on the flyer, from the day before, swam into his vision and he spun from the window burying his head in his hands. What the hell had he done?

Moments later, Catherine arrived home. "Daddy, you was mean to my friend."

"I'm sorry, sweetheart. I didn't intend to be. I'll apologise later. I promise."

CHAPTER FIVE

I spent the rest of the morning cleaning the house, although I found it odd, with the family's obvious wealth, that they didn't have a cleaner or gardener. My contract said those chores were down to me. Not that it was any real hardship—I was glad for the distraction to be honest.

Afterwards, I filled two washing-up bowls, one with coconut shower gel scented water and one with clean warm water then carried them through to Charlie's room one at a time.

Moving him over onto his side expertly, I slid a waterproof sheet underneath him and, while he was still in that position, I sponged down his back and dried him before rolling him onto his other side and pulling the sheet over. Once he was on his back again, I cleaned his eyes first with the rinsing water, using cotton balls. Starting with his hair, I began washing him methodically, cleanest parts first ending at his genitals.

I'd done this procedure thousands of times during my career, but the patients had been nameless, faceless people. This was Charlie Maidley for Christ's sake, and I felt a little awkward, not to mention a tad perverted. I shook my head. "Pull yourself together, you fool," I chastised.

After lunch, I checked on Charlie before heading into the front garden to weed the flowerbeds. The sun was shining, and I couldn't face another minute cooped up inside.

Although I'd never professed to be green-fingered and was uncertain on a few occasions whether I'd actually pulled out a weed or a plant, I enjoyed the change of scenery and the fresh air.

"Afternoon." The voice came from close beside me.

Shading my eyes, I could only see the silhouette of a man peering down at me—the glaring sun behind him blinded me. "Hi." I staggered to my feet.

He held his hand out towards me. "Nigel Mason. Pleased to meet you."

"Lizzi." I could now see he was a small man in his late fifties or early sixties.

"I've been meaning to pop over and welcome you to the area. My wife and I saw you arrive last week in the ambulance. We thought something had happened to Miriam at first."

I smiled and nodded. "No, Miriam's fine. She's just gone away for a few weeks on business."

"And you're looking after the house, are you?"

I smiled. "Yeah. Lucky me. Which is your house?" I wanted to change the subject around to him.

He turned and pointed to a double storey detached house opposite. "Not a patch on this one, but we like it." His tone was clipped, and I wondered if I'd managed to piss him off in even fewer words than I had with Phil. What was wrong with me today?

"It looks lovely. And I'm very pleased to meet you, Nigel. Apart from Kate, I don't have any friends around here."

He smiled. "You should meet my missus, Joan. She's a lazy bitch and sits at home all day. Call in for a coffee any time."

Shocked by the way he spoke about his wife, I nodded but had no intention of setting foot in his house. He gave me the heebie-jeebies.

"Have the police called in to see you yet?"

I shook my head. "No. Why would they?"

"Looking for that German tart."

"I don't know what you mean. Has someone gone missing?"

"Yeah." He rolled his eyes dramatically. "The new teacher from the primary school. I told Joan she was trouble as soon as I laid eyes on her. You know the type; short skirts, open neck blouse, cleavage up to here." He put his hand under his chin. "Not someone you'd want teaching your kids, I can tell you."

"I see. Do you have kids, Nigel?"

He barked out a laugh. "Me? No way. Can't stand them. So, you're a nurse, right?" He rummaged in his trouser pocket, and I was certain he was rubbing his cock.

"I am." I took a step backwards towards the house. "What do you do for a living?"

"I'm a bus driver. Have been for the past thirty-five years."

"Oh, cool. I don't know how you can drive all day like that. I'd be falling asleep at the wheel."

"That's the easy part."

"Really? What could be more difficult than that?"

"Dealing with the public has got harder and harder over the years. Cheeky teens are the worst—brought on by too many do-gooders in the world. The kids of today could do with a bloody good hiding, I can tell you. In my day, we'd never answer an adult back—we'd have got a backhander. And if a copper caught you up to no good, he'd give you a clip around the earhole and march you home to your parents—then your dad would finish the job for bringing trouble to his door. These days' kids have nothing to be scared of."

I just nodded, liking this man less and less by the second.

"You want to see what they do on the buses. Young kids—girls no more than fourteen—having sex in full view. They don't give a toss who can see. No respect." He blatantly rubbed his cock this time.

"Gosh." I took my gloves off. "Oh, well, it was nice to meet you, Nigel, but I'd best get on. These weeds won't pull themselves."

"Oh, I meant to ask, who are you caring for in there?" He nodded towards the house.

"A member of Miriam's family. He's a very sick man."

His eyebrows drew tight together. "Nothing contagious, I hope."

"Yeah. So do I." I scratched at my face and neck.

This had the desired effect and Nigel backed off into the road. "I'll see you around." He turned and rushed back towards his house.

Laughing, I returned to the flower bed.

The sound of a car pulling up close by a short while later was followed by running footsteps on the pavement.

I looked up as Kate appeared around the hedge and bounced towards me. "Hello, you," I said to the red-faced little girl.

"Look what I've got for you." She handed me a box of chocolates.

"For me? Whatever for?"

"To say sorry."

"Sorry? You don't have to say sorry for anything, lovely."

"She doesn't, but I do."

My head snapped up to see Phil standing a few feet away, looking sheepish. "Oh, hi."

"Hi." He smiled his cute, cockeyed smile.

"Tell her, Daddy," Kate said, excitedly.

He rolled his eyes. "I'm sorry for being rude earlier. Can we start again?"

I got to my feet and wiped my grubby hands on my jeans. "Of course, we can. Cuppa?"

"I'd love one."

"Yay!" Kate said, clapping her hands.

CHAPTER SIX

I led Kate and Phil down the side of the house to the back garden. "Take a seat." I indicated the garden table. "It's too nice to be cooped up inside."

"Can Thomas come out?" Kate asked with a pleading tone to her voice.

"I'll send him out." I turned back to Phil. "Tea? Coffee?"

"Coffee. Black, no sugar, thanks."

Once I'd let the dog out, I filled the kettle and rushed through to check on Charlie. "Wish you could join us outside, buddy. The sunshine would do you so much good," I said to his sleeping form. It bothered me he was wasting what was left of his life drugged up to the eyeballs in bed. I squeezed his hand and sighed.

Back in the kitchen I finished the coffee and poured a glass of pineapple juice for Kate. After placing everything on a tray, I headed back outside. "It's only instant, I'm afraid. Miriam has a fancy coffee machine, but I need to learn how to work it."

"Instant's fine," Phil said.

"Did you go anywhere nice earlier?" I asked, handing him a mug.

"To the park. That's all."

I glanced at Kate who was once again rolling on the grass with Thomas. "Glass of juice for you, Miss Kate," I called.

Phil winced.

"Have I done something wrong? Is she not allowed juice? It's sugar free."

He shook his head. "No, it's not that." His cheeks flushed red.

"What is it then?" I was keen not to piss him off again especially so soon.

"My wife used to call her Kate. It brings back so many memories when I hear you call her that."

It was my turn to gasp. "She told me that's what her friends call her."

"Really?"

I nodded. "Is that not true?"

"Not that I know of."

"Oh, I'm so sorry. I wonder why she said that, then?"

"Because I like it," Kate said suddenly standing beside me. "Don't make her stop, Daddy, please."

"Well…" He shrugged, clearly at a loss what to say.

"Juice?" I picked up the glass and handed it to Kate… Catherine, or whatever I was meant to call her now.

"Thank you, Lizzi," she said, taking the large, half-filled glass in her delicate little hands.

"Can you manage?"

She nodded as she drank causing me to laugh.

Phil also laughed and shook his head good-naturedly.

"Do you work around here, Phil?" I asked, trying to get the conversation back on track.

"I'm a builder by trade, but I've been renovating properties and renting them out for a few years now."

"Really? I love watching *Homes Under the Hammer* and would love to get into something like that. Not that I've ever tried renovating anything."

"Yes, those kinds of programs are popular these days."

"Do you rent them out as holiday lets or permanent rentals?"

"Mainly long term."

"How many do you have?"

"Eight done and rented out, another two are sitting empty at the moment. The plan used to be to have a portfolio of at least twenty by the time I'm fifty."

"Wow!"

"I don't know if that'll happen though. I've not done much of anything since Sam died. It's difficult with the kids. And besides, the income from the ones I already have keeps me afloat."

"That was lucky."

He squinted his lovely brown eyes as he looked at me in confusion. "What was?"

"That you had a job that gives you an income whether you work or not."

"Yeah, I guess so. I never really thought of it like that."

A silence passed between us, and I glanced back at Kate who was now sitting on the concrete, her back against the brick wall of the house with Thomas fast asleep on her knee. "Aw, look at them two."

Phil smiled at the sight of his daughter, but the smile didn't reach his eyes. Instead they were filled with immense sadness, which tore at my heart.

Something about him totally intrigued me even though he was proving difficult to get to know. It was as though he had a brick wall built around him.

He drained the last of his coffee. "We'd best get off. Thanks for your hospitality."

"Anytime."

We both got to our feet.

"Come on, rascal. Elizabeth needs to get back to work."

"Lizzi, please."

"Is Daddy your friend?" Kate said, gently pushing Thomas off her knee.

"Erm…" I raised my eyebrows at Phil. "Yes. I guess he is."

"Is he your *boy*friend?" she giggled.

"Oi, monkey." Phil laughed, his face transforming for a split second, and then he took off chasing after his daughter.

Thomas began barking and bounded after them.

Phil caught Kate around the waist, tackled her to the ground, and began tickling her tummy while Thomas licked her face.

Kate's squeals caused laughter to bubble in my belly. It had been almost five years since I spent any amount of time in the company of a child, and I'd forgotten how infectious their laughter could be.

"Dad?" a male voice came through the hedge.

Phil stopped tickling his daughter and got to his feet, as though feeling guilty for allowing himself to relax for a second. "Yes?"

"Can I go to Kev's for a while?"

Phil looked at me and rolled his eyes before pulling Kate up from the grass. "Hang on. We're coming home now."

"Aww, Daddy. I don't wanna go home. You never laugh at home."

A sadness settled in his eyes again. "Don't be silly, baby. Of course I laugh."

She looked at me and shook her head. "No, he doesn't."

CHAPTER 7

"What were you doing next door?" Ben asked as they entered the kitchen.

"Your sister wanted to see Thomas."

"And Daddy wanted to see Lizzi." Catherine giggled again.

Phil couldn't help but grin at his cheeky daughter.

"Did you? Do you like her, Dad?" Ben's eyebrows furrowed.

"Not like that." He ruffled Catherine's hair and turned back to Ben. "Are you okay?"

He nodded, but Phil still sensed something was wrong.

"Just tell me, mate. Is something on your mind?"

He shrugged. "I could hear you laughing and…"

Phil's heart raced. "And what, buddy?"

"It's just been so long since I heard you laugh like that." Tears filled his eyes.

"Hey. Come here." He pulled Ben into his arms, surprised how tall he seemed all of a sudden. "I'm sorry I've been so down lately. I promise I'll try harder in the future."

"I know… but Mum…"

"Your mum was the sweetest, most amazing woman I've ever met, but she wouldn't want us moping around forever."

Catherine grabbed his legs and buried her face in his jeans, suddenly sobbing.

He patted Ben's back before bending to Catherine. "And from now on..." Phil waited until he had their attention. "Catherine will be known as Kate. Is that alright with everyone?"

"Kate?" Ben said, clearly confused.

He nodded and raised his eyebrows at his son. "Yes. Kate." He kissed her on the top of her head. "Right, come on, sweetheart. Let's drop your brother off and you can help me prepare dinner. How's that sound?"

Once I'd waved goodbye to Kate and Phil, I felt suddenly bereft.

Maybe taking this job hadn't been the best idea. Since splitting with my ex, Sean, I'd thrown myself into my work, but this job afforded me far too much time to think—too much alone time.

Wiping away a flurry of sudden, unexpected tears, I fed Thomas and then strolled back through to Charlie.

"Well, Charlie-boy. It's Saturday night. What do you fancy doing? We could go to the movies. Nope? Dinner? Nope? How about we order in Chinese food and watch Netflix?" I sighed. "That settles it then. I hope you like chicken fried rice. My treat."

Stroking my fingers along his jawline, I sighed. "Who made the call to keep you drugged up like this, Charlie? It seems a crime and such a waste of a life."

He was one of the UK's top celebrities—a household name in every home across the country—and rich as hell if the tabloids could be believed. Yet here he was living his remaining days in an induced coma and for no apparent reason.

Once I'd topped up his meds and fed him via the tube, I drew the curtains, flicked on the lamp and headed back through to the kitchen in search of the food delivery leaflets I'd seen earlier.

Phil poured himself a brandy, grabbed his cigarettes, and stepped out onto the patio. He shivered. The evening temperatures were much colder than even a week ago. Winter would be here before he knew it.

He hated winter. The bleak, freezing cold months seemed to go on and on.

He lit his ciggie, pulled out a wrought-iron chair from the matching table, and sat down, exhaling noisily. He found the evenings the worst to cope with since Sam. Once Catherine was tucked up in bed, he rarely saw another soul until the morning. On the odd occasion he did see Ben, it was short and sweet and comprised of a series of grunts. He'd stayed at his mate's house tonight, so there was no chance of bumping into anyone until tomorrow.

Suddenly, next door's outdoor light came on and Lizzi appeared. "Be quick, Thomas. Do your business and hurry up back."

Phil smiled. Something about her appealed to him. Not that he'd act on it. He and women didn't mix—his latest dalliance with Erin proved that.

After greedily tucking away a huge Chinese meal that would easily have fed a small family, I snuggled onto the sofa feeling sleepy. But Thomas had other ideas for me—he began squeaking at the back door.

I groaned, forcing myself to my feet. "Alright, alright, I'm coming."

Thomas must've been bursting as he shot out of the door as soon as the gap was wide enough for him to slip through. "Hey, wait for me, buster," I laughed before following him to the end of the garden just beyond the reach of the outside light. One minute he was there, the next he'd gone.

"Bloody dog!" I hissed. "Thomas, come back here at once, you little nuisance."

There was no telling where he'd gone, and I had no intention of going through the hedge after him. I had no idea what was back there, but the area looked dense with trees and bushes, and I could also hear the sound of running water not too far away.

"Thomas," I hissed again, not wanting to wake the neighbours.

"Has he done a bunk?" Phil's voice made me jump out of my skin.

"Jesus, you frightened the shite out of me."

He gave a throaty chuckle. "Sorry."

"Yeah, Thomas has taken off. This is the second time today. What's even back there? Do you know?"

"Just a steep bank of trees leading down to the creek."

"Thomas," I hissed again, louder this time.

Phil put his finger and thumb to his mouth and let out an ear-splitting whistle.

I winced, covering my ears.

A rustle from the bushes alerted us of Thomas's return and the little rascal burst through the hedge.

"There you are!" I bent and gripped hold of his collar before he could vanish again. "Oh, my gosh, he's soaking wet."

"Maybe there's a bitch in heat across the other side of the creek? That would explain it."

"Yeah, there must be. Thanks for your help." I smiled at Phil. "Although you've probably woken the neighbourhood."

"It's not that late. Anyway, do you fancy a nightcap? I was about to pour myself a glass of wine."

"I can't leave my patient."

"Oh, yeah, and I can't leave Cath...er, I mean Kate either."

I screwed my face up. "Maybe another time?"

"Or I could grab us a drink and we could chat over the bushes?" he said.

I laughed. "I can't see any problem with that. Let me put our furry friend back inside. I don't fancy a repeat performance. Do you?"

"Meet you back here in two?" he said, scooting through the gap in the hedge.

"Come on, Thomas. I hope you've done your business because you're going back inside." I led him into the kitchen and towel-dried his muddy little feet and underbelly. Then I placed a bath-towel on the sofa and left him cleaning his bits while I checked on Charlie.

Back outside, Phil handed me a glass of red wine over the hedge.

"Cheers," I said, holding the glass up for a sec before sipping the contents.

"Don't you get a day off?" he asked, nodding towards Charlie's bedroom window.

"No. Not until Miriam gets back."

"I would've thought full time care would need to be split between at least two nurses."

"With an agency it would, but this is a private arrangement. And to be honest, it's a doddle. The easiest job I've ever done. All I'm required to do is administer his medication, keep him clean, and massage his legs once a day."

"Who is he?"

"I'm not sure. A close friend of Miriam's is all I've been told." I hated lying, but there was no way I'd let it slip to anyone exactly who lay beyond the curtains.

"If he's so bad, why isn't he in hospital?"

"I don't know the answer to that either. You'd have to ask Miriam."

"No, thanks." He chuckled. "You've seen how she acts where I'm concerned. I don't know what she's got against me."

I shook my head. "Nothing. In fact she said you're an okay bloke. But I don't suppose she needs a reason to be horrid to anyone—I can imagine her being quite temperamental. Have you known her long?"

"Six years, since we moved in. Not that anyone knows her very well. She's always invited to the community get-togethers, but she never attends. What's wrong with the patient anyway?"

"He has a brain tumour."

Phil gasped. "Poor bugger. So he's not compos mentis?"

I shrugged. "Not with the drugs he's on, no."

He scrutinized my face. "What was that look for?"

I shrugged again. "Oh, nothing."

"Go on. You can tell me."

"I just think it's a waste of a life. Yes, he's dying, but why can't we manage his pain with meds and let him live out the rest of his days? The state he's in, he may as well be dead already."

"That's disgusting. Who made that call?"

I shrugged. "I've no idea. As far as I know it was the hospital. I need to talk to Miriam about it when she gets home."

"Maybe he's loopy—away with the fairies, or in a lot of pain?"

"That's what I thought but..." I paused, annoyed with myself for saying too much.

"But, what?"

"Oh, it doesn't matter."

"Go on..."

I shook my head and sighed. "Promise you won't tell anyone?"

"I promise. Come on, spit it out."

"I made a mistake one night last week and messed up his meds. I couldn't believe it when I woke up the next morning and he was awake."

"Oh, shit. What was he like?"

"More lucid than I'd expected. He didn't appear to be in any pain at all." I didn't mention the damage he'd done to himself by tearing out his catheter.

"Why the hell would they dose him up like that if he doesn't need it? It makes no sense."

"Tell me about it. I panicked and pumped him full of drugs right away, but we had a lovely chat before he zonked out again."

"So, what are you going to do?"

"Not a lot I *can* do. I'll have to wait and talk to Miriam, I guess."

"But she might not be back for weeks. In the meantime, that poor bloke's festering away in his bed instead of enjoying his last days. You owe it to him to do the right thing."

"But I might lose my job."

Phil shrugged. His mouth was set in a firm line. "Be that as it may, at least you'll be able to live with yourself."

He was right. I'd been battling with myself all week and his words just confirmed it to me. "Okay. I'll reduce his meds in the morning and assess the situation from there."

A short while later, I drained my glass and handed it back to him. "I'd best get back inside. But thanks so much. I needed that, and I enjoyed our chat."

"Me too. It sure beat feeling sorry for myself in front of the TV. How my life has changed."

"What do you mean? Since your wife?"

"Yeah, and no. I meant, a few years ago, Saturday night used to be the highlight of my week."

I nodded. "I know what you mean. I would have a bottle of cider to get me in the mood while I was getting ready, and I was always half-cut before I even made it to the pub."

"Those were the days." He laughed.

"Well, you may scoff, but this has been the highlight of my week."

"Mine too. I've enjoyed it. Maybe I'll see you tomorrow—I think my daughter has plans to visit you and the pooch in the morning, if you don't mind?"

"Not at all, I'll make breakfast if you like?"

And so it was settled. A few minutes later, I was back indoors with everywhere locked up behind me.

I checked on Thomas who was still on the sofa with his legs in the air giving me a not too pleasant view of his gonads. I laughed and then padded through to Charlie.

"Okay, matey. I suppose I'd best give you your meds." I contemplated giving him a light dose but the thought of him waking during the night and damaging himself again prevented me doing that.

The next morning, I put Thomas on his lead and took him into the garden.

"Don't look at me like that, you rascal." I laughed. "I can't trust you not to run off again."

Once he'd done his business, we headed back indoors.

I dished up Thomas's breakfast before checking on Charlie.

"Good morning, my friend. I have some good news for you. How do you fancy waking up for a few hours?" I'd been pondering on it all night. If I reduced his morning meds, then he should be awake by dinner time.

Going about my business, it took the best part of an hour to wash him from top to toe and change his pajamas and sheets. I gave him a thorough going over, checking for any hot spots that might lead to bed sores. Then I trudged through to the laundry and put a wash on.

I'd worked up an appetite and was relieved when the back door opened, and Phil and Kate peered inside.

"Knock, knock," Phil said.

"Oh, hi. Come on in. I'm just making a pot of coffee. Would you like some?"

"I'd love some," Phil said.

"And what about you, Miss Kate?"

"I'm not allowed coffee."

I grinned. "How about juice?"

She nodded and slumped to the tiles making a fuss of Thomas.

"Take a seat," I said to Phil who was busy scanning the kitchen and as far into the rest of the house as he could see from where he stood.

I poured a small glass of juice and placed it on the table. "Here you go, sweetie. Now, who's for pancakes?"

"Me, me, me," Kate said.

I laughed. "How about you, Phil?"

"I shouldn't. I'm watching my waistline—but go on then. You twisted my arm."

"Can I take Thomas into the garden?" Kate asked.

"I'm sorry, sweetheart, but Thomas is grounded."

Kate's tinkling laughter made me chuckle. "A doggy can't be grounded. Can he, Daddy?"

"He can if he's a naughty doggy," Phil said, seriously. "Thomas ran away last night and Lizzi couldn't find him."

She gasped and looked at me.

I nodded confirmation. "He's grounded until further notice." I slid the last of the pancakes onto the pile and walked them over to the table. "Okay, let's tuck in."

It was a wrench to get Kate up off the floor to eat her pancakes, but, when she finally gave in, Thomas seated himself beside her, his head on her feet while he gazed up at her adoringly.

Both Phil and I laughed.

Kate babbled on and on about him between mouthfuls and cooed at each pathetic expression he gave her. She gobbled up her pancake in record time and moments later was back on the tiles with him, laughing—in her own little world.

"These are lovely," Phil said, nodding at his plate. "I've had to learn how to cook since... you know. But pancakes are still something I mess up time and time again."

"I could give you some lessons if you like?" I offered. "I used to work in a café part time when I was at Uni."

"I couldn't ask you to do that." A grin lit up his face. He was really quite lovely in a dark and moody sort of way.

"Why not? It's not as if I have much else to do at the moment." I glanced across the hallway to Charlie's room.

"Have you decided what you're going to do about that situation?"

I nodded. "Yeah. I've reduced his meds today. I'll be in breach of my contract, but I can't continue to do this. The poor guy needs to be allowed to live out any time he has left."

"What if…? He shook his head, "Nah. Forget it."

"Go on. Tell me."

"Well, how do you know he's sick at all? What if Miriam is a nutter?"

I barked out a laugh. "Boy! You have some wild imagination."

"But, really. How do you know?"

"I know because he was in hospital and I saw his notes. My boss is a friend of Miriam's, and he asked if I wanted this job."

Phil shrugged. "Ah, well. Maybe I should stop reading those psyche thrillers." He grinned. "What will you do if he wakes and he's in agony?"

"I'll have his meds on standby, and besides, I've given him his pain meds so hopefully he'll just wake up, albeit groggily. I should be able to talk to him at least and ask him what he wants me to do."

"Good idea. Poor bloke, it would be terrible to be in his boat."

"To be honest, he won't be aware of a thing with the amount of drugs he's been on. But that's not the point. It's the morality of the whole situation. If he died without ever waking again, I'd never be able to forgive myself."

"Right then…" He drained the last of his coffee and placed the cup on top of his empty plate. "Come on, Catherine, we need to get on. Thank Lizzi for feeding us."

"It's Kate! And aw, Daddy, do we have to?"

"Sorry. Kate." He rolled his delicious eyes at me and grinned. "Yes. We need to go food shopping early." He turned back to me. "There's a storm heading this way, apparently. Do you want me to grab anything for you from the supermarket?"

"I'm fine thanks. I intend to place an online order and have it delivered, but I have plenty in for now."

"Come on then, squirt," he said to his daughter.

She harrumphed.

"What did I say earlier?" His voice was stern.

"That I must come home without a fuss."

"Exactly. So what do you say to Lizzi?"

"Thanks, Lizzi," she mumbled.

"You're very welcome, Kate." I stroked her pretty curls once she'd climbed to her feet. "But you must promise to come back soon. Thomas is really quite smitten with you."

"I promise." She brightened.

———

After tidying the kitchen, I settled at the dining table with the laptop and made a list of groceries online using the account Miriam had set up for me. Afterwards, I changed the sheets on my bed and did a load of washing. I'd planned to do some more weeding, but the weather had turned nasty and, as Phil predicted, by lunchtime the squally, wet wind battered against the kitchen window.

Settling on the sofa under a blanket to read my kindle for a couple of hours, I was surprised when I woke a while later to the sound of Thomas's whimpers.

"Oh, sorry, fella. Do you need a piddle?" I staggered to my feet.

The weather, now even worse, blasted me backwards as I opened the door. I slammed it shut again.

Thomas looked at me and continued to whimper.

"Sorry, pooch. We can't go out there, it's awful. Can't you cross your legs for a while?"

More squeaks came from the desperate looking dog.

"Well, you'll have to go alone then. Hurry back." I opened the door and Thomas flew through it and out of sight.

I rushed to the kitchen window and saw the back of him darting through the bushes at the back of the garden once again. "Oh, no!" I cried. "What's the bloody attraction down there?" I had no intention of following him, not in this weather. And besides, I doubted he'd want to stay out very long. It was terrible out there.

I headed through to check on Charlie—he was still zonked out.

"Hey, buddy," I said softly. "Are you with us yet?"

Nothing.

I turned him onto his side, stroked his hair and pulled up his duvet. The temperature had dropped a lot since earlier.

Heading back through to the kitchen, I peered from the window again. Just then, the sun umbrella was lifted out of the table and flung to the end of the garden. "Bugger!" I hissed, angry with myself for forgetting to put it away. I had no choice but to brave the elements and go to retrieve it. I only hoped it wasn't already damaged.

In the garage I dragged on a raincoat and a pair of knee-high rubber boots. They were far too big but would have to do.

My shoulder jarred as the wind tried to snatch the door from my hands. Dense grey clouds had blocked out the daylight casting the garden in premature twilight. The rain lashed down and crashed against the hood of the raincoat temporarily deafening me.

Once I'd secured the umbrella in the shed, I decided to venture a little further to find that pesky mutt.

The gusting wind swirled all around me, the sky was leaden and the boughs of the trees above me swayed and creaked. It wasn't just rain; it was a downpour as heavy as any I'd ever seen. Walking through a waterfall couldn't have got me any wetter.

I called Thomas from the end of the garden and tried to whistle like Phil had last night, but my feeble attempts could scarcely be heard by my own ears.

Forcing my way through the small gap in the hedge, I cried out when a sharp branch scratched painfully across my right cheek. "Fuck!" I roared, clamping both of my frozen, wet hands to my face.

I couldn't see much in front of me—the trees and shrubbery had taken what little daylight the storm had left behind. "Thomas!" I yelled, inching my way forward one half-step at a time. The ground was spongy underfoot combined with the odd treacherous tree root that threatened to trip me up and send me flying down the rugged bank. Stumbling, I reached out and steadied myself on the trunk of a large oak tree and tried to take stock of my surroundings.

A few feet ahead, the ground fell away sharply, and the dense shrubbery continued down with no obvious path to follow. I had no choice but to shove my way through.

A branch snagged the hood of my jacket and ripped it from my head just as the branches above me shook in the ferocious wind and showered me in huge droplets of water that ran down my neck.

"Thomas!" I was close to tears and wished I hadn't bothered attempting to find the naughty dog. He'd soon return home once he was cold and hungry enough.

I glanced behind me from where I'd just come, contemplating just heading back to the house, but the creek couldn't be too far below me now. I could hear the splash and bubble of gushing water.

"Thomas, please." I stepped down the bank a little further, trying to keep myself upright on the slippery surface and failing miserably. I landed on my backside with a bang and began to slide down at a rapid rate of knots. I clawed out at any passing shrubbery I could, but it was no use. All I ended up with was handfuls of leaves and twigs—nothing would stop me. That is until another huge tree jumped out in front of me. I slammed into it, whacking my head on the trunk and sandpapering the skin off my forehead on the rough bark.

I froze for a second, hardly breathing for fear that any movement would propel me forwards again, but I seemed pretty secure slammed up against the tree.

After touching my tender forehead, I winced and checked my fingertips that were covered in blood. "Fuck! Can this day get any worse?" I was soaked to the skin, covered in slimy mud and cut to bloody ribbons. That dog had a lot to answer for.

"Thomas!" I screeched, my voice sounding like it had come from a crazed woman. And it pretty much had.

The faint sound of yapping gave me hope.

"Thomas. Here, boy."

Struggling to my feet I braced myself again, not wanting to take another slippery trip but into the water this time.

Slowly I stepped down, holding myself steady on the trunk of the tree. Certain I was close to the water now, it sounded as though it was just beyond the next row of bushes.

"Thomas?"

A couple more yaps confirmed the troublesome dog was no more than three feet away from me.

I gripped hold of the branches of the bush below me, terrified of going head first into the creek, which, after all the rain, sounded more like a river.

Pushing through the bushes, I spied Thomas, ankle deep in the water. He was staring at me, his ears pointing up and I could swear he had a smile on his face.

"Come here, you naughty doggy." The next words stuck in my throat as my eyes wandered to the side of Thomas.

My screams, when they came were drowned out by the driving wind and rain.

CHAPTER 8

The young woman was submerged at the edge of the creek—her head on the rocks and her body deeper into the water. The short, white cotton dress she wore, made transparent by the water, showed she was naked underneath—she was also barefoot. A mane of black, matted curls were spread out over the rocks behind her, but it was her lifeless eyes that freaked me out the most. The last lightning strike had painted her up like a picture.

As a nurse, I'd seen my fair share of dead bodies, but nothing like this. The terror in her final expression was still evident on her face.

I lunged for Thomas, grabbed him by the collar and dragged him back up the bank—almost faster than my trip down, which was saying something considering I'd slid down half of it. My heartbeat thudded in my chest and my breath came out in short, noisy pants. As I pushed through the boundary hedge, I cried out in relief to be back in the familiar garden.

Shoving Thomas inside, I dumped the boots and jacket at the back door before following his muddy paw prints through the kitchen to the living room.

My thoughts were in a riot. In the safety of the house I began to question what I'd seen. Could it have been a dummy? I hadn't got too close, but I could still see the haunted expression on the girl's face. Although her skin was as white as alabaster, I was certain she'd been real.

Grabbing the phone off the stand, I dialled 999.

Phil and Kate returned home just as the heavens opened.

As Phil carried the last of the shopping bags into the kitchen, he thought he heard someone shouting, but, after peering from the window, he decided he must've been hearing things.

Ten minutes later, he saw Lizzi, dressed in wet-weather gear, running up next door's back lawn and into the house, with Thomas tucked under her arm.

"Oh, you little swine!" he muttered, guessing the dog had gone walk-about again.

Once I hung up the phone, I stripped off my sodden clothing and wrapped myself in my robe while I waited for the police to arrive.

My entire body shook uncontrollably. I didn't know if it was because of the shock or the cold but figured it must be a mixture of both. I poured myself a glass of neat brandy from Miriam's stash and downed it in one.

A short while later, the sound of a vehicle pulling up outside had me on my feet and rushing to the front door. I gasped at how many uniformed officers and plain-clothed detectives had congregated at the entrance to the driveway.

"Elizabeth Yates?" a tall, well-built, detective, who appeared to be in his late fifties, approached me.

I nodded.

"I'm Detective Inspector Joel Karlson and this is my colleague Detective Constable Sharon Jones." He stepped to the side and a petite blonde woman came into view.

I nodded and tried to smile. "Thanks for coming so soon."

"Do you mind if we come inside, miss?" he asked.

I stepped backwards to allow them access and led them through to the living room. I took a seat on the closest armchair and the detectives both sat opposite me on the sofa.

"Now, if you could tell me exactly what you found and where?"

"Of course." I took a deep breath and exhaled in a controlled blow. "The dog ran off, and I followed him through the back hedge to the creek. There's a woman's body in the water."

The detective glanced at his partner and she nodded before ducking out of the room.

"Did you recognise the woman?" he asked.

I shook my head. "No. I'm not from around here—but she's not very old, mid-twenties. I thought I was seeing things at first."

A frantic knocking at the front door startled me. Phil appeared in the doorway.

"Oh, thank God you're okay," he said. "What's happened? Why all the police?"

The detective got to his feet. "And you are?"

"Philip Mathews. I live next door." He parked himself on the arm of my chair and reached for my hand. "Are you okay?"

I glanced back at the detective, who was heading to the door.

"I'll see how my colleagues are getting on, Miss Yates. I'll be back shortly."

Once he had left, I turned back to Phil and, for the first time since seeing the poor girl's broken body, tears filled my eyes. "Oh, Phil, it was awful."

"What was? You're scaring me now."

"I found a body." My words were barely audible.

"A what? A body?"

I nodded, poking at my eyes. "Where are the kids?"

"I left Ben looking after Catherine. I almost died when I saw all the police marching down the side of the house and through the garden."

"I'm sorry, I didn't think. I should've come to you first, but I was in a right state."

"Understandable. What a terrible shock."

"At least I now know why Thomas keeps running off. The little darling was trying to get us down there all along."

"Do you know who it is?" Phil asked.

"I don't—although I wouldn't be surprised if it was that missing teacher."

He gasped. "Really?"

"Just a guess, but who else could it be?"

Someone tapped on the front door again and the two detectives stepped inside. "May we come in?" DI Karlson called out.

"Yes, yes of course."

Phil jumped to his feet. "I'd best go and check on the kids. I'll call back later, if you like?"

"Please do." I smiled gratefully.

Phil passed the detectives in the hallway.

I waved him off and then turned back to them. "Did you find her?"

DI Karlson nodded. "We did. We've made a bit of a mess of the hedging, I'm sorry."

I shrugged. "Can't be helped, I guess. At least it's stopped raining. It was treacherous down there before."

"It's no better now, to be honest," DC Jones said, still rubbing her shoes on the doormat.

"Oh, you poor things. Can I make you a cuppa?"

"I'd love one, please," she said.

Her colleague rolled his eyes and then smiled. "That's very kind of you, thanks."

They followed me into the kitchen and sat at the table while I filled the kettle.

"Is it the missing teacher?"

"We're not certain at this stage," DI Karlson said.

"But it might be?"

He nodded. "But I'm going to have to ask you to keep this to yourself until we announce it."

I gasped, my hand flying to my mouth. "I already told Phil, the neighbour."

"We'll have a word with him before we go," he said. "Can you tell me who lives with you?"

"Oh, this isn't my house. I only work here—I'm a nurse. My boss is out of the country, and I'm caring for her brother who's terminally ill."

"Do you have your boss's details? We'll need to be in touch with her about the damage."

"Yes, of course." I placed a teapot and three cups down on the table before reaching for my handbag hung on the hook by the door. Finding Miriam's business card, I handed it to DI Karlson. "I'm not sure you'll get hold of her, but she promised to call me soon and I can pass your details on to her."

"How long have you been staying here?" DC Jones asked.

"This is my second week."

"Have you seen anything suspicious—anyone hanging around the property, at all?"

"No. Nothing."

"You said you had a dog. Has he alerted you of anything happening outside?"

"No. He's been with me most of the time. But, thinking about it, there was a night at the beginning of my stay where he barked and howled all night. He was in his cage in the garage. He's slept with me most nights since then." I poured the tea into the cups and grabbed the milk from the fridge.

"And that was the only time he barked?"

I shrugged. "You can't hear very much when he's in the garage. I mean, you and your lot are here now, but we haven't heard a peep from him, have we?"

I thought about the night Thomas had been barking in his cage and my heart missed a beat. He'd clearly been barking and howling because Charlie was creeping around the house, but to admit that would be admitting my incompetence as a nurse.

"Is something wrong?" DI Karlson asked, deep furrows between his eyebrows.

"No. Why?"

"You looked worried as though you'd remembered something."

"No!" I snapped, reaching for a cup and splashing some milk into it. "Milk?" I glanced from one to the other.

"Yes, please." DC Jones smiled, taking the plastic container from me.

"Have you ever seen this woman?" DI Karlson placed a photograph of a young, vibrant-looking woman. I recognised her immediately as the girl in the creek.

"Is that the teacher?" I asked.

He nodded.

"It's her. I'll never forget that face although she looked completely different to this. It's definitely her."

"And you've never seen her before today?"

"Never. In fact, the only people I've met are Phil and his kids and the weirdo from across the road."

His eyes popped open at this and he glanced at his colleague before turning back to me. "Weirdo?"

"Yes. I can't remember his name... oh, actually, I think it was Nigel. He's odd—and a bit sleazy. I caught him perving at me, and he made me feel uncomfortable. He also said the missing woman deserved all she got as she paraded around in short skirts all the time."

"Did he indeed?"

I nodded. "Hey, you won't tell him I told you that, will you? I'm staying here on my own and wouldn't want to cause any problems for myself."

"Don't worry, we won't." DI Karlson got to his feet and placed the cup on the kitchen worktop. "Thanks for the tea. I needed that. And I apologise in advance for any disturbance tonight. It will be a little while before we can remove the body."

It took all Phil's self-control to walk from the house and down the path in a calm, controlled way. Once home, he raced up the stairs and threw up in the toilet bowl—visions of Erin's beautiful face swam before his eyes. Surely it can't be her? What were the chances of her being found dead at the end of his garden?

After a few minutes, he swilled his face and headed back downstairs. Although his head spun, he fixed a smile to his face and went through to check on the kids in the living room.

"Can I go out now, Dad?" Ben asked as soon as Phil appeared.

He considered telling him no—wanting more than anything to keep his loved ones safe under his roof, but he didn't want to arouse any suspicions. "Where are you going to?"

"Kev's!" he snapped irritably.

"You can go, but don't be back late. Promise?"

"Promise." He legged it from the house as though his tail was alight.

Phil rolled his eyes. Oh, to be young without a care in the world. "Shove up, Catherine," he said, squeezing onto the armchair beside his daughter.

"It's Kate!" she said for the umpteenth time that day.

"Sorry, Kate. It's going to take me a while to get used to the new name. Will you be patient with me?"

"Depends."

"On what?"

"Will you watch TV with me?"

He groaned. "Let me guess... Frozen?"

She nodded excitedly.

"Oh, go on then. Get it ready while I make a drink."

He rushed through to the kitchen and peered from the window at the activity next door. His heart rate escalated at the sight of all the people coming and going dressed from head to toe in white overalls and black booties.

A knock at the front door caused him to jump out of his skin.

He took a deep breath and cleared his throat before going to answer it. The two detectives he'd met earlier were standing on his doorstep.

"Hi, guys. What can I do for you?"

"Can we have a quick word, sir?"

"Yeah. Come on in." Adrenalin coursed through his veins. What the hell were they here about?

"Miss Yates has just informed us she told you about the body she discovered earlier today. We'd like to ask you to keep it quiet for now, if you don't mind, sir."

Phil nodded. "Don't worry. I'll keep schtum. Is it the missing teacher?"

"Early days yet, Mr..."

"Mathews," he said. "Phil Mathews."

"Ah, yes, of course. You already said. Well, it's early days yet, Mr Mathews. So we can't possibly say."

"Of course. How terrible. I can't believe something like this has happened around here."

"Likewise," the male detective said. "Anyway, we need to get on. We appreciate your cooperation on this matter."

I watched the detectives head next door to Phil's house. Moments after closing the door behind them, and returning to the living room, the doorbell rang again.

"Bloody hell," I grizzled, desperate for a few minutes to myself. Turning on my heels, I headed back to the front door to find a young man wearing an orange dayglow.

"Where do you want it, love?"

I shook my head, confused.

"Your delivery," he said. "Although it's going to take a while. I had to park down the street."

In the excitement, I'd forgotten all about the grocery order I'd placed. "Oh, gosh. Erm… just in the kitchen, please."

I followed him out to the van and helped him carry the bags back to the house. On my return, I noticed the usually immaculate front lawn was all churned up after the torrential downpour and steady stream of cops wading in and out.

"What's happened?" the guy whispered, once he'd dropped the last of the bags on the kitchen tiles.

"I'm not allowed to say."

"Really? Is it something bad?"

"I'm sure it'll be on the news later." I walked him to the door and sighed as I closed it behind him. Just that morning I'd complained to myself how every day was like groundhog day—but not anymore.

"Hello?"

Startled, I held my breath. Where the heck had that come from?

"Is there anybody there?"

I gasped, suddenly remembering Charlie, and rushed through to his bedroom finding him awake. "I'm so sorry," I said, checking he was still hooked up to everything. "It's been a mad house around here today. I'm your nurse, Lizzi. How are you feeling?"

"Groggy. How long have I been asleep?"

I didn't want to go into the specifics. "A good while. Are you in any pain?"

He shook his head. "I don't think so."

"Good. I adjusted your meds so you could wake up, but I was afraid you would be in pain, so that's a relief."

His eyebrows furrowed. "Why would I be in pain?"

"Because of your brain tumour. Miriam doesn't want you to suffer."

A wry grin covered his face. "Miriam doesn't want herself to suffer, you mean. Sickness and bad publicity are her worst nightmares."

"Bad publicity?"

He nodded and began to cough.

I waited until he'd finished, then I raised the head of his bed and plumped up his pillows. "Better?"

"Much better. Thanks."

"Good. Can I get you anything? A glass of water perhaps?"

"I'd love one. My throat is all scratchy."

I rushed to the kitchen and brought back a jug of iced water and a glass.

"Where's Miriam?"

"She's on a business trip overseas. I'm not sure when she'll be back."

He took a sip of the water I offered then began fingering the tube going up his nose. "What's this for?"

"It's a feeding tube."

"Can you take it out?"

"I shouldn't. In fact, I'm probably going to be in big trouble for reducing your meds. But let's see how you get on. If you can eat and drink on your own, we can make that call then."

His eyelids began to close.

"You sleep now. I'll keep your meds at this level for now, but please, promise me if you feel any pain or discomfort you'll let me know."

Once the groceries were put away, I made myself a sandwich, surprised to find it was 7pm already. The back of the garden was floodlit, and a steady stream of people dressed in white coveralls went backwards and forwards down the side of the house.

"Shit!" I slammed my plate on the table—I'd forgotten about Thomas in amongst all the excitement. I popped my head in to check on Charlie, and was relieved to find him sound asleep, then continued to the garage and released the whimpering pooch from his cage. "I'm sorry, little fella. Come on, I'll take you down the street. Your usual stomping ground is out of bounds, I'm afraid."

With Thomas on his lead, we walked to the large patch of grass at the end

of the street. The air felt crisp and fresh after the storm, and slightly chilly too. I let him off his lead and he ran to a tree sniffing and cocking his legs like boy dogs do. The poor thing was bursting.

"What a relief you're okay," a man's voice boomed behind me causing me to cry out, and my feet left the ground.

I spun around to find Nigel standing a little too close for comfort. Everything about him unnerved me. "Of course, I'm okay. Why wouldn't I be?"

"We saw all the police and wondered what was going on…" He paused and licked his lips, one eyebrow cocked as though waiting for me to fill him in.

I recoiled inwardly but tried to mask my reaction to him. It wasn't his looks as such that made my skin crawl. Although not the most handsome man around he wasn't bad looking. But it was as though he had an ugly soul and it shone right out of his piercing dark eyes. "I-I can't tell you, I'm sorry. The police made me promise."

He sneered. "Come off it. Something bad's happened. Just tell me."

"No. I can't." Was I being unreasonable? The detective had asked me not to blab but I would've told someone else, just not him.

"Is it your patient? Did he die?"

"No! It's nothing to do with him either."

"Someone must've died. You don't get that kind of attention for anything else."

I shrugged. "I honestly can't say. You need to ask the detectives in charge." I called for Thomas and fastened him to his lead. "I'd best be off." I smiled and edged my way around him, dragging a mightily pissed off dog as I went. I could feel Nigel's eyes on me all the way to the house.

Back inside, I shuddered and my heartbeat hammered in my chest. That man gave me the absolute creeps.

CHAPTER 9

Phil was beside himself.

He stood at the kitchen window watching the comings and goings in next door's garden. The two detectives had left. They didn't seem to suspect him of anything, but it seemed from their questions they thought the dead girl might be Erin.

He paced the kitchen, all his nerve endings clanging. There was nothing to connect him to her. He hoped not anyway. He guessed they would've questioned him sooner if they knew anything.

"What's going on?" His son's voice startled him.

"Jesus, Ben. You freaked me out then. When did you get back?"

"Just now. Why are you so jumpy?"

Phil tried to laugh, but it sounded empty and fake. "I'm not jumpy. I was just miles away, that's all."

"So, what's happening?" He nodded at the lights at the end of the garden.

"They've found a body in the creek."

"Who?"

Phil shrugged. "Not sure. A woman."

"From around here?"

He shrugged again. "I don't know—she could've come from anywhere, I guess. There was a lot of rain earlier."

"So, you think she could've fallen in and been washed down the creek?"

Phil rubbed his stubbly chin and turned away trying to avoid his son's eyes. "Who knows, but it's possible, I guess. Can I make you something to eat? We had meatballs, there's some left."

"No, thanks. I had sausage sarnies at Kev's."

"Okay, well you'd best get yourself ready for school tomorrow. Have you finished your homework?"

"I didn't have much, so I did it on my break on Friday."

Phil eyed him suspiciously. "I hope you're not telling lies, buddy. I'll find out if you are."

Ben sucked his teeth and sneered at his father, "Why do you never believe me?" He turned and headed for the stairs.

"It's not that I don't believe you. I worry, that's all." But his words landed on deaf ears and, moments later, he heard Ben's bedroom door slam. "Little shit," he murmured.

I carried a tray holding a bowl of tomato soup and a slice of toast through to Charlie's room. "Hungry?" I asked, placing the tray down on the bedside table.

"A little," he said groggily.

"Here, let me help you sit up a little." I used the remote to lift the head of the bed and then fluffed up his pillows to make him comfy.

"Thanks."

"You're welcome." I moved the tray onto his knees. "Shall I feed you? There doesn't seem to be an over-bed table."

"Would you mind?"

"Of course, I don't mind. Here you go." I handed him a slice of toast then perched on the side of his mattress and proceeded to feed him.

"What's all the noise outside?" he asked in-between mouthfuls.

I rolled my eyes. "It's the police—I discovered a body this afternoon down by the creek. I was hoping you wouldn't notice. Are they disturbing you?"

"A body? Who is it?"

"I suspect it's a German teacher who's been missing for a few days. Poor darling. She wasn't very old." I held out another spoonful.

"That's terrible," he said, then opened his mouth.

"Thomas found her. He's been running off down there every chance he got, so I suspect she's been there a few days." I offered him another mouthful, but he shook his head.

"I'm not hungry—sorry."

"That's fine. I'll top you up via your tube."

"Do you think I'd be able to get out of bed tomorrow?" he asked.

"I don't know about that. Let's see what tomorrow brings, shall we?"

"I'm desperate for some fresh air."

"Let's take it slowly—I could bring the TV in here for you though, if you like? You could catch up on your sport."

"No, thanks. I hate sport."

I laughed. "You're joking, right? How can you hate sport—you're a top football player."

"I like playing it, but I can't stand watching it. It bores the pants off me."

"I can understand that. I've never been into sport either—playing nor watching. But aren't you keen to know how your team have been doing?"

He shrugged, a faraway look in his eyes. "I don't think I care, to be honest. I haven't played for almost a year now."

"Is that when you got sick?"

"That's when I was diagnosed with an inoperable brain tumour, but I had been sick for six months or so before then."

"How the heck did you keep it out of the papers?"

"I didn't tell anyone except Miriam. I sponsor the hospital, so Imran Singh was more than happy to keep it quiet."

"Were you in a lot of pain when you were admitted to the hospital?"

"To be honest, I don't remember. In fact, I can't remember much at all."

"Miriam said you had to be highly medicated at all times, which I find really strange considering you seem perfectly fine to me."

"What made you go against her?"

"Do you remember waking up last week? I almost died when I realised I'd missed giving you your meds. I'd got you back in bed and dosed up before I'd realised you didn't appear to be in any pain. After that it haunted me. I mean, how could I justify drugging you when you might not need it?"

"And where is Miriam now?"

"She's abroad—Atlanta, I think she said. She's gone for two weeks."

He nodded, his eyes growing heavy again.

"I'll just give you your meds, and then I'll let you have a rest."

He rubbed his temple. "Why are you giving me meds? I thought you said..."

"Don't worry. I'm only giving you half a dose just to see how you're feeling. If you still appear okay tomorrow, we can look at reducing it further, and maybe we can get you out of bed for a while."

A couple of hours later, I took Thomas out for a final run before bed. Although I was wary of seeing Nigel again, I had no choice but to go back to the grassy area. There was still a lot of activity happening in the back garden and beyond, but I didn't see a soul out on the street. In fact, Nigel's house was in total darkness. However, that didn't stop prickles forming at the nape of my neck. I was certain someone was spying at me from behind the curtains.

CHAPTER 10

The news of the body was all over the TV the next morning. Although unconfirmed, it hadn't taken a rocket scientist to connect the body with that of the missing teacher.

"Are they still outside?" Charlie asked as I placed his breakfast tray on his lap.

"Just a few stragglers remain. They must've taken the body away before it got light."

"Poor soul. I feel for her parents."

I nodded. "Me too. I can't imagine anything worse. Talking about parents, are yours still alive?"

"No. They died when I was nine years old. Miriam was nineteen—she brought me up."

"Gosh! That's awful. What happened?"

"Double suicide."

"What?" I shook my head, totally shocked that a couple could choose to kill themselves when they had children.

"Afraid so. Selfish bastards." He popped a spoonful of boiled egg in his mouth.

"Do you remember them?"

He closed his eyes in a prolonged blink. "I remember Mum

was a snivelling wreck most of the time—downtrodden would be how I'd describe her now. She was scared of her own shadow."

"And your dad?"

"A bully—the total opposite. I have no doubt he forced her to do it."

"But why? It doesn't make sense."

"I've puzzled on that all these years. He wasn't depressed, or not so you'd notice anyway. He had a few financial problems but nothing too bad. He'd taken voluntary redundancy from work and was due to be paid out, which would've paid off his debts, so it's a mystery."

"Do you think that's why Miriam didn't marry and have kids of her own? I mean, that's pretty devastating to have to deal with the death of her parents at that age and have to bring up a nine-year-old as well—must've been really difficult for her."

"I don't know. Maybe. She focussed on her career from an early age and was never really interested in men—or women for that matter."

"Hasn't she ever had a partner then?"

"Not that I know of." He finished his egg and placed the spoon back on the plate before picking up his mug of tea.

"And what about you? I heard about your girlfriend going missing. That must've been tough."

He closed his eyes and inhaled deeply.

"I'm sorry. I shouldn't…"

"It's okay. Laura vanishing like that still upsets me. I just wish I knew where she was. If she's safe—you know?"

I nodded.

He shook his head as though trying to rid himself of his painful thoughts. "Do you think I'd be able to get out of bed today?"

I sighed heavily. "I suppose so. I'll remove the feeding tube and the catheter. You can have a shower then, if you feel up to it?"

His cheeks reddened.

"What?" I asked.

He shook his head, avoiding my eyes.

"What?" I asked.

"I know this will sound silly after you've been caring for me all this time already, but the thought of you taking out the catheter is embarrassing."

"Don't worry. I'll close my eyes."

Charlie chuckled.

The schoolyard was a hive of activity when Phil arrived to drop Catherine off. It didn't take long before he heard the whispers—the missing teacher's body had been found.

His heart plummeted to his boots. Nobody knew of his connection to the German woman, he was certain of that. He'd told her how important it was not to tell a soul. However, he couldn't help but worry that the guilt was written all over his face.

Once Catherine was safely in her classroom, he made a dash back to his car. He should get some work done, but his heart wasn't in it. He headed home instead.

As he pulled up outside, he checked his watch—just after nine. He wondered what was happening down by the creek, and, instead of heading down his own path, he went next-door.

Lizzi opened the door moments after his knock. "Oh, hi, Phil. Come on in. Do you fancy a coffee?"

"Would love one, thanks." He followed her to the kitchen. "I just wanted to check how you are after your shock yesterday."

"I barely slept a wink. I couldn't get the image of the poor girl out of my mind."

"I can imagine. Have they finished back there now?"

"Yeah, I think so. I haven't seen anything for a couple of hours anyway." She filled the kettle and took two cups from the cupboard.

"I was watching them toing and froing until the early hours of the morning. I didn't see them remove the body though."

"I didn't either, but I presume they must've—they wouldn't leave her down there alone, would they?"

"I guess not." Phil got to his feet and moved to the window. "What do you think happened to her?"

"I don't have a clue, but I'm hoping it was just an accident. The thought of a killer walking amongst us freaks me out."

He spun from the window. "I'd best be off. I'll pop back later."

"What about your coffee?"

"Can I take a rain check? Oh, how did you get on with your patient? Did he wake up?"

"Yes. He seems fine. He's just having a nap and then he's going to have a shower."

"So, you did the right thing then?"

She shrugged. "Miriam might not agree."

"Who gives a shit what that old battle-axe thinks? She's out of order drugging him if he doesn't need it. You could report her."

"I hope it doesn't come to that."

I turned the TV off and jumped to my feet when I heard Charlie calling my name. "Coming," I called, rushing through to his room. "How are you feeling? Still fancy a shower?"

"Can't wait. Who was here earlier?"

"Phil. The neighbour. He's my friend."

"The widower?"

"Yes. Do you know him?"

"No. Just what Miriam has told me about him—plus I've seen him a couple of times in the back garden when I was visiting."

"He's nice. He lost his wife recently and they're still trying to come to terms with it—must be so difficult for the kids. But you'd know all about losing parents at an early age." I blushed, suddenly feeling a tad silly.

"Yes, it's the most unnatural loss of all. Your parents are supposed to be there for you till you grow up."

I wanted to disagree. The most unnatural loss of all was a parent burying a child, but I didn't intend to disagree. "Life doesn't always work out that way, unfortunately."

"Are your parents still alive?" he asked.

I nodded. "Yes, I'm lucky. I have experienced loss though— unnatural loss." I don't know why I said that. I wanted to bite my tongue as soon as the words were formed.

"Who have you lost?" Came the inevitable question.

"Oh, heck. Less of all this maudlin talk. Are you going to have that shower or what? It'll be bedtime again if you don't get your skates on." I set about unhooking him from the tubes.

Ten minutes later he was showering himself happily on the other side of the bathroom door.

CHAPTER 11

Phil peered from the living room window as a car pulled up onto his drive. His stomach dropped to the floor as he saw the two detectives had returned.

Taking several deep bracing breaths, he headed to the front door. "Detectives, what can I do for you?" He smiled as he swung the door wide open.

"We'd like to have another chat with you, if that's okay?"

"Certainly. Come on in." He led them through to the living room. "Can I get you anything—tea, coffee, juice?"

"Actually, I wouldn't mind a cold drink," the cute female detective said.

Her colleague nodded.

"Be right back." He retreated to the kitchen, his nerves clanging. Placing both hands on the work surface, he leaned forward, breathing heavily, trying to calm his raging heartbeat.

"Do you mind if I use your bathroom?"

The woman's voice startled him, and he spun around to see her standing in the doorway.

"Yes, yes, of course. Up the stairs, first door on the right." If she'd seen him, she didn't show it. If he was going to pull this off, he needed to be more careful. He poured two glasses of apple juice and carried them back through to the dining room. "Right then." He placed the glasses down on the table. "What can I do for you, detective... sorry, I can't remember your name."

"Detective Inspector Joel Karlson and this is Detective Constable Sharon Jones." He nodded at his colleague as she descended the staircase.

"Ah, yes. Sorry. I'm shocking with names."

"As you know, we're investigating the death of Erin Lieber, the schoolteacher."

"Yeah, I get that."

Detective Jones took a seat and picked up one of the glasses, drinking deeply.

"Can you tell me of any connection you had with her?" Detective Karlson said.

"None. Sorry, I didn't know her."

A confused glance passed between them. "Really?"

"Yeah. Why would I? What seems to be the problem?"

"We've been going through Miss Lieber's phone records, and we see there were several calls made between you and the dead woman."

Phil laughed. "You're kidding right? That's impossible. I didn't know her."

The detective pulled a notepad from his pocket. "August 28th, at 7:03pm. The call lasted over fourteen minutes. Then again on the 3rd September at 5:15pm lasting nine minutes. Another call was made by you on the 7th September lasting five minutes and finally on the night before her disappearance on the 12th September at 5:23pm lasting three minutes."

"Shit, man. Are you serious? I really don't know..." He paused and scratched his head. "Hang about, let me check my diary." He went into the lounge for his briefcase and pulled out his work diary. "Ah, yeah. Here it is. I had a call from someone called Emily —a foreign girl. She was looking for a place to rent. I told her I had no vacancies, but I expected to have some vacancies coming up in the next few days. She said, if she hadn't found anywhere, she'd call back, which she did—several times."

"Didn't you have any vacancies in the end?"

"No, I did. I called her and told her one had become available, but she would need references. She said she'd get back to me once she sorted them out, but I couldn't hold it for her. She rang back a few days later saying a friend of hers would go guarantor. She wasn't very happy that the flat had been rented out to someone else."

"So, you never met her?"

"No. I've already told you that. I didn't even know she was a teacher—I knew nothing about her other than her name was Emily."

"But it wasn't Emily, Mr Mathews. It was Erin."

"My mistake. But that hardly makes me a suspect does it?"

"Suspect? For what?"

"Murder."

"Nobody said she's been murdered, Mr Mathews. We're just trying to piece together her life before she went missing. That's all."

Phil shrugged and swallowed hard. "I just surmised she'd been murdered because you're sniffing around here. And besides, what was a young girl doing down at the creek?"

"That's what we intend to find out, Mr Mathews. Thanks for the juice." He got to his feet and drained his glass before handing it back to Phil, a knowing look in his eyes.

"You look like a new man!" I said as Charlie emerged from the bathroom dressed in grey jogging bottoms and a blue Adidas T-shirt.

"I must admit, I feel it. But I'm knackered again. I'm going to need another lie down."

"It's the meds. If you want, we can halve them again."

"Yes, I want. If I don't need the drugs, I'd rather avoid them."

"Let's get you back to bed, then. Have a rest before lunch."

"Can I just lie on the sofa instead? If I have to go in that room again, I'll go stir crazy."

"Of course. But what if somebody calls by?"

He shrugged. "Tell them I'm asleep on the sofa. It's the truth."

The phone rang as Phil watched the tail end of the detective's car drive away. "What now?" he growled, stomping to answer it.

"How's my gorgeous brother-in-law?" a husky female voice said.

"Alexis? Is that you?"

"Yes, it's me, you plonker."

"Where the hell have you been?" His sister-in-law had been on the missing list for the past two years. Not officially of course. Her parents knew her of old, but he'd been searching for her since Sam died.

"Long story, babe—I'll fill you in later. I'm so sorry to hear about Sam. I came as soon as I could."

"You came? Where are you?"

"I've just landed at Manchester Airport. I've got to hire a car, and I'll be on my way."

"You'll be staying here?"

"Yeah. That's alright, isn't it?"

"I guess so. Would've been nice to be asked though."

"Don't get shitty, Philip. I'm asking you now, aren't I?"

"Whatever. See you when you get here—if you don't get waylaid that is."

"Sarcasm doesn't suit you, lovely. See you soon." The phone went dead in his ear.

"For fuck's sake—that's all I need," he said, slamming the handset down on the base. Alexis had always been the same. Self-centred was her middle name. Her parents had said she'd turn up like a bad penny, and they'd been right again. But he wondered what problems she was bringing to his door this time.

He sat down on the sofa and buried his head in his hands. It was all such a mess. He contemplated calling his wife's parents but decided against it for now. He'd wait till he had the full story. Alexis may be the older of the two sisters, but she certainly wasn't wiser. If she was home, there would be a major reason behind it, of that he had no doubt.

"I've made ham salad sandwiches for lunch," I said, popping my head around the living room door. "You think you're up to it?"

"Sounds lovely," he said groggily.

"Do you feel any better?"

"A little. I'll be glad to get the drugs out of my system. I feel like a zombie."

"Yes, that's a natural reaction, I'm afraid. Shall I bring the food through, or do you think you can manage the dining table?"

"I should be fine to make it to the table. Then, when it's dark, I wouldn't mind going outside."

"Would it matter if you go out in the daylight? The back garden is only overlooked by Phil's family, and I'm certain he won't say anything."

"No. It wouldn't matter to me, but Miriam will have a fit. She's always insisted we keep my identity a secret."

"Why is that? Don't you think that's odd?"

"A little, but I'm used to her by now."

I shook my head in amazement.

"What?"

"I'm astonished you'd still protect her after what she's done to you, to be honest."

"What can I do about it? It's not like I can report my own sister."

"I know. But…" I shook my head. "Don't worry about it."

"Go on, spit it out."

"I don't want to speak out of turn, but I definitely wouldn't be dancing to her tune anymore. Then again, I'm pretty sure I won't be around for very long once she discovers what I've done."

"I'll employ you myself if I have to, so don't worry about it."

"We'll see."

CHAPTER 12

Four hours later, Alexis still hadn't arrived and Phil had to leave to pick up Catherine from school. He was glad he hadn't bothered to tell her parents after all. He figured she must've had a better offer on the way over—the selfish cow.

After considering whether or not to leave the door unlocked, he decided against it and bolted the back door from the inside—they didn't have a key, and it was usually left unlocked, but, if she happened to arrive while he was out, she would just have to bloody well wait till he got back.

"So, shall we do this?" I paused, one hand on the back-door handle.

"I'm game if you are," Charlie said, a mischievous grin on his face.

"Are you sure you don't want to wait till I've spoken to Phil?"

"No. I trust your judgement. And besides, I'm desperate to breathe in some fresh air."

"Okay then." I pulled the door open and stood back allowing him to step outside.

"Brrrr! Where did the summer go?"

"You know what the great British summers are like—blink and you'll miss it. Although this summer hasn't been bad, to be fair."

"Typical, and I missed it."

"Shall I look for a coat in the garage?"

"No, it's okay. I won't be out long."

I stepped out onto the path and followed him down the garden. Thomas had been desperate to get out there, almost as desperate as Charlie, but I didn't trust he'd behave yet. I'd taken him to the grass down the street a few more times, and thankfully I hadn't seen sight nor sound of Nigel.

Once around the garden and I could tell Charlie was flagging.

"Had enough?" I asked.

He nodded. "Wouldn't mind a drink."

"Come on. I'll put the kettle on."

"I didn't mean tea. I meant something a little stronger."

"Dream on, mister." I shook my head in mock disapproval.

"Okay, tea it is, then."

Suddenly, a woman I'd never seen before popped her head over the hedge. She had a shock of strawberry blonde curls and big blue laughing eyes.

I gasped and jumped in front of Charlie.

"Sorry, I didn't mean to startle you. I'm looking for my brother, Philip. Have you seen him at all?"

"Not since this morning, sorry. Maybe he's gone to pick up the kids from school."

"Ah, yes, that will be it. Never mind, I'll hang around till he gets back."

I nodded and turned towards the house.

"We were just about to make a pot of tea, if you fancy?" Charlie said.

I spun around to glare at him, my mouth agape.

"What I wouldn't give for a decent cup of tea. Turkish tea is nice, but it isn't a patch on good old English teabags."

"Oh, have you been away? That explains the tan," Charlie wittered on.

"Yeah. Just back after a two-year break."

"How exciting." He bent the hedge aside, giving her enough room to step through. I couldn't believe he was breaking all his own rules.

A little part of me suspected it was something to do with the pretty face and the amount of golden-brown cleavage on show. I caught his attention and rolled my eyes at him.

He grinned at me once again.

Leaving them to it, I entered the house to fill the kettle. The giddy chatter from them both was irritating the shit out of me. But they followed close behind.

"... and the sun is lovely, but it does get a bit boring after a while," she said.

Charlie shook his head. "I can't imagine that. I hate the cold."

"Plus, I missed the food here. Fish and chips. I've been dreaming of battered cod for months now."

It suddenly occurred to me she hadn't recognised him—unless she was faking, of course. But something told me this woman wouldn't notice anything if it wasn't about her.

"Take a seat." I gestured to the table. "I'm Lizzi. Sorry, I didn't catch your name."

"Alexis." She reached for my hand and pumped it enthusiastically before turning to Charlie. "And you are?"

"Charlie," he said, reaching for her outstretched hand. "Lovely to meet you, Alexis."

CHAPTER 13

Two cups of tea later, and Charlie and Alexis were getting on like a house on fire. Her cackling laughter made the hair stand up on the back of my neck. But Charlie didn't seem to mind it. Or maybe it was the jiggling excess flesh that had won him over. She'd definitely been at the front of the queue when they were dishing out boobs, whereas I had been at the far end.

Glancing down at my semi-flat chest, I felt my shoulders curl in self-consciously. I got to my feet to clear the table.

"You feeling okay?" I asked Charlie. He seemed fine, and I'd never seen him so animated, but I was worried he might be over-doing it.

"I'm fine," he said quietly, eyeballing me.

I reached for my phone and texted Phil.

Your sister's here. Pop in when you get back

I strolled to the front of the house and peered from the window. The sight of Nigel standing on the pavement directly outside startled me. He was staring in the window straight at me.

I jumped backwards, not sure if he could actually see me through the tinted glass, but what the hell was he looking at?

Keeping to the side of the window, I peeked around the curtain and realised he wasn't looking at me at all. He was staring down the side of the house into the back garden. Why would he be interested in what was happening back there? Goosebumps travelled down my entire body.

Just then, Phil's car pulled up alongside Nigel startling him and causing him to turn on his heel and march across the road towards his house.

Phil, Kate and Ben appeared on the drive moments later.

I opened the front door just as Phil rang the bell. "That was quick." I grinned.

Alexis suddenly rushed from the kitchen squealing like a lunatic.

Ben and Kate joined in with the squeals and launched themselves into her open arms.

Phil stood stock still, his mouth wide open, no sound coming out. What the hell was wrong with him?

I turned to see what he was looking at and spotted Charlie standing in the kitchen. It suddenly dawned on me. Unlike his sister-in-law, Phil had recognised him immediately.

I caught Phil's attention and placed a finger to my lips indicating he keep quiet then beckoned him in further.

He nodded and turned back to stare at the footie star, doing as I asked.

"Phil, Charlie—Charlie, Phil," I said, trying to keep the situation as normal as possible.

Phil shook Charlie's hand enthusiastically. "Hiya, mate. Pleased to meet you."

"Likewise. I've heard a lot about you."

Ben, Kate and Alexis were still talking excitedly, not paying the least bit of attention to the two men in the other room.

"Where's Thomas?" Kate suddenly asked when she heard the little dog yapping.

I stepped back into the hallway. "He's in the garage in his cage."

"Aw, poor doggy. Why is he in a cage?"

"His bed is in there, but, between you and me, he doesn't like being locked up." I winked at her.

Her cute little forehead furrowed. "Then why did you do it?"

"Because I can't trust him not to run off. I tell you what, if you want to come back later, we could take him for a little walk."

"Can I, Daddy?"

"If you're sure you don't mind," Phil said, looking at me.

"I'd enjoy it."

"Great. I'll send her over after dinner if that's not too late?"

"It would be perfect."

"Right. Let's be off and leave these good people to get on with their day," Phil said to everyone. "Thanks for looking after Alexis for me."

"No problem." I forced a smile to my face and opened the front door. Moments later they'd gone.

"Phew!" Charlie said as I returned to the kitchen. He was suddenly pale.

"Are you okay? That was a little chaotic, wasn't it?"

"I'll be fine. I might have a lie down though."

"Good idea. I'll give you a shout when dinner's ready. Did you see Phil's face when he saw you? He was hysterical—I was dying to laugh."

"I did. He won't blab, will he?"

"No. Although I can't vouch for Alexis. But to be fair she seemed oblivious—she's clearly only interested in herself."

"Ooh! Bitchy!"

I felt my cheeks flush. "No. Just an observation, that's all. Now go and lie down while I let Thomas out. You won't get any rest with him yapping his head off."

Phil was astounded to discover Lizzi's patient was none other than Charlie Maidley—the footballing legend. He had no idea what possible connection Miriam had to Charlie, but he was determined to find out. He intended to quiz Lizzi later.

Alexis was still talking ten to the dozen as she always did, but she'd put a smile on Ben's face and so he couldn't complain.

"Can we have fish and chips for dinner? My treat," she said.

"I guess so. I'll go and pick it up if you like?"

"No, it's okay. I'll go. Will you come with me, Ben?"

Ben nodded, beaming from ear to ear.

"I'll butter us some bread and make a pot of tea," Phil said, heading into the kitchen.

"Bliss," Alexis threw over her shoulder.

"Can I come too?" Kate asked.

"Why don't you help me instead?" Phil suggested, trying to distract his daughter. He hoped Ben would open up to his aunt if they had some quality time together. He'd not seen him so relaxed in months.

"Aww, but I've not seen Auntie Lexi in a long time." Kate's stroppy attitude warned him she was about to blow a gasket.

"Neither have I. And do you know who else hasn't?"

Kate shrugged.

"Nana and Gramps. How about you give them a call and tell them the good news?"

His daughter's face lit up and she nodded wildly.

Phil dialled his in-laws number and handed the phone over to her.

"Hello?" He could hear Eric's deep voice booming from where he stood.

"Hi, Gramps. It's Kate."

"Catherine, my dear, how are you?"

"I'm called Kate now. Daddy said it's okay."

"Alright. I'll try to remember that. How have you been?"

"Good. Did you hear about my teacher? She's dead."

"I did. Although I didn't realise she was *your* teacher. How terrible. Are you very sad?"

"Nah. I didn't know her very well."

Phil cleared his throat to catch her attention and then nodded at her to remind her of the reason for the call.

"Oh, Gramps, I've got something to tell you."

"Go on," he said, suddenly serious.

"Auntie Lexi's here. She's been somewhere that sounds like meat, and she's brown and a little bit fat."

"Catherine!" Phil said, laughing. "Maybe I should take over from here."

"Kate! Not Catherine." She scowled as she handed him the phone.

"Hi, Eric. How are you both?"

"We're fine. But what's all this about Alexis?"

"She turned up today. Apparently, she'd been in Turkey for the past two years—not got much more than that out of her yet as the kids have been around, but I thought you needed to know she's safe and well."

Eric grunted.

"You okay?"

"No doubt Viv will be overjoyed."

"But you're not?"

"You know how she is. She's nothing but trouble that girl. You mark my words—she'll turn us all upside down and then take off again, without a care in the world, leaving me to pick up the pieces and console her heartbroken mother again."

"I know, Eric. But she might've changed."

"When was she intending to call her mother?" This question proved his point.

"I don't know. But I'll tell you what—I'll get her to call after dinner if that's okay?"

He exhaled noisily. "It'll have to be, won't it?"

The phone went dead in his ear. "I don't know—talk about shoot the messenger."

"Did he shoot someone, Daddy?"

Phil laughed. "No. Not literally, anyway. But he's a little grumpy. Come on, let's butter the bread—they'll be back in a minute."

Ten minutes later, the tea was brewing, plates warming in the oven and a huge pile of bread and butter sat in the middle of the table.

Ben and Alexis returned, still talking each other's socks off. Phil smiled, relieved to see Ben with a spring in his step finally.

"Grub's up." I gently prodded Charlie who was lying on the top of his bed, snoring loudly.

Snorting like a pig, he sat up abruptly and wiped the drool from his chin.

"Sorry, I didn't mean to startle you. I made us some cheese on toast."

"My favourite." He ran his fingers through his short fair hair and swung his legs off the bed. "How long have I been asleep?"

"A couple of hours. I had forty winks myself, and now I'm ravenous."

We walked through to the kitchen and took our seats at the table.

Charlie began devouring the food as soon as his backside had hit the chair. It was as though he hadn't eaten for a week, but I knew he'd polished off a huge lunch earlier.

"After this, I'll be taking Thomas down the street for a walk. Do you fancy coming?" I asked.

"I'd love to, but I might need a coat or a jacket. It sounds horrid out there."

"I've seen something in the garage that should fit."

Once we were both wrapped up and ready for the off, I clipped Thomas to the lead and opened the front door.

"Ooh! I need to pay a visit—won't be a tic," Charlie said, turning and heading for the bathroom.

"I'll wait for you outside."

The wind sounded worse than it actually was, and I was surprised to find it was much milder than I expected. Stepping from the garden to the street, I stopped in my tracks as I almost collided with Nigel.

"Bloody hell, you frightened the life out of me then."

"No doubt you'll be on the phone to the cops, any minute, grassing me up for stalking you," he spat.

"Why? Is that what you're doing?"

"You know I'm not. I don't know what's wrong with women nowadays—a man just has to glance in their direction and he's in danger of getting done for sexual molestation."

"Do you really think trying to look down my top and stroking your cock through your pocket is harmless? Because if you do, you need to get a lesson in what is and is not acceptable in this day and age."

The expression on his face was priceless. "When? I didn't do anything of the sort. Women like you get off on pulling the rape card—no wonder the world is in such a mess."

"Women like me?"

"Yeah," he sneered. "You're all the bloody same."

I wanted to knock his teeth out. "The same as the type who are murdered because they wear short skirts, I suppose? You know, just like the dead teacher."

He spluttered. "Now you're putting words in my mouth. I didn't know she was dead when I said that."

Thomas began growling at him and baring his teeth.

"And that matters, does it? Fuck-off back to your own side of the street and stop coming over here trying to cop an eyeful." I heard the front door close behind me and remembered Charlie, but I didn't blink or drop my gaze for a second. Men like Nigel were used to intimidating women, and I wouldn't allow him to see how unnerved I was.

Nigel turned on his heels clearly lost for words.

"What the hell was that all about?" Charlie said, appearing behind me once Nigel had reached the other side of the road.

"He's just a nasty bully who needed putting in his place. Don't worry. I gave him as good as I got."

"You're telling me! I was about to intervene when I realised you were doing perfectly well on your own."

"I hate men like that. They have nothing better to do with their lives than intimidate women. I wouldn't allow him to drive a school bus if it was up to me." I was livid and intended to do exactly as he'd suggested and call the detective to update him as soon as I returned home. "Pull your hood up. If he gets wind of who you are, I can guarantee he'll tell the world."

We turned and began to stroll towards the grassy area.

"What did he say to you to cause that dressing down?"

"He was angry because I'd mentioned to the police that he'd made some inappropriate comments about the dead woman. That was before we actually knew she was dead. He's a sleazebag. It's his poor wife I feel sorry for."

"He's married? I bet he goes home and kicks seven bells out of her now because of you."

I gasped and my hand flew to my mouth. "Do you really think so?"

He grinned. "No. I'm kidding. But he *was* mightily pissed off. I bet he's never been spoken to like that before—especially by a woman."

"I've been scared of him for days, and something just snapped inside me. Maybe I was a little harsh, but I'm not sorry." My cheeks throbbed with the heat from my embarrassment.

"He'll certainly think twice before he approaches you again."
Charlie laughed.

"Shut it, you." I shoved him in the shoulder. "Or else you'll
be next."

"No! No! Please. I'll be quiet."

I shook my head, rolling my eyes to the heavens. "Idiot." I
grinned.

Nigel stomped home, absolutely livid. He'd only intended asking
the crazy bitch about the dead woman, and she'd almost bitten his
head off.

He slammed the door of his double-storey upside down house
and Joan appeared at the top of the stairs. "What the fuck are you
looking at, you fat cow?" he barked at her.

"Dunno—they don't label shit," was her retort.

He punched the bowl of knickknacks on the side table, and
sent everything flying, knowing it would drive her potty, then he
marched into his bedroom.

There'd never been much love lost between him and Joan. He
detested her and had done for years, but he didn't relish divorcing
her—splitting everything down the middle didn't appeal to him in
the slightest. He wanted the lot, but, short of killing her, he would
have to wait until she carked it of natural causes.

"Pick that up!" she screeched at him, but he slammed the door
muffling the sound.

Flinging himself on the bed, he closed his eyes and imagined
running up the stairs and punching her in the middle of her fat
fucking face. The only thing that stopped him was the fact that
she weighed three times more than him—he knew she'd beat him
hands down in a fight. The gobby bitch across the road, however,
was another story—he could easily overpower her. He slid his
hand down the front of his slacks and began stroking his rock-

hard cock, all the while imagining the snooty cow's eyes bulging from her face as he choked the life out of her.

A few minutes later, Charlie and I turned for home. My stomach dropped when I saw the silhouette of a man standing beside our front gate.

"Oh, shit. I think he's back," I hissed, feeling suddenly sick.

"More fool him," Charlie said.

As we approached, I played out the scenario in my head. I planned to create a fuss to give Charlie plenty of time to pass him by and hide in the house. My heartbeat raged in my ears.

Working myself up, I was determined not to let the nasty bastard intimidate me. I was over men thinking they could treat me like a metaphorical punch bag. As the man turned to face me, I exhaled noisily realising I'd not been breathing for a little while.

"Bloody hell, Phil. You scared me then."

"I did? Why?"

"Long story. Fancy a cuppa?"

"I'd prefer something a little stronger." He produced a bottle of red wine from his pocket.

"Now you're talking my language," Charlie said, patting Phil on the back.

"You're not having any." I laughed. "You're sick, remember."

"No, I'm not. You said I couldn't have any alcohol while I'm on drugs, but I haven't had any today, *remember?*" He mimicked me.

I shook my head again. "Impossible! Come on in, Phil. I'll get us some glasses."

We all went inside, and Charlie joined Phil in the living room while I went to grab a couple of glasses.

"Where's mine?" Charlie asked when I returned.

I rolled my eyes. "You can have *one*—a small one, mind. You are still my patient. Agreed?"

"What choice do I have?"

"Agreed?" I pressed.

"Okay, agreed. Cripes, you're bossy."

I half-filled one of the glasses and handed it to him, but I could tell he wasn't too thrilled with me.

He tipped the wine down his throat then turned and headed to his room. "I'm going for a lie down."

"Why didn't you tell me who you were looking after?" Phil hissed once we were alone.

"I was sworn to secrecy, and I'll have to ask the same of you, please. This can't get out."

"Don't worry, my lips are sealed. But I can't say the same about Alexis. If she gets any inkling of who Charlie is, she'll sell her story to the highest bidder. She's got no morals that woman."

"Seems a funny thing to say about your own sister."

"Sister-in-law. We're not blood related, thank god."

My stomach flipped. I'd seen the green-eyed monster where Charlie was concerned, but I was even more jealous knowing the voluptuous sex pot was sleeping next door with Phil, and they weren't actually related. "So, you don't get on, then?"

"We get on, I guess. But I wouldn't trust her as far as I could throw her, to be honest."

"Well, let's hope she doesn't get wind of who Charlie actually is then, otherwise we'll be bombarded with the press."

"She won't hear it from me, I promise." He made a lip-zipping motion. "But Ben is a massive fan of Charlie Maidley. I'm surprised he didn't see him earlier. He would definitely recognise him."

"Bloody hell, I didn't even think about the kids. But of course, why wouldn't he? Boys are football mad at that age."

"Ben definitely is. He'd die if he saw his idol was living right under his nose."

"Aw, maybe he can meet him one day. I can ask Charlie anyway."

"Have you asked him about the disappearance of Laura Sanders? She was my favourite page three girl, if it's not too un PC to admit."

"Briefly, but I don't want to pry—it's none of my business."

"Spoilsport." He grinned.

"Fancy another?" I reached for the bottle and poured the dregs into his glass. "I have another bottle in the kitchen."

"Why not? Would be rude not to." He laughed.

I hurried through to the kitchen and grabbed a bottle of Merlot from the wine rack. Then I turned and straightened my hair in the reflection from the kitchen window, not entirely happy with the results—not a patch on Alexis.

"Here you go," I said, returning to the living room.

"Lubberly-jubberly." He took the bottle from me and reached for the corkscrew.

"Tell me more about Alexis."

"What do you want to know?"

I shrugged. "What made you say all those things earlier? She seems a livewire."

"She's that and more. Alexis is nothing like Sam was—opposite ends of the spectrum, to be honest. She's got zero regard for her family and never has had. Did she tell you she did a moonlight flit over two years ago, and her poor parents have been out of their mind with worry? And then today, she just calls up out of the blue as though she's not got a care in the world."

"She did say she'd been in Turkey, but no, she didn't tell us anything else. That's terrible."

"That's Alexis." He cocked one eyebrow. "She didn't even come back for her sister's funeral."

"Really? Did she know?"

He shrugged. "Not sure. She said she'd heard once it was too late. But I don't believe her."

"Surely she'd have come back if she knew? Sam was her sister after all."

"Family has never been important to Alexis. She treats them as a hindrance."

"That's not how it looked earlier when she saw the kids. She was all over them."

He half smiled and nodded, a distant expression in his eyes. "Yeah, but it won't last. The only person Lexi loves is Lexi."

His forlorn expression broke my heart. "What was Sam like?"

He closed his eyes and took a deep breath before turning to face me. "She was perfect. And I know everybody says things like that about the dead—people seem to forget all their bad points and focus on their good. But in Sam's case it's true. She was the most selfless person I've ever met."

"You must miss her terribly."

"I do, although I went through a phase where I felt immense anger. A rage I never thought possible bubbled under the surface, and I thought I might explode with the intensity of it. But now I'm back to feeling sad."

I thought about my own doomed love life and sighed. At least I hadn't had a death to deal with—my ex was still alive and kicking, more's the pity.

"How about you? Do you have a significant other back home?" Phil asked as though reading my thoughts.

"Not anymore." I smiled, trying not to give anything away in my demeanour. "We're divorced."

"I'm sorry."

"Don't be. I'm not." I topped up his wine.

"Hey, go easy—I'll never get up in the morning," he said, still holding his glass out till it was full.

I giggled and topped up my own glass, feeling a little tiddly already.

"So, what happened?" He took a sip of his wine before placing the glass back onto the coffee table.

"With what?"

"Your marriage."

"Who knows? Not compatible, I guess." I closed my eyes and saw myself cowering on the kitchen floor while my husband kicked our unborn baby to death. I shuddered. I couldn't speak about that. It was still too raw, and maybe it would remain that way. Some things stay with you forever, and that was one of them for me.

"So, what will happen with Alexis now? Is she planning to stay?"

"She hasn't said. I asked her to contact her parents while I'm out, but I bet she hasn't. Alexis has always been a free spirit. Anything for a laugh. She seems to travel from one wild party to another, never tiring or stopping to think of anyone else. I can only imagine something's happened to cause her to come home to lick her wounds for a while. She's not here for us, no matter what she says. However, Ben seems happy to have her staying with us, and that can only be a good thing. He took the death of his mother extra hard, and I've been worrying about him. Tonight he seems back to his normal self."

"That's good then. Let's hope she doesn't just vanish and mess him up again."

"That's what I'm worried about. Both Ben and Catherine have struggled lately, and woe betide anyone who hurts them. That's all I can say."

CHAPTER 14

"So, he's gone then?" Charlie said, seeming a little pissy for some reason.

"Yes. Are you okay?"

He shrugged.

"What's that supposed to mean?"

"Well, would you actually care if I wasn't? You only had eyes for lover boy."

I was stunned. Was he joking? He didn't appear to be.

"Phil and I are just friends. What's wrong with you?"

"He'd like to be more than just friends, believe me," he said, his face twisted into an ugly version of himself.

"Well, to be perfectly honest, it's none of your business who I'm friends with, or more than friends with come to that. Your sister tried to warn me off him too, and I wouldn't accept it from her either."

"That's me told." He looked down at his feet.

"Would you like a drink?" I asked, begrudgingly.

"So long as it's not wine, eh?"

"Don't be like that. You know why I don't want you to drink alcohol."

"Yeah, well, it seemed you just wanted me out of the way earlier."

"Nonsense. You were more than welcome to stay."

"But you were happier when I left?"

I sighed, shaking my head. "Do you want a drink or not?" I snapped.

"Not."

"Fine." I flounced into the kitchen and filled the kettle, more than a little pissed off with the way everyone thought they could control my every movement. Well, I'd rather walk out than have to put up with any more of their shit.

Alexis and Ben were still up talking when Phil arrived home a couple of hours later.

"Hey, buddy. It's pretty late," he said, glancing at his watch. "Come on, you know the rules. It's a school night."

"It's my fault." Alexis smiled apologetically. "I didn't want to be left here alone."

Phil bit his tongue. This woman took the biscuit! She'd travelled the world on her tod. Why the hell couldn't she be left on her own for an hour? "Well, I'm back now. So come on, Ben, bed!"

"See you in the morning, Auntie Lexi," Ben said, kissing her on the cheek before heading off up the stairs.

"Fancy a nightcap?" Phil asked, indicating the drinks cabinet.

"Not for me, thanks. But I wouldn't mind a cocoa."

He almost choked on his own tongue. "A cocoa? Okay, who are you, and what have you done with my piss-head sister-in-law?"

She laughed. "Maybe I've grown up?"

"Pull the other one. It's got bells on."

"Seriously. I hardly ever drink anymore."

He peered at her through narrowed eyes. Alexis was the only woman he'd ever known who could put most blokes to shame with the quantity she could put away and still remain upright. "Since when?"

"Four months, give or take. I don't smoke either."

Now he knew she was taking the piss, but the more he looked at her the more he could see that she was indeed different, although he couldn't put his finger on what exactly.

"Did you go next door?" she asked.

He nodded.

"Are you sniffing around the lovely Lizzi?"

"No, I am not. We're just friends."

"Alright. Don't get on your high horse—it's a fair question. Is she knocking off that Charlie bloke?"

"No, I don't think so. He's her patient, nothing more."

"Oh, goody. He's hot. I wouldn't mind having a crack at him myself." And there she was, the Lexi of old.

"He's sick. Very sick. My advice would be for you to stay away from him. Do you hear?"

"Since when have I listened to advice?"

"Probably never. Which reminds me, did you call your parents?"

"No. I couldn't face their interrogation tonight. I'll call them tomorrow."

"Alexis, I promised your dad I'd have you call them tonight."

"And I will, tomorrow. Now are you going to make me that cocoa, or do I have to get Ben up again?"

———

In bed that night, I tossed and turned unable to get comfortable. My brain wouldn't settle. I couldn't get over the cheek of Charlie. Where did he get off speaking to me like that? I was his nurse, not his property.

As I watched the bright red numbers of the clock roll closer to morning, I made my decision—I would contact the hospital and arrange for someone else to take over from me. But how could I? I'd gone against Miriam's wishes. Any replacement would wonder why the heck they were caring for someone around the clock who appeared perfectly normal in every way.

And then what would happen when Miriam got back from her trip? She'd complain to the hospital about me, no doubt—then again, I could report her for keeping her brother drugged up when he clearly didn't need to be. I could go to the newspapers myself if they fired me. Let them all explain why they'd done what they did to a sporting hero.

I finally dropped off, only to wake with a start when Thomas jumped on the bed a couple of hours later.

"Shh, lie down, that's a good boy." I stroked his head and prayed it would have the desired effect. But chance would be a fine thing, Thomas licked my face excitedly. I loathed the stench of dog breath. "Okay, okay. I'm coming."

Dragging myself out of bed, I pulled on a fleece nightgown and followed the pesky mutt through the kitchen to the back door.

"Now, I'm trusting you again, sunshine. Don't you make me regret it." I opened the back door wide and watched as he ran outside and cocked his leg up against the table. Then my stomach dropped as the little terror took off towards the back hedge like a bat out of hell and vanished through the gap that had been made bigger by the toing and froing of the police.

"You are joking!" I cursed, stamping my bare feet.

"What's wrong?"

I whirled around to see Charlie standing directly behind me. "Thomas has shot off down the bank again," I said once I'd recovered.

"He'll be back. Shall I make you a coffee? Peace offering?"

I shrugged. Surprised he'd mention last night's performance. I had a feeling he might try to ignore it and continue as though it hadn't happened at all. I closed the door worried about leaving

Thomas outside alone, but I had no intention of following him down there again. Not a chance.

Charlie set about making a fancy coffee on the state-of-the-art machine, and I watched with interest. Dressed in white shorts and a fitted T-shirt he whistled as he went about grinding the coffee beans, and I took the time to check him out while he was preoccupied. Although much shorter and less muscly than the type of man I was usually attracted to, I found him incredibly handsome. His taut, compact physique was clearly built for speed on the football pitch and, even after being left to waste away in bed for a time, his shoulders still filled his T-shirt beautifully. Slight men weren't normally my thing, but I would make an exception in his case, if I was in the market for a man, that is. Fortunately, I wasn't —especially after his nasty display last night. I'd had enough of temperamental men to last me a lifetime.

"Milk?"

Startled out of my reverie, I nodded. "Just a drop, please." I got to my feet and scanned the back garden through the window still stressing about Thomas. I hoped he'd come back once he realised there was no longer a body down there.

Charlie placed two steaming cups on the table and sat down.

I reluctantly returned to my seat—still miffed and awaiting some attempt at an apology.

The sound of the newspaper delivery broke the silence, and Charlie jumped up to grab it, clearly feeling uncomfortable in the heavy atmosphere. His shocked face, when he returned, startled me.

"What is it?"

"This girl. I knew her." He pointed at a close-up image of the young woman I recognised immediately as the dead teacher.

"Really? Where from?"

"I'm trying to think. But I definitely know her from somewhere."

"But how? You've been here for ages and the hospital before

that. She's only been in the country for a few short weeks. Maybe she just resembles someone you know."

He shook his head. "I'd put money on knowing her. And I'll remember." He rubbed his temples. "But I need another lie down. I'm feeling quite woozy." He staggered and reached for the table to steady himself.

I jumped up, linking my arm through his and guiding him to his bedroom. "Maybe you've been overdoing it? You do have a brain tumour when all's said and done."

"Maybe. And Lizzi, I'm sorry about being a dick last night. I don't know what came over me."

"Don't fret. Let's get you on the bed before you fall down." I was concerned as he'd turned deathly pale all of a sudden. It must've been the shock of seeing the face of someone he recognised in the newspaper.

I got him onto the bed and stroked his clammy brow. "Shall I get you something to make you feel better?"

"No drugs. I just need to sleep."

"Are you sure?"

"I'll be okay. I promise."

Still smarting from that nasty bitch's comments last night, Nigel got ready for work. He knew he wasn't a popular guy, but it wasn't often anyone would stand up to him. In fact, he'd never had someone calling him out on it like she had done, other than his wife that is. Thinking about how his wife spoke to him triggered an instant rage.

"You still here?" Joan said, as he climbed the stairs to the kitchen.

"The fuck's it got to do with you?"

"Who's rattled your cage?" she sneered.

He jumped forward, grabbing her by the throat and slammed her into the fridge door.

Joan yelped like an injured puppy and her weakness spurred him on. His lips twisted in disgust. "You watch your fucking mouth when you speak to me, woman. I'm warning you. You hear me?"

Joan gripped his hands, her eyes bulging under the pressure.

Suddenly realising he'd gone too far, he let go and watched as she slid to the kitchen tiles as though her bones had turned to jelly.

Humming to himself, he straightened his shirt, stepped over her, and set about making a slice of toast for his breakfast.

CHAPTER 15

Phil handed the box of cereal to Kate. "Eat your breakfast, sweet-heart. We're running late."

"That's not very healthy, is it?" Alexis said, sipping her coffee. "Isn't it full of sugar?"

He rolled his eyes. "An expert all of a sudden, are we?"

"No. But I don't mind doing a bit of cooking to earn my keep. I could be on breakfast duty."

"Cereal's fine. It never did me any harm."

She glanced at his paunch and grinned as he sucked it in a bit.

"So, are you going to see your parents today?"

"God, no. I said I'd call them, not visit. That will require much more mental preparation."

"I don't know why you think like that—they're lovely and will be thrilled to see you, their only living child. I can't begin to tell you the effect Sam's death had on them, especially your mum."

It was her turn to roll her eyes. "No pressure, then."

Suddenly furious, Phil jumped to his feet. "I don't know how you can be so cold. They're good people and you've put them through hell. Tell me, Alexis, when the fuck do you intend to grow up?" He stormed up the stairs.

A few minutes later there was a tap on his bedroom door. Alexis popped her head inside. "I'm sorry, Phil. You're right. And, for the record, I do want to see them, but I know Dad will have a go at me. I know. I know. I deserve it, but I'm home for good this time, although I have no real place to call home. But, I mean, I intend to stay around here now."

Phil shrugged, taking her apology with a pinch of salt. "Until something more exciting presents itself, you mean."

"No. I'm serious. It's time I grew up and found a bit of stability in my life, but I don't blame you for not trusting me. I know I've been a bitch in the past, but I promise I've changed."

Phil looked at her long and hard. He had been a little surprised she hadn't touched a drop of alcohol or a cigarette since she'd arrived, but it was still early days. Could someone change so drastically overnight? He wasn't so sure. However, he was willing to give her the benefit of the doubt. "You can stay here as long as you like, you know that. But your parents still have your bedroom set up, and they might be offended if you don't want to go back there."

"But I'm thirty-eight years old, Phil. I don't want to live with my parents at my age. Besides, there's something I haven't told you."

"Oh, here we go." He braced himself. "What is it?"

"I'm pregnant. I'm going to be a mum!"

CHAPTER 16

I sat at Charlie's bedside watching him sleep. This was the first time in days he'd actually looked as ill as his hospital notes suggested. I contemplated administering his meds again. I wasn't his doctor, and, although I'd cared for hundreds of people over the years, it didn't give me the right to overrule the experts' decision. What had got into me? I would see how he felt later on, and, if he was no better, I'd give him a light dose. It seemed a shame though. I'd enjoyed his company, apart from last night's episode. He was charming and fun to be around.

I'd still had no correspondence from Miriam—not that I intended to tell her what I'd done over the phone or by email, but it was wrong of her not to check on us. I had her email address, and I suppose she thought I'd be in touch if there was a problem, but still.

The doorbell rang startling me from my thoughts.

I jumped to my feet and, with one final glance at my patient, I went to answer it. I was relieved to see Phil's face through the glass panel.

"Time for a cuppa?" he asked as I opened the door.

"Always." I smiled, stepping back and gesturing for him to

enter with a sweeping arm movement. "Have you just got back from the school run?"

"Yeah, and I can't face going next door yet. Alexis dropped a bombshell this morning."

"Let me put the kettle on, and you can tell me all about it."

He followed me through to the kitchen, and I set about making a pot of coffee. As I poured out two mugs, my stomach growled. "Have you eaten?" I asked.

"I had a slice of toast earlier."

"Fancy some scrambled eggs?"

"You can't keep feeding me." He laughed.

"Why not? I like looking after people, and, besides, it beats eating alone."

"Where's Charlie?"

"He had a funny turn earlier. He's sleeping, but I'm now questioning whether I was a little hasty stopping his meds."

"What does he say?"

"I haven't asked him, really." I got the tray of eggs out of the fridge and cracked four of them into a jug. "But he said he didn't want any drugs earlier."

"What will you do?"

"See how he is later. What more *can* I do?" I placed the jug in the microwave and set the timer for sixty seconds.

"So, what actually happened?"

"He seemed fine one minute, and then he recognised the dead woman on the front page of the paper, and it seemed to send him spinning."

"He recognised Erin—the teacher?"

I nodded.

"How? Where from?"

"I dunno. He doesn't remember where he knows her from, but he's pretty adamant he does. Then he went faint. It was a struggle to get him back to his bed, to be honest." I finished buttering a few slices of bread and placed them on the table.

"Hasn't she only been in the country for a few weeks? How could he possibly know her?"

"Yeah, that's what I said. Maybe she just looks like someone he knows."

The microwave beeped and I shared the eggs between two bowls and handed one to Phil. "So, what happened with Alexis?"

"Didn't I tell you there had to be a reason she'd come back?"

"Yes."

"I've been surprised how well she actually looks. She's put on a little weight, but it suits her—I've never seen her look so good, to be honest."

My stomach dropped. I'd hoped he was oblivious to the sex appeal of the beautiful, curvaceous woman he had staying in his house, which surprised me. If I wasn't interested in him, why would I be so bothered?

"She's even given up smoking and drinking, which seems too good to be true, but this morning she told me the real reason behind it all."

"Go on."

"She's pregnant."

"Ah—makes sense then, I guess. But why's that so bad? Who's the dad?"

"Some Turkish bloke. She's done a runner from him, and she doesn't want him finding her, so I'm sure she's not being totally honest with me about him yet."

"What will she do? Surely it will be easy for him to find her if he puts his mind to it." I shoved a forkful of eggs into my mouth.

"I've no idea. I've told her she can stay with me for as long as she needs to, but I'd prefer her to go home to her parents. It would be just what they need—a little baby to distract them from everything else."

I knew he meant the death of his wife. "Do you have enough room for her *and* a newborn baby?"

"She can have the spare room—it's big enough for a cot if she decides to stay, and she can help me with the kids. Ben really loves having her around at least. These eggs are really good, by the way."

I nodded, unsure of how much I should interfere. "It's one thing having a family member visit for a while, but quite different altogether to have them move in permanently, especially with a baby."

He scratched his cheek with the end of his fork. "We'll have to play it by ear. I still don't believe she's changed—it's too drastic. She's selfish. Always has been."

"Motherhood has been known to soften the hardest of hearts." I touched my painfully empty stomach still overwhelmed by the love I'd felt for the child I'd lost.

"I know, which is why I'm willing to give her the benefit of the doubt."

"Hey. How are you feeling?" I asked Charlie a couple of hours later.

"Better, thanks. Sorry about that this morning. I don't know what came over me."

"You're a sick man. I guess we need to expect you to feel less than wonderful on occasion. Do I need to up your meds again?"

"No. I'm fine now. And I remember where I knew that girl from."

"Really? Where?"

"She was kissing and canoodling with your neighbour when I visited Miriam a few weeks ago."

"My neighbour?" My first instinct was Nigel. But why would a young, attractive woman be kissing that horrible old man?

"Phil," he said. "I watched them through his kitchen window when I was out walking Thomas. It was definitely her."

My heart stopped.

Leaving Joan spark out on the kitchen floor, Nigel strutted from the house his head high and his chest expanded like the cock of the north. That would teach the old battleaxe not to give him attitude. He'd had about as much as he was willing to take from her and also intended to wipe the smug smile off that bitch's face across the road. He sniggered. No more mister nice guy.

Phil headed to the current renovation project he'd been avoiding since Sam died, even though he still wasn't in the mood. However, the prospect held far more appeal than returning home did.

He wondered if Alexis had called her parents like she'd promised. He could imagine Viv would be sitting on top of the phone willing it to ring.

He'd hated the way Alexis treated them in the past and prayed she'd turned a corner like she said she had.

I was stunned. How could it be possible? Phil hadn't mentioned knowing Erin when we'd discussed it. In fact, from the conversation, I presumed he'd never laid eyes on her.

"You must be mistaken."

"Well, I'm not. I may be many things but mistaken isn't one of them. I have a photographic memory when it comes to faces. Believe me, that girl was all over your mate like a rash in his kitchen a few weeks before she died. I suggest you call the old bill."

My legs suddenly felt weak, and I gripped the chair before plonking down on it. "Maybe I should talk to him first? There could be some reasonable explanation."

"Not a good move, Lizzi. You could be his next victim."

"Ridiculous! You *actually* think he killed her? You're off your rocker!"

Charlie shrugged his shoulders. "Well, somebody did, and, let's face it, he's not exactly being honest about his involvement with her, is he? Let the police decide. I'll call them if you like?"

My mind was in a spin. How could I allow him to call the police without discussing it with Phil first? "Can you give me a couple of hours to get my head around it?"

"You're going to call him, aren't you?"

I shook my head, but I could tell he didn't believe me. "Look, it's almost one o'clock. Let me go and see him when he gets home, and I'll ask him a few questions. I won't tell him what you said. I promise. I just want to ask him outright if he knew her, that's all."

"And then you'll let me call the police afterwards?"

"I promise."

———

At just before four I heard Kate in the back garden.

"Okay, Charlie. I'm heading next door. Won't be long."

"If you're not back in half an hour, I'll send out a search party." He grinned.

"Don't be silly. I'm sure you have this all wrong."

Shaking his head, he rolled his eyes. "Whatever. See you when you get back. Unless you want me to come with you?"

"No, you stay here. I don't want to arouse any suspicion. If you *are* right, I just want to act as normal as possible and see his reaction."

"Good luck."

Moments later, I was knocking on Phil's front door. Alexis opened it with a whoosh startling me.

"Oh, hi. Is Phil home?"

"Not at the moment. He won't be long though. Come on in,

and I'll make us a cuppa. I've been meaning to invite you over for a chat."

"Really?" I stepped inside and into the dark hallway realising I hadn't actually been inside before.

"Come on through," Alexis said walking ahead of me through a door at the end of the hall.

I noticed the sway of her behind–everything about her was designed to be purely sexual. I'd presumed she'd put it on for Charlie's benefit the other day, but now I realised it was all natural—another reason for me to hate her.

"Lizzi!" Kate said as I entered the huge square kitchen-diner. "Did you bring Thomas with you?"

"I didn't. He's asleep on the sofa. You could come over later though, if your dad says it's okay." As the words left my mouth, I realised how unlikely that was. If Charlie did indeed call the police, there would be no more friendship.

"Tea? Coffee?" Alexis said, indicating I take a seat at the large wooden table next to Kate who was busily colouring in an intricate-looking butterfly picture.

"Tea sounds nice. So, where did Phil go to?"

Alexis shrugged as she placed two teabags in a pot. "He's not been back all day. He called me to pick up Kate from school and said he was on his way home and wouldn't be long."

"Auntie Lexi is making dinner, but I don't want it."

Alexis rolled her eyes to the ceiling. "Don't start this again, Catherine. I promise you'll love it."

"I told you. My name is Kate!"

I pressed my lips together in amusement. "What are you making?" I asked Alexis.

"Fish finger sandwiches," she said proudly.

I laughed. "What's wrong with fish finger sandwiches?" I turned to Kate.

"I don't want to eat fish's fingers." A look of disgust crossed her face.

"They're not really fish's fingers. You do know that, don't you?"

"That's what Auntie Lexi said. But I don't believe her."

"But fish don't have hands, so how can they have fingers?"

Kate paused her colouring in as though in deep thought. "So, if they're not fish's fingers, what are they then?"

"Just fish made into delicious finger shaped sticks."

"I've craved fish finger sandwiches since I moved to Turkey. The food just wasn't the same over there. I've bought all the ingredients—mayo, tomato sauce, white bread—it has to be white bread. Nothing else will do."

"Sounds scrumptious."

Alexis smiled, clearly thrilled. "Stay for dinner, if you like?"

"Oh, will you, Lizzi?" Kate squealed.

"I can't, I'm sorry. I have to make dinner for Charlie. He's not been too well today."

"What's wrong with him?" Alexis asked.

"I shouldn't really say, patient confidentiality and all that. I'm sure he'll tell you himself if you ask."

"Can't believe he's single. He's a real catch. Unless..." She looked at me, her eyebrows raised.

"No. Nothing like that between us."

"Oh, good. I mean, I wouldn't want to step on anybody's toes. We got on like a house on fire the other day."

"Go for your life." I smiled, thinking she wouldn't be so keen once she discovered what Charlie had in store for her brother-in-law.

"Oh, good. I might pop in to see him later and take him one of my fish finger butties."

I grinned and nodded. For all of her sexiness and huge baby blues, she was not a patch on me in the culinary department.

"Daddy's home." Kate jumped off the chair just as the kitchen door swung inwards.

"Hey, squirt. That was a nice welcome. I'll have to come home late more often if that's the fuss I get." He dropped to his knees and pulled her into a bear hug.

"Hardly late." Alexis reached for the kettle. "It's not even five o'clock."

"This is late for me. I'm usually at the school gate. Thanks for picking her up, by the way."

"My pleasure." She held up the teapot. "Fancy a brew?"

"I'd love one, thanks." Phil stepped further into the room and suddenly spotted me. "Oh, hello. I didn't see you there. How are you?"

"I'm fine. I was just at a loose end and thought I'd visit you for a change."

"Only, you weren't here and so she had to make do with me, instead." Alexis grinned and handed him a cup.

"I hope you pulled out all the stops?" He gave me a cheeky wink.

"Of course. We were perfect hostesses, weren't we, Catherine —er, Kate?"

Kate nodded. "Did you know fishes don't have fingers? They don't even have hands!"

Phil barked out a laugh. "Well, you learn something new every day."

"And we're having fish's fingers butties for dinner tonight, aren't we, Auntie Lexi?"

"We certainly are, sweetheart." Alexis looked pleased with herself.

"Where's Ben?" Phil asked.

"He's not come home yet."

"Really?" Phil looked at his watch. "He usually calls if he's going to be late. I'd best call him." He stepped back into the hallway.

I took the opportunity to get the conversation started about Erin. "Did Phil tell you about the dead teacher?" I asked Alexis.

"He certainly did. Isn't it terrible? I can't believe something like that can happen around here. You found her, didn't you?"

I nodded. "Well, Thomas did. It was quite a shock, I can tell you."

"What was?" Phil said, reappearing in the doorway.

"We were just discussing Erin," I said quietly, nodding at Kate who had returned to her colouring book on the table.

"Ah, yes. Nasty business, that was. But don't worry about Ben —he's gone to his mate's house for dinner."

"That's good," I said. "I guess everyone must be on pins now with someone you all know being murdered like that."

Phil nodded.

"Did you? Know her, I mean."

"I knowed her," Kate said.

I looked at Phil again. He appeared uncomfortable and struggled to return my gaze. "Nah! I didn't know her. Why do you ask?"

"No reason. I just realised I hadn't asked you. I told you this morning Charlie thought he recognised her, and he thinks he saw her around here when he paid Miriam a visit." I could've bitten my tongue off—I'd always been a crap liar—the truth was bound to burst from my mouth sooner or later.

Two deep grooves appeared between his eyebrows. "Really?"

"Apparently so." I felt disappointed at his response, and I actually didn't believe him. Now I had to go back and admit to Charlie he was probably right after all.

CHAPTER 17

"So?" Charlie said as soon as I was through the door.

"As I thought, he said he'd never met her."

"He's lying. You agreed I could call the police, and I think I need to."

I shrugged. "Do what you must."

He picked up the handset and headed through to his bedroom. I could hear his muffled voice through the door. Ten minutes later, he emerged, a self-satisfied grin on his face.

"Well?"

"They were very interested. Let's see if they act on it or if they were just paying me lip service."

Anger bubbled in the pit of my stomach. How could he be so smug about getting someone he knew into trouble? "How would you feel if someone pointed the finger at you for Laura's disappearance?"

"Whoa! Where did that come from?" He put his hand to the centre of his chest dramatically.

"Just saying! You don't have to be so fucking pleased with yourself."

"I'm not pleased with myself, Lizzi. And, for your information,

I was questioned at length after Laura vanished, and they soon realised they had nothing on me."

I exhaled noisily. "I know. I'm sorry. I shouldn't have said that. It was wrong of me."

"You're defending your friend, I get that."

Nodding, I jumped up and busied myself, tidying the cushions.

A movement outside the window caught my attention. Nigel sauntered past the driveway eyeballing the house. He was another problem I had. I seemed to be making enemies left, right and centre. Maybe it was time for me to pack my bags and leave for home.

CHAPTER 18

Nigel could see her silhouette through the living room window. Did she think he couldn't? Fucking high and mighty bitch needed taking down a peg or two.

He crossed the road dreading what awaited him at home since his spat with Joan that morning. He regretted his actions now. Not because he hadn't enjoyed showing his wife who was boss, but because he knew not to underestimate her. Theirs had always been a volatile relationship, but he was usually the underdog, and he knew it wouldn't go down well with her. He imagined her sitting at the top of the stairs waiting for him with a pan or a baseball bat raised over her head. She'd always been a nasty, simmering bitch, while he was the opposite—a flare of temper and then he calmed down.

This was the reason he'd stayed away all day—hoping she would've had the chance to calm down by now. After his morning schoolbus run, he'd paid a visit to the local casino where he'd blown an entire week's pay. Then he'd returned to school to do the afternoon run.

As he approached the house, his nerves were getting the better of him. He'd felt so cocksure of himself earlier when the adrenaline had been buzzing through his veins. Why couldn't he keep that level of intensity? March straight in there and tell her to back the fuck off and just deal with it. He was the man in the relationship, not her.

He opened the door and stepped inside. "Hi, honey. I'm home," he called up the stairs sarcastically.

No answer.

Taking off his jacket, he trudged through to his bedroom and threw it on the bed, emptied his pockets, placing his wallet and keys on the hallstand then headed upstairs to face the music.

As he reached the top step, his heart stopped dead.

Joan was still lying in the same position he'd left her in hours ago. What the hell had he done?

Dropping to his knees beside her, he fumbled at her bruised throat, relieved to feel a faint pulse.

"Joan! What the heck? Come on, my love. Wake up." He slapped her cheeks, hoping for some response. There was none.

"For fuck's sake, Joannie, what have you done?" He got to his feet and reached for the phone dialling 999, but, before it could connect, he hung up. How could he call the police? He'd be blamed regardless of the cause, especially with the definite finger marks around her neck. He replaced the handset and returned to her side, wringing his sweaty hands in distress. He tried to lift her, but her humungous bulk was far too heavy for him. He grabbed her by the feet instead and dragged her into the living room. Her head managed to connect with every object along the way and a sickening smack off the antique sewing machine table made him pause and try to be a little more careful. "Why do you always have to be so fucking awkward?" he ranted. As he glanced back to where he'd dragged her from, he noticed a wet trail followed her sprawling body.

"Have you pissed yourself?" He shook his head in disbelief. His fucking day couldn't get any worse. "Honestly, why can't you be like any other woman and take a hiding for what it is? A reminder of who's boss. You've got away with things for far too long, by the way. But now it's going to look as though you're the victim! Have you ever heard anything so fucking hilarious? All these years I've put up with your backchat and nagging, and now *you're* the victim! Typical! Fucking typical."

Once he had her lying in the centre of the room, he unfastened the buttons on her huge cotton nightie, realising it was sopping wet with not only piss, but a smear of disgusting runny yellow shit too. "You're a fucking disgrace, woman. You hear me?"

He couldn't believe it. What a mess. How unlucky was he? Any other time he'd be reaching for the phone to call an ambulance, and would get someone else to clean her up, but any other time she wouldn't have huge blue bruises covering her neck. He'd be hauled over the coals for this, without a doubt. He had no choice —he would need to care for her himself for a while, at least until the bruising faded. She'd come right—he was certain.

CHAPTER 19

Phil walked Lizzi to the door and waited until he heard her front door close behind her. She'd definitely seemed preoccupied by something—maybe she'd wanted to talk about Charlie but couldn't because of Alexis. He'd call in to see her later, maybe.

"Lizzi said I can go over there after dinner to see Thomas," Kate said as he returned to the kitchen.

"We'll see, squirt." He stroked his daughter's head. "Why don't you go on upstairs and get out of your uniform and wash your hands for dinner?"

"Aw, but…"

"Come on. You know the rules—uniform first."

She jumped from her chair and stomped up the stairs.

He turned his attention to Alexis who was dressed in a long, flowing gypsy-style dress and was busy arranging fish fingers on a tray as though the precise placement of them would alter the flavour somehow.

"Did Lizzi seem okay to you?" he asked.

"Yeah. Fine. Why?"

He shrugged. "No reason. I just sensed something was off. That's all."

"Not that I could tell—I thought she seemed fine. Right, I'm going to prepare my very own sauce for these beauties." She got a huge jar of mayonnaise from the fridge and a bottle of tomato ketchup from the cupboard.

Phil watched as she made a production of mixing equal quantities of each into a bowl and stirring it to within an inch of its life. Hardly her own sauce, but who was he to knock it—at least this meant he didn't have to make dinner tonight, which was a plus, so he'd just go along with things. "Wow! I've never seen that before," he gushed.

"Really? Didn't you know this was how to make your very own thousand island dressing?"

He wanted to laugh out loud but curbed his amusement by pressing his lips together and bending to untie his shoelaces. "No, I didn't. The second thing I've learned today. But if you've got dinner covered, do you mind if I go and have a shower? I feel grimy."

"Of course not—dinner will be ready in twenty minutes."

"Fantastic! Thanks, Alexis."

Once he'd cleaned his wife's most intimate of places—somewhere he hadn't been near in years—he propped several pillows under her head and covered her with the duvet off her bed.

"Right, Joannie, that must feel a little better—don't say I never do anything for you." He lifted one of her eyelids and noticed the eye was severely bloodshot. Had he actually done that? Surely not. It must've been a stroke or a heart attack, maybe after he'd left for work. Trust her to do this to him—fucking inconsiderate bitch.

He went into the kitchen to start preparing dinner. He needed to feed her if he was to keep her alive and well until the bruising cleared up. Forty-five minutes later, he dished up two plates of mincemeat and onions, with a dollop of mashed potato on each.

"Right, Joannie, grub up," he said jovially, as he entered the living room again. Turning on the TV, he settled down to eat his meal—shame to let it go cold while he tried to feed her. She wouldn't notice any difference hot or cold so she could wait.

The sound of a car pulling up outside his house had him back up on his feet, and his heartbeat quickened when he saw a police car. "What the hell?"

He turned back to his wife. "Come on now! You've had your fun, Joan. The fucking cops are here, and I need you to wake up." He nudged her with his foot.

She didn't respond.

"You're just an evil fucking bitch, aren't you?" he snarled.

Heading down the stairs, he took two steps at a time, hoping to be able to head the police off before they reached the house— guessing his earlier call had registered somehow. But the police car was empty, and there was no sight of them up or down the street.

Realising they hadn't been there for him after all, he trudged back upstairs to eat his now cold dinner in peace.

Half-an-hour later, he shovelled a spoonful of mashed potato and gravy into Joan's mouth. "Swallow it. That's a good girl."

But she didn't.

He held her mouth closed and covered her nose, trying to encourage her to swallow.

Still nothing.

"If you don't swallow it, you stupid bitch, you'll die—is that what you want? Do you want to fucking die?" he yelled into her face.

Holding her by the shoulders, he shook her violently.

"Suit yourself! Go without. See if I care."

As he stepped out of the shower, Phil heard the doorbell sound.

Grabbing the towel, he dried his hair and then wrapped the towel around his waist.

Footsteps running up the stairs were followed by a tap on the bathroom door. "Phil?" Alexis hissed through the door. "The police are here, and they're asking for you."

A feeling of dread landed between his shoulder blades. Had they finally discovered his connection to Erin? For the first few days following her body being found he'd expected it, but only this morning he'd thought that maybe he'd dodged a bullet. He should've known better. "I'll be right down," he called.

Waiting till he heard her descend the stairs, he ran across the hall to his bedroom and dressed in grey jogging bottoms and a white T-shirt. Taking a deep, bracing breath, he plastered a smile on his face and headed down to face the situation head on.

The male detective from the other day was standing by the kitchen window while Alexis was fawning all over his sidekick—a handsome, dark-skinned young man.

"Gentlemen, what can I do for you?" Phil asked, trying to keep his voice as upbeat as possible.

"Hi, Mr Mathews, Remember me? DI Joel Karlson and this is my colleague DC Wayne Campbell."

"Yes, of course." He shook hands with both officers. "What can I do for you?"

"We'd like to ask you a few more questions, if that's okay?" He eyeballed the hallway at the sound of Kate bounding down the stairs.

"Why don't we go through to the living room?" Phil led the way.

Once they were seated, DI Karlson took charge while his colleague took notes.

"When we questioned you the other day, you indicated you'd spoken to Miss Lieber, but you hadn't actually *met* her—is that correct?"

"That's right." Although he tried to keep his voice from quivering, he was conscious of a definite tremor. He hoped they couldn't hear it.

"We have reason to believe that not only did you meet her, but that you knew her intimately—what do you say to that?"

His mouth suddenly dry, he tried to swallow but a lump caught in his throat.

"Mr Mathews?"

"I-er..."

"Mr Mathews, I think you need to accompany us to the station. Do you need to arrange childcare?"

Phil nodded. "My sister-in-law will look after the kids. I'll just get my shoes and coat."

CHAPTER 20

I couldn't relax. The sight of the detectives marching Phil across the road to their car had sat uneasy with me. Surely they didn't think he could be guilty of murder? But they must—otherwise why would they arrest him?

"Satisfied now?" I barked at Charlie as he emerged from the bathroom wrapped in a towel.

"Not particularly. Why? What's happened?"

"They frog-marched Phil off to the station, that's what happened. But don't worry yourself about it. I hope you enjoyed your soak in the bath."

"I'm sorry, Lizzi, but I have a right to inform the police of something I've seen, whether you like it or not. It's a murder inquiry for Christ's sake."

"Did you though?"

"Did I what? Have a right to…?"

"No, stupid. Did you actually see the dead girl with Phil or is this just another of your petty jealousies?"

"I refuse to get into this with you. And may I remind you of the fact you're staff, and if you feel you can't trust my motives then you're welcome to get out of here whenever you please."

I saw red. "And may I remind you, you'd be drugged up and out of it still if it wasn't for me. I'm suddenly understanding why your lovely sister might want to do that to you. It's all starting to make sense now." As the words left my mouth, I regretted them, especially when I saw the hurt expression on his face. "I'm sorry. That was uncalled for. I just feel bad for Phil, but I shouldn't be taking it out on you. Forgive me?"

Charlie looked me up and down, disapproval pouring from his eyes, and, without another word, he turned and entered his room, closing the door firmly behind him.

CHAPTER 21

Nigel woke with a start when the TV remote slid off his lap. It took a few seconds before he remembered where Joan was. She hated him sleeping in front of the TV and would always prod him to go to bed even if he dozed off for a second.

Groaning, he got to his feet and moved to her side. "Did you swallow your food yet?"

He placed his little finger into her mouth and pried her jaws open. Brown mashed potato covered the end of his finger. That enraged him.

"For fuck's sake, Joan, this is ridiculous now—you've made your point." He knew he had to get something inside her, or he'd be done for murder, not just battery. He had no choice but to remove the food from her mouth in case she choked on it.

Opening her jaws again, he hooked his forefinger inside and scooped the food back into the bowl. It took several attempts to clear her mouth out completely. How the hell was he going to get her to eat something?

Maybe water would work?

He took the plates through to the kitchen and filled a glass from the tap before returning to her side. "Right, Joannie, come on. I need you to play ball with me this time." He lifted the glass to her lips and tilted it slightly.

The water entered her mouth then dribbled out again and down her chin in two rivers, pooling on the duvet.

He thought she'd swallowed some, but he couldn't be certain. What he needed was a syringe or a turkey baster. Something he could aim at the back of her throat.

Back in the kitchen, he searched the utensil drawer for something, anything that might just do the trick, but he couldn't find anything.

Spying the washing up liquid bottle, he pounced on it, emptying the contents into a cup, he gave it a quick swill under the tap before filling it with cold water and rushing back to Joan's side. He placed the pop-up lid inside her mouth and squirted a small amount of water at the back of her throat. He couldn't believe it when he saw a slight movement and watched the water vanish.

A relieved sigh escaped him. "Thank Christ for that! You had me worried there, Joannie, that you did."

He repeated the action several more times until he was satisfied she'd drunk enough. Then he removed the damp towel from between her thighs and replaced it with a clean one and kissed her on the forehead. "Goodnight, my love. See you in the morning."

Phil couldn't believe it. How the hell had they worked it out? He'd told no-one and neither had Erin, as far as he knew. It wasn't as if they were serious or anything—at least he hadn't been serious, anyway. She'd surprised him how uninhibited she was for her age. Clearly girls were far more promiscuous and had looser morals than back when he'd been dating.

He sat in the police car going over and over what he should tell them. Whatever he said now would sound like a crock of shit—he should've just been honest with them from the start. But he'd been aware how it would look. He was almost twice her age.

When they arrived at the station, the detectives took him in through the back door and up a flight of stairs to a stark white-painted interview room housing nothing but a table, four chairs and *the* most annoying clock in the history of man. The loud tic, tic, tic was certain to drive him mad. Then they left him stewing for an hour.

When DI Karlson eventually returned, he was accompanied by the female detective from last time. He carried a mug of milky tea, which he placed in front of Phil. "I hope you don't take sugar," he said.

Phil shrugged feeling it didn't need a verbal response.

"You remember my colleague, Detective Constable Jones, don't you?"

"Of course." Phil nodded. "Am I under arrest?" The time alone had given him the chance to think, and he'd decided the truth was the only way forward. It wasn't as though he'd done anything wrong—although young, she'd been a consenting adult for Pete's sake.

"No, you're here to answer a few questions, that's all," DI Karlson said.

"Do I need a solicitor?"

"That's entirely up to you. I can call one for you if you like?"

"No, that's okay—I've got nothing to hide."

"So, Mr Mathews," Detective Jones said.

"Please, call me Phil."

"Phil." She smiled and looked down at her notes. "Maybe you can fill us in on your involvement with Erin Lieber and the reason you failed to report it earlier."

"It was as I said—she'd called looking for somewhere to rent when she first arrived from Germany. Someone she knew had rented a room off me a while back and gave her my number."

"So, what happened?"

"I told her I had nothing available, but she sounded desperate. I said I had a room above my workshop, but it was a bit fumey as I store all my paint and stuff there. Like I said, she sounded desperate, and I felt sorry for the girl. We met the following afternoon at the workshop. But she'd been offered a room in town above the bookies by then, so she didn't need it."

"Then what?"

"She was very beautiful and a real flirt. She made me feel good, and so I asked her if she wanted to meet for a drink—the kids were due to go to their grandparents for the weekend. I arranged to pick her up on the Friday night. I took her for a Chinese, then we went back to my place."

"What date was this?" DI Karlson asked.

"I can't remember off the top of my head, but it was the first weekend after she arrived in the country."

He pulled a pad from his pocket and flicked through a few pages. The Friday after she arrived was the 30th August—does that sound about right?"

Phil nodded. "Yeah, I guess so."

"What happened then?"

"She stayed the weekend and I dropped her in town before I went to collect the kids at around 2pm on Sunday afternoon."

"And that was it?" Detective Jones asked. "You didn't see her again?"

Phil contemplated lying again and then thought better of it. He shook his head. "As you know, she called me a couple of times after that, but I told her I didn't want to get into anything serious. She was persistent, I'll give her that."

"You mean she kept calling?" Jones said.

Phil shook his head. "No. She turned up late one evening. Tapped on the kitchen window and almost scared me out of my skin with her face squished up against the glass all distorted—her nose pressed to the side of her face. We both laughed hysterically at that and, in a moment of weakness, I let her inside."

"And she spent the night?" She raised her eyebrows suggestively.

"No. I didn't want the kids to see her. They're still mourning their mother—especially Ben. That's why I told her to stay away in the first place."

"Then why let her in?"

He shrugged. "I dunno. Lonely, I guess. She just caught me at the right time."

"How long did she stay?"

"An hour or two. We had a passionate half hour, then a couple of glasses of wine in the living room after that."

"Was that the last you saw of her?" DI Karlson asked.

"Sadly, no. I bumped into her at the school. I almost shat a brick when I saw her in my daughter's classroom. She approached me but I gave her a warning look and backed off. But when I picked Catherine up that day, she cornered me at the gate."

"What did she say?" Detective Jones edged closer in her seat, clearly thinking she was about to get a breakthrough.

"That she wanted to see me again—no strings. I told her to forget it. Especially now I knew she was my daughter's teacher. From then on, I dropped Catherine off at the gate and waited for her in the car. I didn't want any more awkward conversations. I didn't see her again. The first I knew about her being missing was when two women from school knocked on my door with flyers— I swear I had nothing to do with her death."

"You know how it must look to us, though?" DI Karlson said. "Surely even you can see it doesn't look good."

"I know it probably sounds like utter bullshit, but it's the truth. I swear."

He nodded his head slowly and looked back at his notes. "Add to that the fact her body was found at the back of your house. Are we expected to believe it was just a coincidence?"

"A total coincidence. The last time I saw Erin she was alive and well at the school gate. I don't know what more I can say to convince you."

DI Karlson rubbed his eyes and groaned. "I've been doing this job for a long time, Mr Mathews, and I don't mind telling you that I don't believe in coincidences. Nine times out of ten, coincidences are brought about by human error and over planning."

"I know, I know. But honestly, it's true. Do you really think I'd dump her body at the back of my house if I had something to do with her death? Grant me with a bit of common sense, *please*. It's obvious you'd look at me. How was the poor girl killed anyway?"

They shot each other a glance and DI Karlson cleared his throat. "She was strangled to death. Someone looked her in the eyes as they choked the life out of her—sick, eh?"

Phil thought about Erin's lovely face and bright eyes filled with life and mischief and, not for the first time since it had happened, he felt immense grief for the loss of the vibrant young woman.

"It is sick. But I didn't do it, I swear."

CHAPTER 22

The next morning, I tried to spy over the hedge desperate to find out if Phil was home. However, other than Alexis buzzing around the kitchen, there was no sign of him. My heart skipped a beat when she suddenly looked directly at me and waved. In my panic, I stepped backwards and almost died when I heard her open the back door.

"Hi, Lizzi," she called.

"Oh, er... Hi." I returned to the hedge and peered through the gap until she came into view.

"Did you want something?"

"Oh, not really. I just wondered if Kate wanted to walk Thomas with me. She said she was going to come over last night, but she didn't."

"Well, between you and me, Phil was picked up by the police last night for questioning."

I forced a shocked expression on my face. "For what?"

"Who knows? They were very tight-lipped."

"And he's still not home?"

She shook her head; her gorgeous blue eyes were bright with suppressed glee—nasty bitch.

"That's terrible! If there's anything I can do, just ask."

"I will do. Actually, I might need someone to watch the kids for an hour or so later as I'm supposed to be going to see my parents. I could take them with me, but I can't imagine it will be a very friendly reunion, to be honest."

"Of course, they can come here—no problem." I gave her my number.

"I'll let you know later. Hopefully Phil will be home soon."

"Hope so." I watched as Alexis headed back inside.

My stomach felt as though I'd swallowed a brick. I knew in my heart of hearts Charlie had done the right thing, but I couldn't help but suspect he'd taken delight in pointing the finger out of jealousy.

I didn't know what I would do. I contemplated calling Miriam and telling her Charlie was awake and well. At least then I'd be able to take the flack, then return home—back to my job. But would I even have a job to go back to? Miriam was a good friend of my boss, and, if he discovered I'd gone against medical advice, I'd be fired on the spot.

What a mess.

I called Thomas, who was rolling about on his back at the end of the garden, and went inside.

"I had a great night's sleep, Joannie. How are you feeling today?" Nigel opened the living room curtains and inspected his wife.

She hadn't moved a muscle, but he could smell an unearthly stench coming from her.

"Jesus, Mary and Joseph! How the fuck have you managed to shit again? You didn't even eat anything yesterday." He lifted the duvet and recoiled at the eye-watering stink. "You make me sick—do you hear me? You dirty bitch." In a sudden rage, he shoved a foot in between her knees and pulled out the sopping wet towel that was, once again, smeared with putrid smelling, yellow shit. He roared and roughly wiped her with the pissy part of the towel. He could cope with most things—in fact he would've said he had a cast iron stomach, but her shit totally floored him. If only the bloody bruises would hurry up and heal, he'd be able to get her to the hospital and get some other fucker to clean up after her.

He carried the soiled towel through to the washing machine and rammed it inside—grateful the shite was watery instead of lumps he'd need to wash off first.

Once his wife was clean again, he placed a fresh towel between her legs, making a mental note to buy adult nappies once he'd finished his morning shift.

Phil shivered and pulled the small square excuse for a blanket up under his chin. How they expected anyone to sleep on the hard, plastic mattress was beyond him. And, if that wasn't bad enough, the entire cell stank of stale piss.

Worrying about the kids, he said a silent prayer of thanks that Alexis had come home when she had, or he'd be in a complete pickle right now. There was no telling how long they intended to keep him locked up. He was aware it didn't look good and wished he'd been honest right from the start.

The sight of Catherine's little face peering from the living room window as the police marched him away broke his heart. His sole purpose for lying in the first place had been to protect his kids but look at what a mess he'd made of that. No kid deserved to go through what they had this past year. Losing a parent at such a young age was devastating, and Ben was only just coming right. What effect would something like this have on them both? Especially if they charged him with murder.

After trawling through his phone last night, they had been able to establish he'd been out with his footy mates, bowling and on for a curry the night Erin vanished. The kids hadn't been home. But his excitement of being let off the hook was short lived when DI Karlson said it made them even more suspicious if anything. They didn't know an exact time she had been killed and that meant it could've happened after he got home that night or in the early hours of the following morning. Basically, he was well and truly fucked.

CHAPTER 23

My stomach was in knots. I'd practically paced a groove in the carpet in front of the living room window while waiting for Phil to return. It was already 2pm, and there was still no sign of him.

The phone rang and my heart skipped a beat as I pounced on it. A number I didn't recognise flashed on the screen.

"Hello?" I answered tentatively.

"Hi, Lizzi. It's Alexis."

I exhaled. "Oh, hi. Any news?"

"Nothing yet. Are you still okay to pick up Kate from school? Ben said he'd make his own way."

"Yes. Of course. Where do I need to be?"

"Just wait at the front gate. She'll find you. Her teacher knows about it."

I gasped. "You told them? About Phil, you mean?"

She chuckled. "No, of course not, silly. She knows to expect you."

Relieved, I let out a long sigh. "Okay then. What time does she need picking up?"

"Three-thirty."

"And I'm okay to bring her back here?"

"If you don't mind. Ben's going to his mate's straight from school, and he has his key, and he'll let himself in if he gets back before me. I shouldn't be too late. Wish me luck. My parents hate me."

"I'm sure they don't, but good luck anyway." I rolled my eyes as I hung up. I don't know why, but she irritated the crap out of me for no real reason.

"Who was that?" Charlie said, suddenly behind me.

"Alexis. She asked if I can pick Kate up from school and bring her here for a couple of hours," I said, tight-lipped.

"Still no sign of loverboy?"

I glared at him but refused to bite. "No, *Phil's* still not home."

"They must have something on him—what did I tell you? They don't keep people banged up for hours if they're innocent."

"Bullshit. You hear of innocent people being kept for days while they interrogate them—so your argument is stupid."

He wiggled his eyebrows. "We'll see."

I tried to scan the faces of the sea of kids swarming through the gate towards me, but it was impossible. I reckoned she'd have more chance spotting me and Thomas, so I pressed my back hard against the railings.

Thomas was in his element as several children dropped to their knees to pet him and he squeaked like a cuddly toy, delighting everybody within earshot.

"Thomas!" Kate squealed, suddenly beside us. She dropped her backpack to the concrete and plonked herself down beside it.

"Hello, Lizzi. How was your day?" I said, sarcastically.

"I'm not Lizzi, silly." She laughed—my attempt at humour lost on her.

"I know." I also laughed. "You should get up off that cold pavement though—you'll get piles." For a moment, I was taken straight back to my own childhood and memories of my lovely gran saying the same to me. We all tend to turn into our parents and grandparents, eventually.

"Hello, ladies." Phil's dulcet tones startled me from my reverie.

I whirled around to see him standing behind us, looking dishevelled and exhausted.

"Oh, my goodness, you made me jump!"

"Daddy, Daddy, did the police let you go?" Kate scrambled to her feet and launched herself into her father's arms.

"Shh." He laughed, glancing around at the disapproving glares of the other parents close by. "Come on, let's get going."

We fell into step, and Kate marched on ahead with Thomas on the lead.

"Where's Alexis, by the way?" he asked.

"She went to see her parents. We weren't sure you'd be home on time—if at all. So, I said I'd pick Kate up."

"I wasn't sure myself. I did try to call her from the police station, but there was no answer at home, and my phone had died. I don't know her mobile number by heart. I got the detective to drop me off at the end of the road just in case she'd forgotten."

"No. She's coped well, by all accounts. How are you anyway?" I was dying to ask him the details but felt nosy. I was sure he'd tell me when he was ready.

"Did Alexis tell you what happened?"

"Just that they took you in for questioning." I didn't let on I already knew the reason why. I figured it was best I keep my mouth shut.

"I'd stupidly omitted to tell them I'd met Erin a couple of times."

"Really?" My surprise this time was real, and I was more than a little pissed off I'd have to tell Charlie he was right all along.

"Yes. I had nothing to do with her death, but it did look a bit iffy for a time there. I had no way of proving I hadn't been involved. And to top it all off—the night she went missing, I'd been out with friends and the kids didn't stay at home, so I had no alibi after eleven pm."

"But they let you go, so they can't think you did it or else they'd have charged you, wouldn't they?"

"No—they don't think I killed her. I've never been so pleased to have huge sausage fingers and monster-sized hands in my life."

"Sorry, I don't get you."

"The killer's hands were small—much smaller than mine."

"Bloody hell. How lucky is that? You might've been facing a murder trial if not."

"Exactly, I was petrified, I don't mind telling you."

"I bet. So, you're off the hook now then?"

"I guess so, although I probably shouldn't book an overseas trip for the time being." He smiled, sadly.

"You look shattered. I can keep Kate for a couple of hours if you want to get your head down for a bit."

We turned into the cul-de-sac.

"Really? I won't say no. I didn't get a wink of sleep last night."

We parted company at the gate and Kate excitedly ran up our path with Thomas at her heels, not a bit bothered about not going home with her dad.

Charlie was standing at the living room window when we entered. "I see your fancy man's home."

I shot him a warning glance and pointed in Kate's direction. "Who would like a nice mug of hot chocolate?" I asked.

"Me, me, me," she chimed.

"Me, me, me," Charlie joined in, his voice flat.

"I'm not sure you deserve one. What do you think, Kate? Can Charlie have one too?"

"Maybe," she said, coyly. "If he promises to be a good boy."

"I'm always a good boy." He grinned and winked at me.

I was able to relax.

Nigel watched the flirty bitch from across the road fawning all over the Mathews guy. Some women had no shame. The man's wife wasn't even cold in her grave, and there she was flinging herself at him—disgusting.

He pulled two shopping bags from the back seat of his trusty old Saab and trudged up the pathway hoping Joan was showing some signs of improvement. Or at least for the bruising to have gone down somewhat so he could call a doctor.

"Hi, honey, I'm home." He'd said the same thing on entering for years and some habits couldn't be broken.

No response. Although he wasn't surprised—trust his wife to milk a situation for all it was worth.

A faint shit smell tickled his nostrils as he reached the top of the stairs, but he was relieved it wasn't nearly as bad as last time.

"I've bought you some liquid meal replacements, Joanie. They should have you back on your feet in no time." He threw a packet of adult nappies onto the sofa and carried the rest of the shopping into the kitchen. "Maybe you'll even lose a bit of weight too," he called. "Can't hurt, can it?"

After putting away the groceries, he opened a packet of rubber gloves and slipped them on. Then he filled the washing-up bowl with hot soapy water. He was getting quite good at this now. He grinned, pleased with himself. And he could seriously get used to the peace and quiet.

Carrying the bowl through to the living room, he placed it beside his wife on the polished floorboards. Then he pulled the duvet back. The towel he'd wedged between her thighs was still in place and, although soiled, was nowhere near as bad as before.

He cleaned her quickly with the washcloth then opened the nappy pack. It took a moment to work out how they were meant to go on., but he worked it out in no time. "Voila!" he said.

Realising he hadn't washed the rest of her, he considered fetching some clean water from the kitchen and then he thought, fuck it, and wiped her face, neck and body with the same shitty cloth he'd used on her arse. Then he covered her up, plumped up her pillows and headed back into the kitchen.

He made up a chocolate flavoured meal replacement in the same washing up bottle he'd used for the water. "Dinner's almost ready, sweetheart," he called through to her.

CHAPTER 24

Charlie was his usual charming self and had Kate eating out of his hands in no time. He even sat in the middle of the living room carpet with her and played a game of fish with a pack of cards while I prepared their dinner.

The doorbell rang moments after they'd sat down to eat. "I'll get it," I said, wiping my hands on a tea towel and heading to answer it.

Alexis stood on the doorstep.

"Oh, hello. How did it go?" I said. Flinging the door open wide, I beckoned her in.

"Tense, emotional on their part, but I'm glad it's all over with, and hopefully we can get everything back on an even keel."

"Oh, good. Did you hear from Phil?"

"Not a word—you?"

"Yes. He's next door. He looked shattered though, and I told him to go home and sleep. Do you fancy a cuppa? Kate's just eating her dinner in the kitchen with Charlie."

"Ooh, that's what I can smell."

"Nothing fancy. Just sausage, egg and chips. I made plenty. Are you hungry?"

"Starving. And it sounds delicious—I've missed good old English comfort food."

"Give me your jacket then and go through."

I was certain Alexis' wiggle was accentuated as soon as she set eyes on Charlie. But I wasn't sure if she was aware of it herself or if it was something that occurred on a more carnal level. Either way, Charlie certainly sat up and took notice—he was practically salivating, and it had nothing to do with his sausages.

"Auntie Lexi," Kate squealed. "Daddy's having a big sleep, and I'm allowed to stay here for dinner."

"How exciting." She stroked her niece's head affectionately.

"Take a seat, Alexis. I'll just fry you an egg."

"Oh, yummy." Alexis didn't need telling twice and plonked down on the chair I'd been sitting on earlier.

"Are you staying for dinner too?" Kate asked. "These sausages are huge!"

Charlie finished his mouthful of food and placed his knife and fork down on the empty plate. "That was delicious, thanks, Kate."

Kate giggled. "I didn't make it, silly."

"I know you didn't, but I'm not usually allowed chips, so, thank you."

I rolled my eyes and felt the corners of my mouth twitch at his childish expression, but I turned my back, not wanting him to know I was thawing towards him.

A few minutes later, I delivered a plate of fried egg, sausage and chips to the table and Alexis practically buried her head in it.

CHAPTER 25

Once I'd cleaned up from dinner, Kate and I took Thomas outside for a walk leaving Alexis and Charlie putting the world to rights.

We walked Thomas to the end of the street, and all the while I kept my eyes peeled for Nigel, our delightful neighbour, but thankfully he was nowhere to be seen.

"I wonder if Ben's home yet," I thought out loud. "Maybe he'd like something to eat. Should we check on him on the way back?"

"Nah," she said.

"Why ever not? He might be hungry."

"Because you're not *his* friend. You're mine."

"It's okay if I'm friends with both of you, you know."

"But he doesn't let me be friends with Kevin. He always goes to his house for dinner and never brings anything for me."

"Well, in this case, with Daddy being so tired, maybe it would be a nice thing for us to do. What do you think?"

She pursed her lips to the side of her cute, angelic face and pondered on it before nodding. "Okay then, just this once."

"Of course. Just this once." I grinned placing my arm around her shoulders.

A few minutes later, we walked up Phil's path and found the

house in total darkness. "Maybe Ben's still at his friend's," I said. "Best not knock as we might wake your dad."

"The back door will be open. It's always open. Mummy lost the key ages ago."

"Really?"

She nodded, all wide-eyed innocence.

"Maybe you should keep that to yourself in future, sweetheart."

"Why?"

"Because what if a burglar overheard you."

"A burger?"

"No, a burglar. Someone who steals other people's things."

She gasped, looking around us at the bushes. "You think a burglar heard me?"

"No. But maybe be a bit more careful who you tell in the future."

"Okay, Lizzi. I'll be more careful, I promise. Are we going inside?"

"You can check if Ben's home, if you like, so long as you're quiet."

I followed Kate down the side of the house to the back door.

The house was in darkness and the moon cast an eerie glow around the place. I suddenly felt as though I was trespassing.

Kate opened the door.

"Hurry back and don't forget to be quiet," I whispered, putting my finger to my lips.

She reached up and turned the kitchen light on and then bounded up the stairs like a fairy elephant—so much for keeping quiet.

Moments later I heard her excited chatter and the upstairs lights came on. Phil suddenly appeared in the kitchen.

"I'm sorry, Lizzi. I was spark out and didn't realise the time. Come in."

"That's okay. I have Thomas with me. I didn't want to wake

you. We were just checking to see if Ben was home. I was going to make him something to eat."

"He's staying at his friend's for dinner, but thanks—that's really kind of you. I don't know where Alexis has got to. I thought she'd be back by now."

"Oh, she's next door with Charlie—she's also been fed, which just leaves you. Are you hungry?"

"Not really, I'm still shattered. I think I'll just go back to bed if Alexis is going to see to the kids."

"I'm sure she will. I'll leave you to it. Is Kate coming back with me?"

"I'll send her down," he said. "Thanks again, Lizzi. I owe you one."

I heard him trudge up the stairs and, before long, Kate reappeared.

"There you are." I grinned. "Whatever happened to you being quiet as a mouse so you wouldn't wake your daddy?"

"Oops." She chuckled.

"Oops, indeed." I ruffled her delightful blonde curls. "Come on, munchkin. Let's get Thomas home."

Alexis and Charlie were still talking ten to the dozen when we arrived back. In fact I'd have been surprised if they'd even noticed we'd gone anywhere.

I hung Thomas's lead on the hook by the back door and filled his water bowl. Then I turned to Kate. "Right, what do you want to do now?"

"Can we watch *Frozen*? It's my favourite."

"Oh, I don't know about that. I don't think Miriam has any children's movies but we could check on *Netflix*."

"What's *Netflix*?"

I'd forgotten how many questions kids ask. "Like a DVD player without the discs. Let's go and check it out, shall we?"

We headed through to the living room and sat together on the sofa.

"We used to have this TV," Kate said as the *Netflix* logo filled the screen. "Daddy cancelled it after Mummy died."

"Really? Well I guess your dad needed to make some changes. Sometimes adults have to make unpopular decisions."

"Did you know my mummy?"

"No. But I'm sure I would've liked her very much."

She nodded. Her sad eyes broke my heart.

"You must miss her very much."

She suddenly launched herself into my arms and buried her face in my shoulder.

"Hey, hey, are you okay, love? I didn't mean to upset you."

"You didn't upset me. I just wanted a hug. Daddy doesn't give good hugs like Mummy used to."

I found that hard to believe. "He looks like he would give pretty awesome hugs to me."

She shook her head. "Mummy's hugs were soft and warm, like yours. Daddy's hugs are hard."

CHAPTER 26

Nigel was fed up. Joan was still showing no signs of recovery and, although he'd got a system going regarding her cleansing and feeding regime, he'd had enough.

Squirting the last of the liquid meal down her throat, he shoved the duvet over the top of her and went to the kitchen to wash the dishes.

"Fucking nightmare," he grizzled to himself as he threw the washing-up liquid bottle into the sink. He'd hoped Joan's bruising would've faded by now, but it was still a mess. It would take months to heal at this rate. "I should've just finished her off when I had the fucking chance." He kicked the rubbish bin and sent ready meal packaging flying across the kitchen.

How unlucky was he? He'd been married to Joan for years, and she'd worn the trousers most of that time, and the one time he grew a pair of balls and decided to stand up to her, she ends up comatose. How was that even fair?

Tired of looking at his wife's pathetic, fat face, he decided to turn in early. He pulled a pair of scanty pink lace knickers from his pocket that he'd found on the back seat of the bus earlier. He rubbed his cock in anticipation and sucked on the crotch.

Kate yawned and snuggled up to me.

I glanced at the clock—almost 8pm. "Oh, gosh, sweetie, it's probably past your bedtime. We'd best give your auntie a hurry up."

"Aw, no. I like being here."

"You can come again. You know that. But you do need to get to bed otherwise Daddy will be angry with me for keeping you up too late."

"Okay." She reluctantly dragged herself upright, rubbed her eyes and yawned.

Thomas jumped up and licked her mouth before I had a chance to stop him.

"Eurgh!" She pushed the pesky mutt away, and we both burst out laughing.

Taking her hand, we went through to the kitchen and found Charlie and Alexis still jabbering away.

"Hey, you two. Kate's tired."

"Oh, gosh." Alexis leapt to her feet. "Where did the time go?"

I smiled and widened my eyes at Charlie. "We'll meet you at the front door," I said, leaving them alone to say their goodbyes. "Let's get your shoes and coat, sweetie."

In the hallway, Kate dropped to her knees to give Thomas a hug. Moments later, Alexis appeared and then they were gone.

"Well!" I said to Charlie once we were alone. "That was intense."

"What was?"

"You two. You got on well, didn't you?"

He shrugged. "Yeah, she's nice. I like her a lot."

I nodded, unable to control the grin I felt spread across my face.

"What's that supposed to mean?"

"What?"

"You know what. You're acting all smug."

"No." I laughed. "Not at all. I'm happy for you both."

"Then you won't mind that I've asked her over tomorrow night. I want to cook for her."

"Oh, okay. And what am I meant to do? Twiddle my thumbs and act like piffy?"

"I don't know what that means."

Shaking my head, I let out a loud breath. "Never mind. I'll make myself scarce."

"If you don't mind. I really like her, you know."

"Did she tell you her news?" I felt a little awful blabbing to him. It wasn't my business after all.

"What news?" His forehead furrowed.

"Oh, never mind. Fancy a coffee?"

"No, thanks. It'll just keep me awake all night. So, what news?"

"It's none of my business, Charlie. Sorry, I shouldn't have said anything."

"Maybe not. But you did. So, spill."

"She's having a baby. Phil told me."

"Ah. That makes sense now. And I did suspect she might be. But I'm fine with it, to be honest."

"Really? It would make most men run for the hills."

"Yeah, well, not me. And besides, I think I might be ready for a child in my life."

"Even someone else's?"

He shrugged. "A baby is a baby, and we're jumping the gun here anyway. I'm not planning to propose. It's dinner, for Christ's sake."

CHAPTER 27

Nigel started awake.

There had been a bang—he was sure of it.

He held his breath and craned his neck to listen. After a couple of seconds, he relaxed back into the pillow allowing his heartbeat to return to a normal rhythm. It must've been a dream.

A series of bumps from directly above him had him springing out of bed and legging it up the stairs. Joan must finally be awake.

As he reached the landing, he could see movement under the duvet and one of her feet was moving. But his relief was short lived when he realised the movement wasn't voluntary—Joan was frothing from the mouth, having some sort of massive fit.

In sheer panic, he reached for the phone and dialled 999. "Quick! I need an ambulance. My wife is having a fit."

Arranging for an ambulance seemed to go on for hours, but in reality it was probably only a matter of minutes.

Joan eventually stopped convulsing.

"Hey, my darling. Don't worry, you're going to be okay. The ambulance will be here shortly. We'll get you sorted one way or another. I promise. Just hang in there, love."

The sound of the approaching siren had him belting down the

stairs two at a time and, once the ambulance had pulled up on the street, he ushered the two paramedics inside, and up to his wife.

"Tell me what happened, sir," the driver, the younger of the two men, asked.

"Erm. She was feeling a little ropey yesterday, so she decided to sleep in the living room last night. I heard a load of banging this morning and when I got up here, I realised she was having a fit."

The older paramedic had dropped to his haunches beside Joan and proceeded to check her eyes and pulse. "Can you hear me, Joan," he said in a loud voice. He shook his head at his colleague, his eyes brimming with concern. "We need a stretcher."

It took a few attempts to manoeuvre Joan down the stairs on the stretcher, but they eventually managed it between them. They loaded her into the back of the ambulance quick smart.

Several groups of people had gathered across the road, and Nigel saw the snooty nurse was amongst them.

"What the hell are you looking at?" he barked.

"Hey! Wind your fucking neck in, grandad," another bint of a woman, with a shock of golden curls and a big gob to match that of her friend's, spat back.

Speechless, he gave them the finger before climbing into the back of the ambulance.

"Cheeky old bastard," Alexis said.

We watched, slack jawed, as the ambulance sped away.

"He's horrible. I've already had several run-ins with him this week," I said.

"Really?" Alexis shook her head, clearly surprised.

"Yeah. He's not my number one fan, that's for sure. Anyway, forget about him. How's Phil today?"

"He seems okay. Quiet though. I left him getting the kids'

breakfast ready. I was getting ready to take them to school when I heard the siren. I'm so nosy."

"Me too." I grinned. "But we're not the only ones." I nodded at several other nosy neighbours. "Anyway, I might pop by and see if he fancies a coffee later, then."

"Phew! I was hoping you'd say that." She swiped her forehead dramatically. "I don't know what to say to him. He won't tell me anything about the dead girl—do you know anything?"

I shook my head. There was no chance I'd betray Phil's trust. "No, sorry. Not a thing. Anyway, I hear you're having dinner with a very eligible bachelor this evening." I grinned changing the subject.

Her cheeks flushed pink. "Only if I'm not treading on your toes."

I shook my head. "No—I already told you, we're just friends —end of."

"Good. Because I really like him."

I smiled and began walking towards the house. "I think the feeling's mutual, you lucky girl." I wondered if Charlie would let her know who he really was, or if he'd try to keep the secret for a while longer.

"He is a catch, isn't he?" She reached out and squeezed my arm.

"Totally. Do me a favour, will you?"

"If I can."

"Ask Phil to pop in as soon as he has a spare moment. I don't want to harass him if he's not up to talking."

"Will do."

The concerned expression that passed between the two paramedics freaked Nigel out.

"Is she going to be okay?" he asked.

"How long did you say she'd been like this?" the older man

asked as his colleague shut the doors and ran around to the front of the ambulance.

"She wasn't feeling too well last night, like I've already said. So, I left her where she was. I called you guys as soon as I found her having a seizure this morning." Nigel could tell they didn't believe him totally, but they'd have to prove he was lying.

The paramedic inspected the bruises on Joan's neck, but he didn't say anything.

Nigel's stomach muscles clenched, but he kept his breathing and his gaze steady. In fact, he was pretty amazed at his own acting ability—it was an Oscar winning performance—the ideal, doting husband for all to see.

At the hospital, they whisked Joan away leaving him to give the details to the receptionist. Afterwards, a nurse led him to an empty waiting room telling him someone would find him as soon as they had any news.

"Can't I just be with my wife?" he complained. It was disconcerting not knowing what was happening.

"As soon as she's been assessed, the doctor will let you know."

The stupid woman then dismissed him and was gone in a flurry of blue uniform and squeaky blue plimsolls.

"Bitch!" he muttered under his breath. Taking a seat, he flicked through several tedious women's magazines, but nothing caught his attention. After a few minutes, he leapt to his feet and began pacing the floor. What if Joan died? Would he be held responsible? At this stage it was his word against theirs but if she died, they'd be able to delve deeper with a post-mortem examination. They could lock him up for the rest of his life if they found he was to blame. Wringing his hands, he suddenly turned towards the door, unable to stand it any longer. He needed to get out of there.

Just then, the door opened and a man, dressed in white, entered. "Mr Mason?"

"That's me." His stomach began doing several back-to-back triple somersaults.

"My name's Doctor Fisher. I've been assigned to your wife's case."

"Okay. How is she?"

"Maybe we could take a seat for a moment?" He gestured to the row of chairs.

Reluctantly, Nigel dropped back onto one of them. "Just tell me, doc. Is she going to be okay?"

"We're still no closer to finding out what's happened to your wife, I'm sorry. We're aware she had some sort of seizure, but can you tell me more about it and what she was like leading up to it?"

"Yes—yes, of course. Like I told the paramedic, she's not been herself for a few days now, to be honest." He figured staying as close to the truth as possible was the safest bet.

"How so?"

"Lethargic, loss of appetite, just generally unwell. She's not been to bed in days, because it would mean her going down a flight of stairs, and she just wasn't up to it. Well, you've seen how big she is. There was no way I could carry her, so we agreed she should stay in the living room."

"Did you not think to call the doctor?"

"Yes, I did, but Joan wouldn't hear of it. She's not the type of woman you can argue with, let me tell you."

"I see. Then what happened?"

"I heard her banging around this morning and thought she must be feeling better. When I went up to check, I found her having a massive fit."

"Was she conscious afterwards?"

Nigel shook his head. "No. She didn't come to in the ambulance either. What do you think caused it?"

"I'm unsure, at this stage, but we'll carry out further tests. I did notice your wife has severe bruising around her throat. Can you tell me anything about that?"

Nigel shifted in his seat. He wondered how long it would take them to get around to asking about the bruises, but he'd done some research of his own and was ready with his answer. "That's private."

"Private? How do you mean?"

"Joan and I enjoy an active sex life."

The doctor's eyes widened. "I see."

"Just because we're close to retirement age doesn't mean we don't have wants and needs like everyone else."

"I never suggested otherwise, but how can a healthy sex life cause such damage?"

"She likes me to squeeze her throat when she's about to orgasm. I don't like doing it, but she can be fairly insistent. It's what gets her off. As you age, the sensations down there aren't as strong. You sometimes need extra stimulation to achieve orgasm." He needed to be careful, he was sounding, word for word, like the website he'd stumbled on last night. "Have you never heard of it before?"

Doctor Fisher appeared shocked. He opened and closed his mouth several times before he could formulate a response. "Of course, I've heard of it, but…"

"But what? She's too old, is that it?"

"No, certainly not. But it's dangerous, and if anything happened to your wife, brought on by the injuries from this extreme act, you could be done for assault at the very least, or even murder."

"Really? Even if she begs me to do it?"

"Even then."

"Oh, gosh." He placed the flat of his hand against his chest. "I never thought about it like that. Thanks for warning me, doctor. I promise I won't give in to her again, no matter how much she threatens to punish me."

"Good plan, Mr Mason."

"So, when can I see my wife?"

"If you like, I'll take you to her now."

"Thanks, doc, you're a star."

CHAPTER 28

I glanced at my watch as Charlie emerged from his bedroom. "You've slept late, are you feeling okay?"

"I'm fine. Just tired. I don't know why though."

I walked over to him. "May I?" I said, holding my hand up to his forehead. "You're feeling a little hot. I hope you're not coming down with something."

"I don't think so. I couldn't sleep last night—things going around and around in my head."

"Things like what? Anything I can help you with?"

"No, not really. Just that I enjoyed spending time with Alexis last night. And then what you told me about the baby. I started thinking about my own mortality. Maybe it's not a good idea to get close to anyone right now."

"Nonsense. You're not dead yet, mate. If having a hot date with Alexis gives you something to look forward to, then go for it, I say."

"Really? You don't think I'm being a selfish prick if I do that?"

"No. Not at all."

"Do you think I ought to be honest with her?"

I shrugged. "Entirely your call."

The ringing of the house phone startled me. This was the first time it had rung since I'd arrived. "Who can that be?" I walked to the base unit and tentatively picked up the handset. "Hello?"

"Ah, Miss Yates, it's Miriam."

Charlie suddenly sprang forward shaking his head and pointing at his chest.

"Oh, hello," I said.

"Sorry I've not been in touch, but I was off the grid at a conference in the middle of the wop-wops. Hard to believe there are still places with no WiFi and telephone signal in this day and age. Tell me, how's my brother?"

"He's fine."

Charlie shot me another warning glance. "Don't tell her," he hissed.

I batted him out of my face with the back of my hand and turned away.

"Any change?" she asked.

"No. Nothing to report where he's concerned although there have been lots of things happening around here."

"Like what?"

"The police need to talk to you. They found a woman's body."

She gasped and the signal faded. Her voice broke up, and I couldn't decipher her reply.

"Hell-o. Miriam. Can you hear me?"

Silence.

I hung up. "She's gone," I said, turning to Charlie.

"What did she want?"

"Apparently she's been out of signal at the conference, so she was just checking in to see how you are. We're going to have to tell her sooner or later, you know."

"I know that, but not yet. What's the point stressing her out if we don't need to?"

"I s'pose. Right then. Where were we?"

"We were talking about Alexis."

"Oh, yes. What do you want to make for dinner? Any idea? I'll go to the supermarket later."

Phil didn't call in until almost 2pm.

"Hello, you," I said as I opened the door. "How are you feeling today?"

"Totally flat, to be honest."

"Fancy a cuppa?"

"No, I'd better not. I need to go to the supermarket before I pick Kate up."

"Ooh! Do you mind if I cadge a lift? I was just about to call a taxi."

"Not at all. Are you ready to leave now?"

"Give me two minutes, then I'm all set."

"I'll wait in the car."

I strode through to the living room and picked Thomas up from the sofa and laughed as he groaned. "Come on, mister. You need to go in your cage for an hour. I'll make it up to you, I promise." I paused outside Charlie's bedroom door. "Charlie?" I called.

"In here." He suddenly appeared in the garage doorway.

"Oh, hi. What are you doing in there? I thought you were sleeping."

"No, I was just looking at Miriam's wine cellar."

"Don't you go drinking it all. She'll blame me."

He laughed. "Don't worry, I'll replenish the cellar before she returns. What did you want me for, anyway?"

"Phil's here. He's taking me to the supermarket. I've got my phone on me if you think of anything else you need." I placed Thomas into his arms before I turned and headed out the front door.

"So, what do you think of the big date?" I asked Phil as I climbed into the passenger seat of his red Honda.

He rolled his eyes, shaking his head as he backed out of his driveway.

"What's that supposed to mean?"

"It means, I've heard about nothing else since I opened my eyes this morning."

"You're not bothered then?"

"Why would I be bothered? I'm glad for them both."

"Me too. Although I don't know what I'm expected to do while they're schmoozing each other. I'll probably just go to bed with my kindle—I don't want to be a gooseberry."

"Come over to mine. Kate would love you to."

I paused, considering his offer. "I'd like that, but are you sure you don't mind? This is the first chance for a bit of time to yourself since Alexis arrived. I'd understand if you'd prefer to have a quiet night instead."

"I'd like you to come to me for dinner—I'll cook for you for a change."

"Ooh!" I clapped my hands in glee.

"Don't get too worked up. It might be disgusting. I'm no cordon bleu chef."

"It'll be nice to be looked after for a change. I'm not fussy—beans on toast will do me."

"I might hold you to that."

When we got to the supermarket, we each grabbed a shopping trolley and went our separate ways. I had a list from Charlie, so I filled my trolley with fillet steak, potatoes, and asparagus spears. I also bought a couple of bottles of wine so he wouldn't be pilfering Miriam's. I couldn't help but think the quality of food was wasted on Alexis, who'd been excited about fish finger butties earlier in the week. A fine-dining palate she didn't have. "You bitch," I muttered to myself.

I wasn't even sure if Charlie was capable of making such a meal, but it wasn't my problem. I didn't mind shopping for him, but I'd draw the line there. I intended to be waited on hand and foot tonight. In fact, I was looking forward to it.

CHAPTER 29

Joan went through a multitude of tests and scans over the next few hours. Nobody said any more about the bruises, and Nigel felt a little more settled than he had when he first arrived. Maybe the gullible doctor had swallowed his story hook, line and sinker. He had no doubts the tale of the randy, perverted pensioners would be bandied about in the staff room, and repeated in homes across Manchester by the morning. But he didn't care about that so long as he wasn't arrested. How Joan would feel about it, if and when she woke up, he had no idea, but he'd cross that bridge when he came to it.

His stomach growled, and he realised he hadn't eaten anything since last night's dinner. He stroked her hair. "I'm going to the canteen, sweetheart. I'll be back soon, I promise."

The young, dark-haired Scottish nurse smiled at him sweetly when he shuffled from the room.

At the canteen, he was relieved to see a selection of old-fashioned meals, and they were reasonably priced too. He was a bit of a skinflint when it came to eating out—he hated wasting money on overpriced fancy nosh, which often wasn't any nicer than anything you could cook at home for a fraction of the cost. He couldn't comprehend today's fast food obsession.

"Liver and onions, please," he asked the homely looking woman dressed in a tabard and white cap.

"Do you want mashed potatoes or chips?"

"Potatoes."

"Anything to drink?"

"A mug of milky tea, please."

The woman shovelled the food onto a plate and placed it and the mug on a tray.

Once he'd paid, he carried the tray to the furthest table in the corner and sat with his back to the room.

Half an hour later, he arrived back onto the ward and his stomach dropped as he approached Joan's room. The crackle of a police radio first alerted him there was something wrong, and then he saw a crowd of people surrounding Joan's bed.

Startled, he jumped backwards and pressed himself back tight against the wall.

"It's impossible to say what's caused it at this stage," someone was saying. "But I'm fairly certain these symptoms aren't all caused by today's seizures. There's definitely more to this than meets the eye."

"Where is the husband now?" said another deep male voice.

"He's gone to the canteen. He should be back soon," said the Scottish nurse.

"I'll wait."

Nigel briskly walked away.

CHAPTER 30

I spent the next two hours pampering myself. After a soak in a bubble bath, I shaved my legs, painted my toenails, moisturised my entire body, and applied a full face of make-up.

I was just appraising myself in the bathroom mirror when the doorbell rang.

Glancing at my watch, I gasped and reached for my jacket.

Charlie was ushering Alexis into the hallway as I breezed from my bedroom.

"Sorry, sorry, sorry. I'll be out of your hair in a sec."

"Ooh, you look nice," said Alexis who was dressed in a tight white dress showing more of her voluptuous curves.

"Thank you. Looking quite the dish yourself." I breezed past them heading towards the front door. "Can you try to remember to let Thomas out for a wee?"

Phil's door was flung open with gusto seconds after I knocked.

Kate answered the door in her pyjamas and welcomed me

inside. "Did you bring Thomas?" She scanned the doorstep behind me.

"Sorry, no. I didn't know he was invited." I grinned.

"Aw, I made him a special dinner—chocolate sponge cake and jellybeans. It was my own invention."

"Aw, it sounds delicious. I'll take it with me when I go. He can have it for supper."

She seemed happy with that, and I followed her through to the kitchen.

"Wow! Aren't you a sight for sore eyes?" Phil said, from his position by the stove.

"Why, thank you, kind sir." I curtsied, suddenly feeling self-conscious and silly.

'Look what I did," Kate said, grabbing my hand and guiding me to the table that had been set with a pretty floral embossed white tablecloth and homemade placemats coloured in by the resident six-year-old.

"Oh, my goodness. Did you make these yourself? They're amazing."

I glanced at Phil. The way his eyes shone told me he was extra proud of his youngest child. "Would you like a drink? We have lemonade, coke, orange juice or corporation pop."

"What's corporation pop?" Kate asked, clearly puzzled.

"Tap water," I whispered in her ear. "Orange juice would be lovely."

He nodded. "I have a cheeky bottle of red for when a certain little lady hits the sack."

"Sounds perfect. Is there anything you want me to do?"

"No, I'm all organised, so just take a seat and keep me company while I be the host with the most."

Kate laughed dramatically, clearly not understanding what he'd said but wanting to be part of the joke.

"What are we having?" I asked. "Am I allowed to know?"

"Chicken, bacon and mozzarella tortellini with a delectable Alfredo sauce, topped with freshly shaved parmesan cheese."

I was gobsmacked. Never in a million years did I expect something like that. "Really? Did you make it yourself?"

"I certainly did, but I reserve judgement until you've actually tasted it."

"Okay. But I'm impressed already. I've never made pasta from scratch so top marks for effort."

We laughed and chatted about nonsense for the next twenty minutes until the oven timer sounded.

"Time to put the pasta on to boil," he said, jumping to his feet.

Ten minutes later, he placed two plates of delicious looking pasta and one plate of chicken nuggets and vegetable fingers onto the table.

"Is Ben not joining us?" I asked.

"No. He's up in his room. He said he's not hungry, but there's plenty left over if he changes his mind."

I was pleasantly surprised by how delicious the pasta parcels were. "Seems you've been telling porkies where your culinary skills are concerned."

"Thank you. I'll take that as a compliment."

After dinner, I insisted on helping with the dishes. The three of us had a job each. I washed and wiped down the sides and scraped the plates into the bin.

"Oh, dear!" I said, turning to Phil, a scowl on my face.

"What?"

I reached into the bin and pulled out a plastic ready-made pasta container and an empty jar of Alfredo sauce.

"Oops, busted." Phil laughed.

"Oops indeed." I couldn't help but laugh too.

We finished cleaning up, and then Phil said it was Kate's bedtime.

"Aw, five more minutes, Daddy, please."

"No, darling. You know the rules. If you don't go to bed on time, you'll be a real grump in the morning."

"Then can you read me a bedtime story, Lizzi?"

"I'd love to, if your dad doesn't mind."

"Go for it!" Phil said.

"Come on, I'll show you my bedroom." Kate grabbed my hand and we walked upstairs together.

"This room is Daddy's." She pointed to the first door on the left. "And this one is the bathroom." She opened the door opposite.

I felt obliged to bob my head inside. "Oh, very nice," I said.

"Ben's room is at the end of the hall, and this one is mine." With a flourish, she opened the last door on the right. "Daddy and Ben don't like pink, but I love it. It's my favourite colour."

"Mine too," I lied.

The bedroom had been lovingly decorated and fitted out with a very pink *My Little Mermaid* theme. Even the headboard was a huge pink clam shell. A large bookshelf held several white wicker baskets lined with pretty pink and white fabric and were all filled to the brim with knickknacks and toys.

"Do you want to choose a book?" I asked.

"Daddy reads me three books every night. Will you read me three?"

"Of course."

She selected the books then climbed up onto the bed, patting the blankets beside her, indicating for me to sit down.

After reading them, I placed the books back on the bookcase. "Now what do we do?"

"Daddy gives me a kiss and sings me a lullaby."

"Okay."

"Will you give me a kiss and sing me a lullaby?"

"I don't know any lullabies."

"Just sing a song."

"Okay." I kissed her forehead and began singing, badly, the only song I remember my dad singing when I was a child.

"You are my sunshine
My only sunshine
You make me happy
When skies are grey
You'll never know, dear
How much I love you
Please don't take my sunshine away"

I stroked her hair once I'd finished. "Goodnight, sweetheart."

"Can you ask Daddy to come and say goodnight?"

I nodded and walked over to the window to close the curtains. Nasty Nigel was loading something into the boot of his car. He saw me and glared, a sneer on his face.

I raised my middle finger defiantly.

Slamming the boot shut, he traced his finger underneath his chin in a throat slitting motion.

CHAPTER 31

I closed the curtain with a gasp, my heartbeat raging. Had he really just threatened me? I'd take it with a pinch of salt usually, but he totally freaked me out. I still suspected he had something to do with the dead teacher so this might not be an idle threat.

"What's wrong, Lizzi?" Kate asked, concern filling her pretty blue eyes.

"Oh, sorry, sweetie. It's nothing. Sleep tight, little one."

As I stepped from the room, I ran smack bang into Ben who was just heading out of the bathroom.

"Oh, hello." I smiled. "I was just reading Kate a bedtime story."

"I know. I heard you."

"Hope I didn't disturb you."

"You're not our mum."

Taken aback, I winced. "I know I'm not..."

But he didn't give me a chance to finish. Instead he slammed his bedroom door in my face.

Scratching my head, I stood there feeling terrible. Ben was clearly still grieving his mother, and me being there had obviously upset him. I wished Phil had told me. Feeling a little deflated, I walked downstairs and found Phil pouring wine into two glasses.

"Your daughter is waiting for a kiss," I said, accepting one of the glasses from him. "Cheers." I clinked my glass on his.

"I'll be right back."

Still feeling a little uneasy about the two events that happened upstairs, I took a deep gulp of the wine. There was nothing I could do about Nigel, but I didn't know whether or not to tell Phil what Ben had said to me. I didn't want him to be angry with his son—the poor boy had been through enough. But if he was mine, I'd want to know how he was feeling.

"Hey, you. Talk about upstaging me—three stories *and* a song!"

"What do you mean? That's what she told me *you* do."

"Seems you've been duped again. I read her one story and absolutely no singing!"

"The little…" I laughed, shaking my head in admiration. "She didn't bat an eyelid—I totally believed her."

"I know. She's a little minx. Shall we go through to the living room? It's cosier in there."

The living room was in darkness until Phil turned on two lamps and closed the thick gold-coloured curtains. It was a lovely room, one I hadn't seen before. He turned on the bluetooth speaker and sounds of Simply Red's greatest hits filled the room.

"I love this," I said, feeling incredibly gooey all of a sudden. It must've been the effects of the wine.

"Me too. I usually have it blasting out from the car, and I sing along shamelessly."

I laughed. "I do the same to Pink."

"I'm maybe a little old for Pink."

"Nonsense. Aren't we about the same age?"

He shrugged. "Really? How old are you?"

"Thirty-nine. It's the big four-oh next year."

"I'm forty-one—you're just a spring chicken."

I laughed. "Hardly."

"How come you never had children?"

His question caught me off guard, and I took a sharp intake of breath.

"Sorry. I shouldn't have asked that—it's rude of me."

I held my breath and then slowly released it. "No, it's okay. Most people ask that once they know my age. A woman approaching forty with no children is an oddity in this day and age—either someone who's too focussed on her career and makes a conscious decision not to have children or the unfortunate ones who, despite years of trying, can't actually fall pregnant."

"Which group do you fall into?"

"None of the above." I grinned. "Sorry to lead you into that, but I said that's what people ask—not that it's always the case."

"Which is?"

"I didn't marry until I was well into my thirties, and, although desperate for a baby, my husband wasn't ready. Then, when he finally agreed…" I paused, shocked I was actually intending to tell him something I hadn't spoken about since it happened, not even to my closest friend. "I fell pregnant straight away. I was ecstatic. But Sean, my husband, was having a bad time at work, not that he confided in me, and he began drinking, which brought out the monster in him."

"Oh, fuck. Why do I think this is going to be horrible?"

"Because it is." I exhaled slowly before continuing. "One night, after returning home from an entire weekend bender, Sean attacked me. I was seven months pregnant."

He gasped and reached for my hand.

"I was in a bad way but, sadly, the baby, who had to be delivered naturally, didn't stand a chance."

"Oh, shit, Lizzi! That's awful. I'm so sorry."

I nodded, feeling tears pricking my eyes. "So that's why I don't have children. Nancy, my little girl, would've been five years old next month. A little younger than Kate."

CHAPTER 32

Phil shook his head. "I'm stunned. What happened to your husband?"

I sighed and closed my eyes for an extended blink. "He was arrested and charged. Served just over a year of a three year sentence and, the worst of it is, he now has two children with his current partner. He still lives in the same village as my parents, and they keep me informed no matter how often I tell them I really don't want to know."

"The bastard. How the hell is that fair? He killed his baby, for fuck's sake. He should've been castrated—prevented from fathering kids ever again."

"I know, but life's never fair, is it? Look what happened to you and your kids—devastating." I felt this was the perfect segue into mentioning Ben. "It must be tough on Ben. He's at that awful age when kids often play up—hormones raging through his system. Life's tough enough as it is. But to lose his mother slap bang in the middle of it—just terrible."

"I do worry about him, more so than Kate if I'm honest. He's struggling."

"He told me off earlier after I'd read to Kate. He said I'm not his mother."

"He what?"

"Don't be mad at him. I understand. It must be so confusing for him to have another woman in his house, no matter how innocent."

"Yeah, but he can't go being rude to guests. It's not acceptable."

"Promise me you won't say anything—he'll think I'm a right blabbermouth and probably never speak to me again."

"I know but…"

"Promise me, Phil. I didn't tell you to get him into trouble. I just thought you needed to be aware he's struggling."

"Alright, I won't say a word this time as long as you tell me if he does it again."

"Deal."

We talked continuously for the next couple of hours, and eventually I looked at my watch and yawned. "I wonder how they're getting on next door," I said. "I suppose I'd best get going."

Phil glanced at the clock on the mantelpiece. "Bloody hell, it's almost ten o'clock! How did that happen?"

"I have no idea. But I'll head off—just sneak in and go to bed. I don't want to disturb the love birds if they're getting it on."

"Surely they won't be! She's pregnant."

I shrugged. "Who knows? But it's none of our business. Thanks for a lovely evening, by the way. I really enjoyed myself."

"Me too. Maybe we can do it again soon."

I nodded. "We'll see. I don't want to upset Ben again."

"Ben won't be here this weekend—they're both going to stay with their grandparents. How about we go out? Let our hair down?"

"I'd like that." I smiled, feeling like a giddy teenager. "Miriam might be back by then, though. Once she discovers I went against her instructions, I'll be out on my ear." I dragged myself to my feet not wanting to go but wary of outstaying my welcome.

"What does Charlie say about that?"

"He said I work for him, not her. Apparently my wages are coming out of his account. He said he'll keep me on. But, saying that, she probably won't want us living in her house."

"Doesn't Charlie have a place of his own?"

"Yeah, he does. But it's miles away from here."

He walked me out and down the path. "I'll watch you get in safely."

My stomach flipped. Being so distracted by him, I'd actually forgotten Nigel and his earlier threat. I spun around and stared at his house—it was in complete darkness, but that didn't stop me from feeling vulnerable, like he could be out there watching me from some dark corner. "Thanks, Phil." I didn't want to tell him what had happened earlier in case he took it upon himself to go and have it out with Nigel.

He stopped at the gate, and I patted his arm awkwardly. "Okay. Goodnight then." I reached the front door and let myself in, then I waved at Phil before quietly closing the door.

"Boo!"

My feet left the floor and I whirled around to find Charlie standing directly behind me with Thomas in his arms. "Bloody hell, you frightened the life out of me."

"Sorry, I couldn't resist. I was just about to let Thomas out. He's been unsettled all night."

"Maybe he's missed me. I'll take over if you like? Then I'll go to bed."

He handed Thomas to me.

"How's it going?" I nodded in the direction of the living room.

"Great. I like her—a lot."

"And dinner?"

"I killed it. And she was well impressed."

"I can hear you, you know?" Alexis called out from the living room.

I winced and laughed. "I'll let you get back to it." Opening the front door, I dropped Thomas onto the mat.

He ran to the middle of the path and began growling at the shadows under the trees—his hackles up.

"Shhh! You'll wake the bloody street up," I hissed.

He ran towards the trees and continued to bark and growl.

Goosebumps covered my body. What the hell was he barking at? I'd considered walking him to the grassy area, but I changed my mind. Maybe Nigel was out there after all, under the trees, waiting for me. "You read too many horror stories," I muttered to myself. Yet I really didn't relish proving myself wrong. "Come on, boy. Do your bloody business, and let's get back inside."

Thomas ran back towards me and cocked his leg up on the plant pot beside the door, then he took off back to the trees barking again. There was definitely something getting him all worked up.

I called him again and picked him up. "Come on, bugger-lugs." I nuzzled my face into his neck. Stepping inside, I shoved the door shut with my foot and took Thomas through to my bedroom.

I couldn't wipe the smile from my face. Although telling Phil about Nancy had broken my heart, it also felt good to finally get it off my chest. Phil was a good man, of that I was certain.

CHAPTER 33

"I should go," Alexis said. "Phil will lock me out if I'm not careful.

Charlie grinned. "Would that be so bad? You could always stay here."

"Hey, cheeky. I'm not that kind of girl." The fact that she used to be wasn't important. Since finding out she was expecting a baby, things had changed.

"Can I see you again tomorrow? There's something I need to tell you before we go any further," Charlie said.

She was intrigued. Phil had told her about his brain tumour. Maybe he wanted to tell her himself. "You can't say something like that then make me wait till tomorrow."

"It's nothing bad. Well, at least I don't think it is, but I'm too tired to go into it tonight."

"Are you okay?" She suddenly noticed he looked a little peaky —he had dark circles under his eyes.

"I'll let you get to bed. Thanks so much for spoiling me tonight."

"My pleasure."

She bent down and kissed his cheek. "Don't get up, I'll see myself out."

"See you tomorrow."

She left the house, pulling the front door closed behind her.

As she walked into the street, she had a feeling of being watched—prickles formed at the back of her neck. She rushed down the side of Phil's house and had just reached the back door when she heard a sound close behind her. She spun around and gasped. "What are you doing here?"

CHAPTER 34

I woke to the sound of Charlie singing. Someone was happy this morning.

Thomas and I joined him in the kitchen moments later. "Good morning. You're bright and breezy considering you had a late night."

"Coffee?" he asked, a beaming smile on his face.

"I'd love one, thanks. I'll just let Thomas out for a little tinkle, and you can tell me all about it." I shrugged into my dressing gown and headed out into the back garden.

"Psst."

I jumped and spun around, relieved to see Phil peering through the gap in the hedge.

"Oh, hello, you," I said.

"I take it they had a good time last night, but I wondered if she's coming home soon? She's supposed to be taking Kate to school for me."

"What do you mean? Didn't she come home last night?"

He shook his head, a grin on his face. "Nope."

"The dirty bugger! No wonder he's got a smile on his face this morning. Hang on a sec, I'll go and ask."

Back in the kitchen I shook my head at Charlie in mock disgust. "You could've told me. I felt a right twit then. Phil wants to know if Alexis is taking Kate to school."

"How should I know?"

"Well, can you ask her?"

"I could, but why doesn't he ask?"

"What do you mean?"

He shook his head, clearly confused. "Hang on, what are you talking about?"

"Phil wants to know what time Alexis will be home. She's supposed to be taking Kate to school."

He steadied himself against the table. "Alexis left here last night."

"Are you sure?"

"Of course, I'm bloody sure."

We both ran out the back door.

"She's not here, Phil. She left for home last night."

The colour drained from Phil's face. "Then where the hell is she?"

CHAPTER 35

I rushed inside and got dressed, then put Thomas in the garage. I ran around to Phil's house.

"Anything?" I asked.

He shook his head. "No, her car's still here, so is her handbag and phone. I don't have a clue where she could be."

I rubbed my face and slumped down on a dining chair. "I should've said something last night."

"About what? What are you talking about?"

"Nigel."

"The neighbour?"

"He's been awful, and yesterday his wife was taken away in an ambulance."

"Yeah, Alexis said, but what does that have to do with anything?"

"Well, last night, when I was closing the curtains in Kate's bedroom, he made a throat slitting motion at me. And then Thomas was going berserk last night at someone in the front garden."

"And you think it was Nigel?"

"I don't know. But we need to tell the police."

"I'll call them now."

"Shall I take the kids to school?"

He rubbed his chin making a rasping sound. "Would you? Ben's already left with his mate, so it's just Kate. I'll call the police once she's gone. I don't want her to know anything's wrong."

"Okay, I'll just go and grab my handbag, and I'll be back shortly. Is she ready?"

"I'll check. See you in a minute."

The phone was ringing as I arrived home. I considered ignoring it, but I guessed it was Miriam and she would think something was wrong and I'd left her brother alone. I picked the handset up. "Hello."

"Elizabeth, it's Miriam. I'm sorry we got cut off the other day. Can you explain to me what you meant about a woman's body being found? Is it Laura?"

I gasped. "No. It's nothing to do with Charlie's ex. It's a German woman, a teacher from the primary school. Thomas found her body down by the creek—she'd been strangled."

"I'm going to ask you something now, and I need you to be truthful. Could Charlie have got to the woman somehow?"

"No." Suddenly, my heart dropped. The night Erin had gone missing was the night he'd woken up. I gasped.

"He did. Didn't he?"

I shook my head, not knowing what to say. Glancing around to make sure Charlie wasn't in earshot before continuing. "He did wake up one night. Maybe it was that night. Why do you ask?"

"Because Charlie's tumour has made him incredibly danger-ous. He's attacked women before, which is why the specialist prescribed the medication. It's imperative he stays sedated. He is still sedated, isn't he?"

I couldn't talk. I fell into the armchair, my thoughts in a spin.

"Please tell me he is."

"Well…" I gulped down a huge lump. What the hell had I done? Could Charlie really be violent?

"Elizabeth! Don't tell me you've not been sedating him. Are you crazy?"

No way was I going to be made a scapegoat. "Well, actually, Miriam, I'm not responsible. You should've been honest with me, but you weren't. In fact, you left me alone with him while you went gallivanting around the bloody world."

"I need to call his specialist, Cecil Bain. Do you know him?"

"Of course, I know him."

"He'll be in touch to tell you where we go from here. But in the meantime, make sure you keep yourself safe. And don't tell him what we've discussed. Promise me."

The sight of a police car pulling up across the road startled me. "I promise. Look, I've got to go." I hung up, annoyed with myself for not getting Kate out of the way before the police arrived. I grabbed my bag and a jacket and ran from the house.

"Sorry, sorry. I had a phone call," I said to Phil.

He looked at me as though he hadn't a clue what I was talking about. "Why, what's wrong?"

"The police—they're here already."

"But I haven't called them yet."

"Really? Maybe Charlie did. I haven't a clue where he is, come to think of it." I didn't want to mention what Miriam had said. I was still trying to process it. "Is Kate ready to go?"

He nodded. "She's watching TV." He called Kate and she appeared moments later.

"Are you taking me to school?" she asked excitedly.

"I am."

"And Thomas?"

"No. Sorry, sweetheart. Thomas is still asleep but you can see him after school."

I didn't even think to ask Phil for his car, so we just started walking.

"Oh, look. The policemans are at Mr Mason's house."

"So they are." I craned my neck to look up the driveway and

saw a uniformed policeman knocking at the door. What would the police want with Nigel? My mind was in a total spin. I still hadn't got my head around what Miriam had said, and I wasn't even sure I believed Charlie could be responsible for Erin's death. But now, with Alexis' disappearance, was I burying my head in the sand? I didn't think so, but I intended to talk to Charlie. I'd have to warn him Cecil, his specialist, would probably be in touch once Miriam had got hold of him.

"Have I done something wrong?" Kate's worried face gazed up at me.

"No, of course not—why do you ask?"

"Because first Daddy, and now you, won't talk to me."

"I'm sorry, sweetheart. We've just got a lot on our mind, that's all."

I dropped Kate off at the school gate and watched while she went into her classroom, then I practically ran all the way back to Phil's.

"Any news?" I panted as though I'd run a marathon.

"Nothing. I popped over to speak to the police and told them Alexis had gone missing, and they didn't seem to care. They said we needed to wait until she'd been gone more than twenty-four hours—they rarely take it seriously until then. He put a call in to register that I'd reported it to him, but I doubt they'll do anything until tomorrow."

"What a crock of shit! I can understand it if she'd gone out and maybe got waylaid, but Alexis hasn't got a thing with her—no phone, no money, no car, and she's pregnant, for Christ's sake. We don't even know if she had a coat on. This is appalling."

"Tell me about it."

"So, what *can* we do?"

He shook his head. "I haven't a clue," he snapped.

"Pardon me for trying to help."

"I'm sorry, Lizzi. I don't mean to take it out on you, but I'm freaking out."

"I know. Have you called her parents? Could *they* know anything?"

"I doubt it. And if they don't, I'd just freak the shit out of them instead."

I scratched my scalp in sheer frustration. "I don't know what else to suggest. I'm terrified that evil bastard across the road has done something to her."

Phil jumped to his feet and began pacing the floor.

"I'm sorry. I'm not helping, am I? Shall I make us a pot of tea?"

"I'll do it," he said, "I need to keep myself busy. Where did you say Charlie is?"

"I don't know. He was in the kitchen making coffee one minute, and then once he'd discovered Alexis hadn't come home he just vanished. Maybe he had to lie down. I'd best go and check on him. He's a sick man when all's said and done—maybe the stress has knocked him off kilter."

He nodded. "Yeah, you go and check while I make a brew."

I ran next door and popped my head into Charlie's room. He wasn't there and his bed had been made perfectly. "Charlie?" I shouted.

Nothing.

Thomas began barking and scratching at the back of the garage door. I opened it, and he ran out excited to see me. He ran about my feet whimpering. "Silly sausage. I haven't been gone that long." I opened the back door for him and stepped into the back garden, but he wouldn't leave my side, which wasn't like him. "What's wrong, boy? Has something frightened you?"

He quick-marched on the spot, looking up at me, whimpering.

Lifting him into my arms, I took him back inside. "Sorry, matey, but you'll have to go back into the garage for a while." I stepped inside the garage and froze. Deep gut-wrenching sobs came from the back of the room. No wonder Thomas was freaked out.

Turning on the light, I saw Charlie curled up in a ball in the corner of the room.

I ran over to him worried sick he was injured or his tumour had caused a seizure or something equally terrible. "Charlie, are you okay?" I dropped to my knees beside him and put my arms around his shoulders. "What's happened?"

His sobs continued. The happy, smiling face of this morning was a far cry from the face before me. It didn't even look like the same man. "Don't come near me," he sobbed. "I can't be trusted."

I gasped and sat backwards onto my bottom in shock. "What are you saying, Charlie?" Miriam's warning came back to me with force. "Is it Alexis? Do you know what's happened to her?"

"I don't know," he cried, snot and tears coated his blotchy, red face. "But it's happened again, just like Laura. Miriam warned me. She said I was a danger to women, but…" He rubbed at his eyes and roared, slamming the heels of his hands into his face several times.

I grabbed his hands and pulled them away so he couldn't do any harm to himself. "Hey, hey—stop that! Tell me what happened?"

"I honestly don't remember, but it must've been me."

"The police investigated you where Laura was concerned—you told me that yourself. They can't think you had anything to do with it, or you'd be locked up now."

"But how else can you explain it? First Laura vanishes then another couple of girlfriends are attacked and beaten within an inch of their lives. Miriam said it was me—because of the tumour. But I honestly don't remember what the hell I've done. That's the reason she had me drugged up. Do you get it now?"

I didn't let on Miriam had already told me. I still struggled to believe he was actually dangerous, but I had to admit it did seem like too much of a coincidence.

"Alexis was here one minute and then she was gone. I fell

asleep in the chair as soon as she left. I was so shattered. What if...?"

"I don't believe that for a second—honestly, I don't. But let's get you to bed. I can give you something to calm you down and help you sleep."

"What if you're next? I'm scared, Lizzi. I'm bloody scared."

"Look at me." I placed my hands on either side of his face and forced his face inches from mine. "I honestly don't believe you've hurt Alexis, or Laura, or anyone for that matter, but, if you're worried, I can medicate you till we know for sure. Not like last time, just enough to take the edge off everything. What do you think?"

He nodded. "Yes. That's what I want. I couldn't bear it if I hurt anyone else. I'd rather kill myself." He glanced down at his side, and I spotted a carving knife tucked underneath his leg.

"Is that what you intended to do?"

He nodded. "But I'm too much of a coward. I'm fucking pathetic, aren't I?"

"No, you're not. Come on, let's get you to bed."

"How do you explain what's happened then? How can you be so certain I'm not dangerous?"

"Because I think it has something to do with Nigel across the road. You said yourself that Thomas wasn't himself last night. He went berserk like someone was out there under the trees. He scared the shit out of me."

"Really? I wish I'd known that. I would've insisted on walking her home."

"I'm so sorry, Charlie. I should've told you."

"It's okay. You weren't to know. What did the police say? It'll only be a matter of time before they start pointing the finger at me. I can't go through that again, Lizzi. I can't."

"They said they won't do anything for twenty-four hours. By then she'll probably be home." I got him to his bed, and he lay on top of the duvet. "Okay, are you sure you want some meds?"

"I don't want them, but I need them. What choice do I have?"

I agreed. I'd feel much better if he was out of it for a while. "Okay. I'll give you a quarter-strength dose. That will make you sleep at least. I'm not going to mention any of this to Phil, but I'll need to be with him. I'll pop back to check on you regularly."

He rolled his sleeve up ready for me to administer the drugs.

I sat with him until he began to drift off. Then I got to my feet and headed to the door.

"Camera," Charlie said softly.

"Sorry?"

"Miriam installed a camera."

"Get some sleep and you can tell me all about it later."

CHAPTER 36

As I stepped outside, I was startled by several loud bangs coming from Nigel's house. Still thinking he had something to do with Alexis, I ran across the road not thinking about my own safety.

But it wasn't Nigel. The police were back and this time they were hammering down his door.

"Miss, stand back," a young, dark-skinned detective said, holding out his ID. "What are you doing here?" He walked towards me, arms outstretched, trying to prevent me from getting any closer.

"My friend's missing. I really think the man who lives here has something to do with it. He threatened me last night."

"If he threatened you, why do you think he's done something to your friend?"

"He's nasty. Honestly, he threatened to cut my throat just last night, and Alexis also had a run-in with him yesterday."

"I see. Well, we're in the middle of something right now. Let us do our job, and I'll come over to take a statement shortly."

"Promise me? I'll be at my neighbour's. Alexis lives there, number seventy-three."

"I'll be over soon. Now I need you to go. I can't guarantee your safety if you don't."

I backed out of the driveway, intrigued and desperate to know what was going on. Why would they be breaking into Nigel's house? I'd been so incensed, needing to get my point across to the young detective, I hadn't even thought about what they could be doing there. And for him to tell me he couldn't guarantee my safety—what the hell was that all about?

As I walked back towards Phil's place, I scanned Miriam's house looking for a camera after what Charlie had said. Something drew my eyes to the top floor. I'd never been upstairs. Miriam had made it clear that part of the house was out of bounds, but I suddenly noticed what could be a camera pointing down at the driveway. "Really?" I shook my head. Why hadn't I seen that before? I couldn't wait for Charlie to wake up.

Phil opened the door seeming a little miffed. "You took your time. The tea's stone cold now."

"You won't believe what happened," I said, following him through to the kitchen.

"Try me."

"I found Charlie in the garage in a bad way. Alexis vanishing like that reminded him of Laura Sanders, you know, the super-model who went missing. It's really affected him. It's understandable he'd think someone was out to get him." I may not have been telling him the entire truth, but I wasn't lying—not really. "It took me a while to calm him down and get him to bed. I even had to give him something to help him sleep."

"Poor bloke. I'm telling you now, if Alexis has just taken off again, I'll kill her with my bare hands."

"She can't have done. Think about it, Phil. If she'd planned to leave, she would've taken her handbag and phone at the very least."

"I know. But she's absconded so many times in the past—I can't help but think she's done it again."

"Well, there's more. The police were back at Nigel's."

"What? Again?"

"Yep. And they were busting down the door, so I went over. One of the detectives promised to come over here later on and take a statement. I don't know what Nigel has been up to, but I'd put money on it being something awful."

"Fuck!"

"I know, right! Then, something Charlie said made me wonder if Miriam had installed a CCTV camera. And, when I was on my way back over here, I think I spotted a camera pointing down at Miriam's driveway. I'm thinking it may have picked up what happened to Alexis with a bit of luck. Charlie hopefully knows how we can access it."

"Bloody hell, you have been busy. I feel a little guilty for begrudging you a measly cup of tea now." He grinned weakly. "I'll make you another—you deserve it after that little lot."

Twenty minutes later, the same detective came over as promised.

Phil ushered him into the kitchen.

"Thanks for coming," I said. "Please tell me you didn't find Alexis locked in the basement over there?"

He shook his head. "No, there was no sign of your friend or anybody else for that matter."

"Can you tell me what Nigel's done?"

"I'm afraid I can't. It's still an ongoing investigation, I'm sorry. However, seeing as I'm doing you this favour, I wondered if you'd reciprocate."

"If I can." I perched on the edge of my seat.

"If you see Mr Mason return to his house, or if you see him at all, can you call me?" He handed me his card.

I nodded. "With pleasure. I couldn't think of anything that would make me happier, to be honest, DC Wayne Campbell," I said, reading the card.

"Thanks. I'd appreciate it. Now, tell me about your friend."

CHAPTER 37

Half an hour later, the detective left, promising to talk to his boss about Alexis' disappearance, mainly because Nigel was already being investigated for something, and he agreed her vanishing like that was definitely odd—especially because she hadn't taken any of her belongings.

"Maybe I *should* call her parents then," Phil said.

I exhaled noisily. "I don't think you have a choice, Phil. They need to know."

He nodded and closed his eyes briefly. "You're right." He pulled his phone from his jeans' pocket. "Hey, Eric, it's me."

I couldn't hear what the man on the other end said, but I could hear his voice jabbering away.

"So, you haven't seen Alexis since then, I take it?"

More intense talking. I didn't know Alexis' dad, but he sounded angry.

"She didn't come home last night. She'd only been to the neighbour's and left before midnight, but she didn't make it back."

More talking.

"That was my first thought. However, she didn't take her

phone, her purse or her car. I can't help but think this time it's serious."

More talking.

"I know. You're probably right. You know her better than anyone, I guess. I just needed to tell you, that's all." He hung up and exhaled, puffing out his cheeks, and rolling his eyes.

"What did he say?"

"That she's playing silly buggers again, and he doesn't believe anything has happened to her."

"Really? I thought they'd be beside themselves."

"I guess they know her of old. She's done this to them so many times in the past, to be honest. I don't blame them for thinking that. But, it's the fact she's not taken her bare essentials that makes me think they might be wrong this time."

"I hope they're not. Did you get the vibe from that detective that he thinks Nigel is dangerous?"

Phil nodded. "I did actually. I wonder what he's done."

"Could he have bashed his wife? She was taken to hospital and hasn't returned. Not that I've noticed anyway."

"Who knows what goes on behind closed doors? Maybe he did. But although losing his rag and beating his wife is shocking, that doesn't mean he'd do it to someone else."

"He's unhinged that one. I can see it in his eyes. I hope I'm wrong, but I wouldn't put anything past him."

He got to his feet. "Are you hungry?"

"A little, but I'd best go and check on Charlie. I'm worried about him." The thought of him trying to cut his wrists freaked me out. "Maybe he shouldn't be alone right now. Do you want to come next door with me, instead?"

"Would you mind? I don't think I want to be alone either."

"Of course not. Come on, let's go."

Phil grabbed his jacket from the newel post and followed me next door.

I quietly entered Charlie's bedroom relieved to see he

appeared to be sleeping. I stroked his forehead and his eyelids flickered then opened. "How are you feeling?"

"Numb. Any news?"

I shook my head. "No. Although I've managed to get the police to take a statement, thank God. I noticed a camera above the driveway earlier. Is that what you were talking about?"

He nodded.

"Do you think that might show who was out there last night?"

He shrugged.

"Do you know how to access the footage?"

"Upstairs. Miriam's PC."

"Will we need her permission?"

He shook his head. "Give me a couple of hours for these drugs to wear off, and I'll go up and check."

"Are you sure?"

He nodded, his eyes already closed again.

The house phone began ringing as I walked back into the living room.

"Aren't you going to answer that?" Phil asked.

I shook my head. "It'll be Miriam. She knows Charlie's awake, and she's angry with me." I waited until it stopped ringing then pulled the wire from the back of the base unit. "I can't be bothered dealing with her shit right now."

"Fair enough."

I actually didn't want to talk to her in front of Phil in case he heard her going on about Charlie attacking women, especially while Alexis was still missing. Maybe it was wrong of me for protecting him, but I really didn't want to be part of a witch hunt —not without evidence anyway.

I made us both a sandwich. I didn't feel very hungry, but I felt lost and preferred to keep myself busy. I didn't tell Phil what Charlie had said about the camera. I didn't want to raise his hopes —after all, it may show nothing at all apart from a fox or a cat in the bushes. Maybe it had just been my imagination, but I'd been certain someone had been out there and hoped the camera had picked up who it was, if nothing else.

Considering we did nothing more than pace the floor and peer from the window, the afternoon flew by. We hadn't heard any more from the police, but I wasn't sure how long an investigation like this took to get off the ground. Or if the cops had decided to wait the allotted twenty-four hours after all.

"I'll go and pick the kids up. Maybe take them for a burger and tell them about Alexis. I can't keep it from them. They'll figure something's wrong. They're not daft."

"Good idea. I'll keep my eyes peeled and call you if anything changes."

I planted myself on a chair at the living room window, keeping one eye on Nigel's house and one eye on next door, but there was nothing to report.

At just after four, Charlie appeared in the living room doorway.

"Feeling better?" I asked.

"Still a little groggy to tell the truth."

"What are you doing up then? Go back to sleep."

"No. It's been on my mind since you came in. I want to check out the camera footage. I'd forgotten all about that. Miriam had it installed last year after someone had tampered with her car. Wish me luck."

"Good luck!" I called after him wanting more than anything to go up too. "Do you need a hand?"

"I don't think so. I'll call you if I find anything."

A niggling doubt crept into my mind, and I couldn't manage to shake it. Miriam's warning played again and again in my mind. What if he saw himself going out after Alexis? Would he delete the footage? I couldn't chance it, so I ran up the staircase after him.

CHAPTER 38

The wide staircase opened up to a large second living room with two rooms off it, which I presumed were the bedroom and bathroom.

"Ooh! Nice," I said, having a nose around. I lifted a photo frame off the bookcase—a very young Miriam and Charlie smiled back at me.

Charlie sat with his back to me at a desk along the back wall. "I thought you were waiting downstairs?"

"I can't. I'm too anxious. Can I help? Please?"

"Don't hover behind me then. Pull up a seat."

The only other place to sit was an armchair with a footstool. I dragged the footstool over and sat down beside him. "Anything?"

"Give me a chance. I've only just managed to open the computer. I had to try a few passwords, but I got there in the end."

"Thank goodness. This is our only chance. I hope it doesn't turn out to be a waste of time."

"We'll soon know. Here's the camera program." He clicked an icon on the desktop. "It looks as though it's live. What time did you come home last night? Let's go straight to that point."

I wracked my brain. "Erm, gosh. I think it was just after ten."

He nodded and typed something into the computer then turned the screen for me to see.

I was surprised at how much the teeny camera picked up. I could see the whole of the driveway, the front door, the hedge and Phil's side path too.

Charlie hit fast-forward and the clock whizzed by. Spotting movement on the screen at 22:12pm, I shouted, "Stop!"

He stopped and rewound slightly.

"There." I watched myself and Phil walk down his path, and then Phil stood on the street while I entered our gate and let myself in the front door. The look on Phil's face made my heart race. He smiled then turned, heading back up his path. Moments later, I returned with Thomas.

"See? Look how he's barking at the trees. He definitely sensed something. Rewind a second."

He did as I suggested and, at the very edge of the screen, I saw a pair of men's boots.

"There. There! Did you see that? I fucking knew it. Who the hell is it?"

He forwarded the tape again and paused as the area was illuminated from the headlights of a passing car showing the silhouette of a man standing in the shadows.

"I feel sick. Do you think it's Nigel?" I said.

He rubbed his chin and pinched at his bottom lip. "I don't know. It can't have been much later than this when Alexis left. I just can't remember."

"Go slow. We'll see her."

He nodded, and the clock ticked over double time. He suddenly stopped the film.

"Did you see something?" I asked.

"I think so." He rewound the tape, and I did notice definite movement in the shadows although it was impossible to see what was happening.

"I think he's just moving around," I said.

The driveway lit up as the front door opened and Alexis stepped outside—a clear spring in her step.

Charlie paused the film.

"What did you do that for?"

"I'm scared," he admitted.

I exhaled. I was so desperate to see what was going to happen that I completely forgot what he must be going through.

"What if I...?"

I shook my head. "I don't believe you would hurt her, Charlie. I don't think you're capable of hurting anyone. Do you? Really?"

"No. But..."

"But nothing. It wasn't you loitering in the shadows was it? Press play." I grabbed hold of his left hand and held it in his lap.

Once again, we watched Alexis leave the house, walk past the mystery man and back up Phil's path towards the back door.

"Look! He's moving!" I gasped.

We watched the shadowy figure step out of the bushes and into the street.

"Who the fuck is that?" I hissed.

Charlie shook his head and paused the image again showing a tall, stocky man with a full, dark beard, and greased back hair. He wore a patterned, long-sleeved shirt and jeans.

"Press play," I urged.

"I don't think I can watch. What if he...? Oh, my God, I'm going to be sick." He ran through the door to the left of me and I heard him throw his guts up.

"Oh, puh-lease!" I mumbled, burying my head in my hands.

"Sorry." He returned, wiping his face on a white hand-towel. "Maybe we should just call the police—let them see what happened."

"You're joking?"

"Whatever happens next might not be... Well, put it this way, we can't unsee it." Tears brimmed in his eyes.

I sighed. "Oh, don't cry. I'll call the detective from earlier—he gave me his number. But if he can't come right away, I'll watch it myself. Deal?"

"Deal."

CHAPTER 39

Detective Wayne Campbell said he was on his way and that he'd be with us within the hour.

I left Charlie upstairs and decided to busy myself in the kitchen—peeling potatoes and frying mince was far more appealing than looking at the back of Charlie's head while he scanned files on Miriam's computer.

When Detective Campbell arrived, I led him upstairs and introduced him to Charlie who was now seated in the armchair, his face drained of all colour.

"Hi, mate," Charlie said. "Thanks for coming."

"Are you okay?" I asked Charlie. "Don't tell me you've already watched it?"

He shook his head. "I didn't watch it. I'm just a little light-headed, that's all."

"Maybe you've overdone it. Can we just...?" I pointed at the computer.

"Sorry, the film is on the screen ready for you to press play. I can't watch."

"No problem." Detective Campbell sat at the desk and, as he

moved the mouse, the image of Alexis standing in the doorway filled the screen.

"Right," I said, pointing at the screen. "You can't see him, but there's a man standing in the shadows, just here. It's not Nigel. We haven't a clue who he is. If you press play, you'll see him."

"Okay. Do you want to watch it?"

I nodded. "I need to see for myself."

"Okay, let's do this." He hit play and we watched Alexis walk from the house, across the driveway, and down the path next door. The man stepped from the shadows and stalked close behind her. She stopped, turned, appeared shocked. Then she spoke. Seconds later, she launched herself into his arms, their faces smooshed together.

"Oh, my God."

"What? What happened?" Charlie said, his face still buried in his hands.

"Safe to say she wasn't kidnapped," I said, shaking my head as I watched Alexis and the mystery man walk hand-in-hand back to the street and out of the shot.

CHAPTER 40

"I'm sorry to waste your time, detective. I honestly thought... well, you know what I thought."

"That's fine. Make it up to me by keeping your eyes peeled for activity across the road."

"I will. I promise."

"Your mate up there, is that Charlie Maidley?"

"It is. But it can't get out where he is. As you just saw, he's not very well at the moment."

"Don't worry. Your secret's safe with me." He climbed into his car.

As he drove off, I noticed Phil's car was back in its usual spot. He must've returned home while I was upstairs. I decided to get it over and done with and headed next door.

My mind was still reeling by what I'd just witnessed. I'd left Charlie upstairs—he'd not moved a muscle since finding out about Alexis which was obviously a relief, but was also upsetting for him considering he'd fallen quite hard for her.

I walked down Phil's path and knocked on the door.

Ben opened the door and let it slam wide open then stomped up the stairs without saying a word.

I stepped inside. "Hello?"

"In here," Phil shouted from the kitchen.

I pushed the door open and found him and Kate doing a jigsaw puzzle on the dining table.

"How were your burgers?" I asked.

"Yummy!" Kate said.

How did it go? I mouthed to Phil.

He shrugged and shook his head. "Ben's just gone upstairs," he said, then mouthed. *He's angry.*

"Okay," I said. *I need to talk to you,* I mouthed.

He nodded. "Kate, why don't you go upstairs and get into your pyjamas?"

"It's too early!" she complained.

"I know, but I thought we could snuggle up on the sofa and watch Frozen."

"Yay!" She slid off the chair and ran from the room.

"What is it?" he asked, once she was out of earshot.

"We accessed the CCTV. In fact, that cop from earlier came around to watch it with us."

"And..."

"And there was definitely a man hanging around in the shadows."

"Who was it?"

"I have no idea. It wasn't Nigel."

"Who was it, then?"

Suddenly, the back door opened, and Alexis and her fancy man fell inside laughing raucously.

CHAPTER 41

"What the…" Phil jumped to his feet as though he'd been scalded.

"Phil, meet Kadri, my boyfriend. He came all the way from Turkey to find me and take me home."

"And you didn't think to tell me? Instead you just vanish in the middle of the night without a trace. We thought you'd been fucking abducted."

"Hey. No curse," Kadri said, in a deep, heavily accented voice.

"No curse? Are you kidding me? Do you have any idea what we've been going through today?"

Hearing raised voices, the kids entered the kitchen, and Ben rushed into his aunt's arms.

"We've informed the police," Phil continued. "And they're out looking for you as we speak."

"The police? Why did you do that?"

"Why do you think?" Phil was clearly furious, and he was struggling to contain it. "You vanish in the middle of the night without your phone, purse or car, and we're meant to think what? Oh, some greasy prick from Turkey has probably found her and they've gone for some sexy time?"

"Greasy prick? I no understand."

"It's okay, Kadri. He's rude."

Kadri nodded, his forehead bunched up.

"Rude?" Phil continued. "I'll tell you what rude is, shall I? Rude is not giving a shit about your family—picking them up when it suits and then dumping them like yesterday's rubbish—that's rude! Going missing for an entire day without telling anyone where the hell you are—that's rude! Turning up with some dude on your arm as though nothing at all is wrong—that's rude! So maybe you need to give lover boy a lesson in the meaning of rude as he seems confused."

I slid off my chair. "I think I'll get going and leave you all to it," I said, extracting myself from the tense environment. "What a day!" I muttered to myself as I ran next door. A slight movement across the road caught my eye and I froze mid-step. Nigel was back.

It took all of my effort to pretend I hadn't seen him and to act normally. I bent to de-head a couple of flowers before taking my time to enter the house.

The young detective answered the phone on the first ring. "Hello, Ms Yates. What can I do for you?"

"Nigel's back. I just saw a movement in his living room window."

"Oh, you star. I'm going to have to pass this on to my superior though as the investigation has been upscaled—but thanks so much for calling me."

"No, thank you for today. I hope this makes us even."

"It certainly does," he said before hanging up.

Charlie wasn't in his bedroom, and, with my heart in my mouth, I ran through to the garage. He wasn't there either. I released Thomas from his cage and let him outside to do his business, then ran upstairs.

Charlie was still seated in Miriam's armchair. He appeared to be asleep.

"Charlie?" I whispered.

"Hmm?"

"Are you okay?"

He nodded and stretched. "I'm fine."

"Good. I'm just gonna dish up dinner, and I think there's about to be a show across the road. Do you want to come and watch it with me?"

"A show?"

"Nigel—he's back. I've just called the detective from earlier, but he said the investigation has been upscaled—whatever that means."

He cleared his throat and stretched. "It seems quite obvious what it means."

"Well, come on then, Sherlock, spill."

"It means the investigation has gone higher—beyond his pay grade. Sounds serious to me."

"I've been telling you this for ages. He's awful. I wonder if he beat his wife up?"

He shrugged. "Quite possibly."

"Come on then. Let's go and get a prime position to watch the show unfold."

He half smiled. "I'll be there in a minute. I promise."

My heart broke for him—he was totally deflated. "I'm really sorry about Alexis, but she's a player. She doesn't deserve you. I'm so relieved you didn't harm yourself earlier."

"Believe me, so am I. And I am upset, but it's not all about Alexis."

"It's not?"

"No." He inhaled deeply. "Go on. I'll follow you soon."

"I'll pour you a drink and dish up your dinner. You've got five minutes, or I'll be back up to drag you down myself."

He smiled. "You're a bloody nuisance, you know?"

"You ain't seen nothing yet."

True to his word, Charlie joined me in the living room a few minutes later.

"We'll have to eat our dinner off our knees. I don't want to miss a thing," I said.

"Are they not here yet?" He approached the window.

"Don't let him see you!" I screeched. "He might scarper."

He jumped backwards. "Bloody hell, aren't you taking this a bit too far?"

I handed him a glass. "Sit down and shut up."

CHAPTER 42

Phil was furious. How dare Alexis waltz in as though she hadn't a care in the world after putting him through sheer hell all day.

He blew his top—mainly because she couldn't see what she'd done wrong.

When Lizzi left, he felt really bad. The kids were all over Alexis like a rash, and he thought he was going to blow a gasket.

He went upstairs to splash his face with water and allow himself to calm down. Was *he* in the wrong?

In his bedroom, he sat on the bed and called Eric to inform him his daughter had showed up safe and sound just like he said she would. Then he went back downstairs.

"Daddy, Auntie Lexi said I can be her bridesmaid," Kate said, as soon as he entered the kitchen.

"Did she now?" He glared at his sister-in-law.

"Don't be like that, Phil. I haven't got long. We're going back to Turkey first thing in the morning," Alexis said.

She made him wild, but this had been the best outcome. It could've been so much worse. But he didn't want to give in so easily. "How do you expect me to be? I was worried sick about you. We had a woman's dead body found at the back of the house just a few weeks ago—or have you forgotten about that?"

"I'm sorry. I got so swept away with the romance of it all, I didn't think. The last thing I'd want to do is upset you. I love you —you're my big bro."

He shook his head. "You're such a twit."

"Yes. But you love me."

"I know I could strangle you. Are you planning to see your parents before you leave?"

She nodded. "Yes. I want them to meet Kadri. I'm sure they'll love him as much as I do."

I glanced over to Kadri who was chatting football with Ben. "But what about the reasons why you ran away in the first place?"

"He wouldn't commit." She gazed across the room at her boyfriend, her eyes sparkling, and it gripped at his heart. Sam used to look at him in the same way, and he saw his wife briefly in her sister's eyes.

"Are you sure you're doing the right thing?"

"Positive. He was just scared. We hadn't discussed settling down and having a family."

"So, what changed?"

She shrugged. "He realized he wants me and bubs in his life. Be happy for me, Phil."

"Of course, I'm happy for you, you silly cow."

He noticed Kadri bristle—the man clearly didn't understand their banter and thought they were arguing again. Phil walked over to him and held out his hand. "Welcome to the family, buddy. I only hope you know what you're letting yourself in for."

As Alexis and Kadri were leaving a little while later, Phil noticed the commotion in the street. Feeling alarmed, he wanted to get

Ben and Kate back inside. He'd had more than enough excitement
for one day.

CHAPTER 43

When the show started, it did so with a massive bang. Four regular police cars, one van and several unmarked cars approached from either end of the street—lights and sirens wailing.

"See? I told you it would be better than a soap opera. I can't wait to find out what he's done. My money is on assaulting his wife—what's yours?"

"Could he have offed the teacher? Seems a little overkill for a domestic."

"I never thought about that. I just presumed it had something to do with his wife after seeing her carted off in the back of an ambulance. But maybe... Ooh! When will it be on the news?"

"Who knows?"

"You seem really sad. I wish I could put a smile on your face—erase ever having Alexis walk into your life. She's a bloody loony."

"Has she turned up yet?"

I nodded. "Yeah. When I was next door. She breezed in as though she hadn't a care in the world."

"Who is the guy?"

"The baby's dad. He's Turkish—they're getting married."

"I'm glad for her."

I breathed in deeply and held it, trying to bite my tongue. "You're a much bigger person than me," I said. "I could've punched her right on the nose—selfish cow."

"Lucky escape, I guess."

"A bloody lucky escape." I clinked my wine glass onto his. "I'll drink to that. But seriously, mate, you'll find someone who deserves you, you'll see."

He nodded, tears brimming his eyes again. I hated seeing men cry and suspected his brain tumour could be the reason he was extra emotional today.

"They're bringing him out!" I squealed, jumping up and leaning onto the windowsill for a closer look.

Nigel appeared flanked by two beefy cops. They shoved him into the back of the van.

"Yuss!" I said, fist pumping the air.

Once the excitement had died down, and the last of the police vehicles had left the street, I carried the empty plates through to the kitchen. Suddenly, I remembered the phone—I'd unplugged it hours ago.

As soon as the phone was plugged in, the shrill peal made me jump out of my skin.

Charlie strode into the room. "I'll get it," he said.

I was relieved. For some reason, Miriam gave me the wild shites.

"Hello," Charlie said, quietly. "Nice to hear your voice too, Miriam." He winked at me. "I think it's time you came home, don't you?"

The way he was speaking unnerved me. And why the hell would he ask her to come home? I'd be glad if she *never* came home.

"I've been on your computer," he said.

I could hear her yelling from where I was across the room.

"Let's just say, we need to talk." He replaced the handset.

"What was that all about?"

"All in good time, Lizzi. But, for now, I'm tired. I think I'll go to bed."

"When did Miriam say she'd be home?"

"She didn't. But I have a feeling it won't be too far away."

"I'm dreading it! She terrifies me. I won't lie. I know you said she can't fire me, but I really couldn't stay on once she gets home —it won't work."

"Trust me. It'll work."

———

Nigel couldn't believe his bad luck. He thought he'd be okay sneaking back to the house after the cops had searched the place, but he'd no sooner got his head down and there they were, hammering down the door. Moments later, several cops, wearing full riot gear, surrounded him. *What the heck?*

They dragged him from the house like a common criminal. He intended to have a word with the superior officer as soon as he got the chance.

He should've continued his journey to France as he first planned, but the ferry terminal had been heaving with police and security. Paranoia had made him turn around and head back.

"How's my wife?" he asked the officer leaning against the wall of the small interview room.

The muscle-bound brute shrugged one shoulder at Nigel gruffly.

It seemed like hours before the two detectives, Karlson and his sidekick Jones, turned up, and he was desperate to know the reason for the arrest. The guy standing over him in his bedroom had barked something at him, but he'd been too terrified to take it all in.

"How's my wife?" he asked as soon as they were seated.

Karlson cocked one eyebrow. "You haven't heard?"

"I wouldn't be asking if I had now, would I?"

"Your wife died, Mr Mason."

Nigel gasped. "Died? My Joanie?"

The detective looked sideways at his partner, and Nigel was sure he saw an eye roll.

"What did she die of?"

"We're hoping you could tell us that, sir."

"Me? Why me? She had a seizure. That's all I know."

"Your wife had been attacked days before her seizure, Mr Mason. She wouldn't have been conscious after that, her injuries were too severe—but then, you already know that, don't you?"

Nigel couldn't hold back the tears. It was over. Joan was dead, and he was screwed. Head down, he buried his face into the neck of his T-shirt and sobbed.

Jones handed him a tissue, but she didn't appear bothered by his tears. In fact, if he wasn't mistaken, she seemed totally bored. What kind of woman was she?

"When you've quite finished, I'll continue," Karlson said.

"It was an accident," he blurted. "We had an argument—nothing big, but she pushed my buttons. Ask anyone what a nightmare she could be."

"So, what are you saying? You didn't mean to do it?"

"Exactly. It was the first time I stood up to her. Maybe I was a little heavy-handed, but I left for work thinking she was just sulking. I couldn't believe it when I got home later that day and she hadn't moved."

"Okay, we'll need to take a full statement. Are you sure you don't want a solicitor present?"

"No point. I did it. Let's just get this over with."

CHAPTER 44

I almost shat myself when I emerged from my bedroom the next morning to find Miriam seated at the kitchen table. Letting out a scream, I almost dropped Thomas to the tiles. "Jesus! You terrified me. I didn't know you were back. Have you seen Charlie yet?"

She shook her head eyeing me with hatred.

I felt light-headed. She was so intimidating. "I'll go and call him."

"Let him sleep," she barked.

"Okay. I'll just…" I held Thomas up and nodded at the back door. I suddenly realised Thomas hadn't batted an eyelid his owner was home, which spoke volumes.

Stepping from the house, I could finally breathe again. I couldn't understand how one woman, and not a very big woman at that, could snaffle every ounce of oxygen from the room. I'd stay outside all morning if I could, but I was dressed in my pyjamas and it was fuh-reezing.

Thomas ran off to do his business but soon returned, dithering at my feet.

"Are you a man or a mouse?" I hissed, picking him up again and heading inside.

I almost jumped for joy when I saw Charlie standing at the sink filling the kettle. "I'll leave you to it," I said, speed-walking through the kitchen.

"I'd rather you were here to witness this, Lizzi," Charlie said.

"Really?"

"Surely she has better things to do than listen to this rubbish," Miriam said.

"Hurry back, please," he said to me.

I nodded. I didn't have a clue why he needed me to support him. Maybe he was as intimidated by her too, and he just wanted some moral support.

I had a quick wash and brushed my teeth before running through to my bedroom where I pulled on my jeans and a long-sleeved T-shirt.

When I returned, Charlie placed a steaming mug of coffee on the table in front of me.

"Oh, thanks." I tried to smile at Miriam's stony face, but my nerves jangled.

Charlie sat beside me with a coffee for himself. I guessed Miriam had declined a drink, which didn't surprise me.

"So," Charlie said. "At what point will loverboy be joining us?"

Taken aback, I first thought he meant Phil, but, I turned and realised he was eyeballing Miriam. What the hell was he talking about?

"Don't be facetious, Charles. It doesn't become you," Miriam sneered.

"That's not an answer. What time can we expect Cecil-fuck-ing-Bain to turn up and save your sorry arse?"

"Cecil won't be joining us. He thinks I'm still in the States."

"Don't bullshit me. I've seen your messages. I know the depth of your intimacy."

"How dare you read my private messages," she said indignantly.

I was completely confused. Charlie had told me Miriam hadn't had any relationships as far as he knew—had he been lying to me?

"I should go," I said, getting to my feet. "This has nothing to do with me."

"Yes, go," Miriam spat.

"Please Lizzi, I'd like you to stay. My sister has a talent for spinning the truth in her favour, and I would like you to witness our discussion."

I shrugged and sat back down noticing Thomas skulking off to the living room and wished I could join him.

"Thanks." He smiled at me. "I should tell Lizzi what I discovered yesterday, shouldn't I, sister dear?"

"Charles, this is silly. Let's go for a walk, just the two of us. We can sort it all out together."

He shook his head slowly. "Not a chance. I'm not going to allow you to squirm your way out of this one. And if you think you can finish the job you started, or try to have me sectioned, you can think again. I've already sent all the evidence, compiled nicely and accompanied by a lovely explanation, to my solicitor and several other high profile recipients."

I looked from one to the other of them, completely baffled.

"Sorry, Lizzi. Where should I begin?" He tapped his lips with his index finger. "How about I tell you about my big bad tumour? This huge inoperable mass that is causing blackouts and, on occasion, makes me attack the women in my life."

He was behaving very strangely. Just yesterday he'd been devastated speaking about the same thing, yet today he was behaving flippant—comedic somehow.

Miriam squirmed.

"Firstly, my girlfriend went missing, Laura Sanders, the love of my life. I intended to marry that woman. She was amazing—beautiful, caring, funny, hardworking—the complete package. But she went out one day and never returned. Had I done something to her? Of course, there was no suggestion back then, but fast forward a few months and a few casual girlfriends later, girl-friends that were apparently beaten pretty badly after I'd fallen asleep or had some sort of *blackout*." He used the first two fingers of each hand to punctuate the word blackout. "It goes without saying, I was devastated. And I paid a lot of money to keep the girls quiet. But when I did it for a third time, my specialist, Cecil Bain, put his foot down and insisted I was to be kept sedated until my death to prevent me hurting anyone else. This is where you came in, Lizzi."

"Okay," I said, not knowing what he expected me to say.

"Thank Christ you had a moral compass and a conscience—if you hadn't allowed me to wake up, who knows what would've happened? I would've wasted away in that fucking bed until I popped my clogs."

"This is boring now, Charles. Can you get to the point of all this." Miriam sighed.

"Didn't he just get to the point of all this?" I said, scowling at her. Because of the way she'd made me feel, I'd forgotten what a terrible thing she'd done and the position she'd put me in, but now I suddenly felt ten feet tall. "You make me sick."

Charlie raised his eyebrows and grinned. "Quite." He nodded at me. "But sadly that isn't even the tip of the iceberg, is it, sis?"

Miriam placed a hand on her forehead, and I was surprised to see she was trembling. Her ice-cold exterior was clearly just an act.

"Now, let's have a little bit of truth, shall we?" He steepled his fingers and balanced his chin on top. "The tumour turns out to be nothing more than a benign growth."

CHAPTER 45

Nigel managed to get a few hours' sleep before Detective Jones led him back to the interview room. "What do you want from me now?" he asked, completely confused. "I've told you everything I know."

"I need to ask you a few more questions, but they're not directly related to your wife."

"What questions?"

"We're investigating the murder of Erin Lieber, the teacher and—"

"Hang on a minute! What's that got to do with me?" His head was spinning.

She ignored his question and glanced at her notes. "Did you ever meet Ms Lieber?"

"Of course, I met her." He gulped, his mouth suddenly dry. "I drive the school bus, don't I?"

"What was she like?"

"I don't know. Just normal, I suppose."

"Did you like her?"

"Didn't know her well enough to have an opinion either way."

"Do you remember saying she deserved everything she got because of the way she dressed?"

"That was taken out of context. She'd not even been found when I said that. She was just missing, and everyone was talking about it—not just me."

"I see. Can you confirm you're left-handed?"

He bristled. "Why?"

"Just answer the question, please."

"Listen. This isn't funny. Just because I admitted what happened with Joan, don't think you can go accusing me of every unsolved murder in the area."

"Can you answer the question, please?"

"Yes, I'm left-handed. So what does that prove? Ten percent of the population are left-handed—that's almost three hundred thousand people in greater Manchester alone. Hardly unique."

"No, maybe not. But I wonder how many people in the area have the same sized hands as you as well as a history of strangulation?"

"I need to call my solicitor."

I gawped at Charlie. "How can that be? I thought you had terminal cancer!"

"Join the club. But no, they lied. Of course, the longer it's left untreated, the bigger it will grow, and eventually it will kill me. It's slow-growing although that wasn't going to cause them any issues, was it, sis? I mean, my specialist had told me I was going to die—there was nothing he could do—who was going to question him? No-one. Not even me. The hospital files show a nasty, aggressive tumour, courtesy of some other poor bugger. It all looks above board on the surface."

Miriam shuffled in her seat no longer eyeing me defiantly.

I was in shock. How could anybody do what she had done and to a member of her own family?

"Then, my whirlwind romance with Laura happened," Charlie continued. "I wanted to marry the girl. We planned to have a baby. The knowledge of the tumour made me want to live my life to the fullest. That freaked out my twisted sister and her partner in crime. They needed me to be single, so I'd have no reason to fight."

"But why?" I asked.

"The forty-two million dollar question. Do you like the way I did that, Miriam? Clever, don't you think?"

"I don't get it," I said, trying my best to keep up yet failing miserably.

"My personal fortune, plus the insurance policy set up by the football club and another insurance policy I didn't even know about, set up by Miriam, was due to go in its entirety to Miriam— my only living relative. However, if I married and had kids, of course my will would change."

Completely astounded I scratched my head. "How did you find all this out?"

"Fortunately, Miriam has never been very tech savvy. She uses her email and social media accounts but, as I discovered yesterday, uses the same passwords for everything. When I found the original diagnosis of my tumour on her desktop, it triggered warning bells. So, I accessed all her messages going back years, then I sent them to myself."

Miriam pinched the bridge of her nose. I was surprised how quiet and calm she was being.

"What's wrong, sis? Did you think coming here at the crack of dawn and deleting everything would be enough? Give me a break." He laughed heartily.

"What actually happened to Laura, then? Do you know?" I asked, dreading the answer, yet desperately needing to know.

"At first they tried to bribe her. Pay her off. Playing on the fact

I was going to die, and it would be a crying shame for her to have to see me like that—unable to care for myself and wasting away before her very eyes. The argument you gave was excellent—top marks, Miriam. But Laura told you where to go. She really did love me, didn't she?"

"She was a money hungry bitch and you know it," Miriam spat viciously.

"There it is. The truth—finally. Which one of you killed her? I don't think it was you. You wouldn't want to get your hands dirty —and although you're a cold bitch, I don't think you're that evil."

"Killed her?" I felt my head explode. Boom! What the actual fuck? I jumped to my feet, not knowing which way to turn. I needed some fresh air, but I didn't want to leave Charlie alone with the psycho bitch for a second. "I've had enough of this." Reaching in my bag, I pulled out my phone and hit redial.

Miriam jumped to her feet in protest.

"Sit down!" Charlie roared, and she fell back into her chair.

The phone answered almost immediately. "Campbell."

"It's Lizzi again, from—"

"Hi Lizzi, what can I do for you this time?" He sounded bored and it irritated me that he might be thinking I'm a crackpot.

"You need to come here. It's to do with Charlie Maidley and the disappearance of Laura Yates."

"I'm on my way."

Charlie smiled smugly. "Nice one. So that gives us, what? Ten minutes or so before the nice young detective comes for you."

"Charles, I'm your sister—you really don't want to do this."

"Don't I?"

"Please. This is ridiculous. I didn't lay a finger on Laura and that's the truth. I admit to the rest and I'm sorry. We never meant for any of this—it just got out of control."

"Boohoo! Tell it to the jury because I'm not listening."

I returned to my seat. "Do you know what happened to the other girls? The ones you supposedly beat up?"

He shrugged. "I think they drugged me. Cecil prescribed my medication, and she force fed me. I'd wondered why she kept coming to my apartment. Thought it was because she loved me and was concerned. How gullible am I?"

"I do love you, stupid boy. None of this would've happened if you'd listened to me in the first place."

"You're a real piece of work, do you know that?" Charlie said. "I treat you like a queen. You're like a mother to me. I've bought you cars, this house, given you money to set up your business. You only need to ask and you could have anything you want. But that's not enough for you, is it?"

She wiped away a stray tear.

"Did the affair with Cecil begin after my diagnosis, or before?"

Miriam gave him the filthiest look. "We met when you went for your initial consultation. He was happy to go along with my plan once he discovered we were talking millions of pounds."

"Are you saying it was all your idea, then?" He suddenly looked deflated.

Her evil eyes sparkled. "You don't know me as well as you think, do you, Charles? It was me. It was all me. Cecil hasn't got the bottle to attack anyone—he's a coward."

"So, you...?"

"With my bare hands—I battered them all—yes, including Laura." She grinned. I felt she'd been pushed over the edge and by the looks of her, she was totally crazy.

"You crazy bitch! How could you? You know how much Laura meant to me."

"How could you?" she mimicked, in a whiney voice. "You were always a cry baby, Charles. That was one thing I couldn't stand about you—you cried for years."

"Our parents died! Of course, I fucking cried. I was a kid, for Christ's sake."

"Oh yeah." She smiled. "They were both cuckoo in their own way."

I suddenly froze feeling sick. "Did you have something to do with their deaths too?"

"Give the girl a prize! You're the first person in over thirty years to ask me that. I always rehearsed my answer to be a massive denial, but what's the point? I'm going to be locked up anyway. *C'est la vie.*"

Charlie was frozen to the spot—clearly struggling to process everything. His own sister had killed his parents. "Why?" he eventually uttered.

"He was a bully. He terrorised Mum, and you, and he... he—let's just say, he assaulted me too. Mum knew what he was doing to me, but she didn't do a thing about it. She was too frightened. He'd beaten her so bad, and for so long she was scared of her own shadow."

"How, though? Even the inquest agreed it was suicide."

"You can convince anybody of anything if you're thorough enough."

There was a knock at the door.

I stood to answer it but turned back to face the table. "Why did you come here today, Miriam? You obviously knew the game was up and Charlie was on to you. Why didn't you just stay away?"

She raised her eyebrows and smiled. "I'd planned the perfect exit for you both. I got back hours ago and intended to break the computer—delete everything, but, considering I'm such a technophobe according to Charles, I discovered you'd sent yourself a message containing all my messages. Then, I discovered you'd sent an email containing these messages from your email address to a further three people. So I called Cecil, and he told me the game was up. He would've either gone on the run or topped himself by now."

"And if I hadn't sent these emails?" Charlie asked.

"You wouldn't have woken up this morning—neither of you."

There was another knock, louder this time.

218 | NETTA NEWBOUND

Stepping away from the table, I was startled by a kerfuffle behind me.

"No!" Charlie shouted.

Thinking I was in danger, I darted sideways covering my head. When I realised I was okay, I turned back towards Miriam who was standing, her arm outstretched, holding a huge carving knife pointed at Charlie.

Charlie stepped slowly backwards. "You don't need to do this, Miriam. Put the knife down."

She did as he asked and, as though the fight had gone out of her, her shoulders drooped. Then, just as suddenly, she smiled at Charlie, raised the knife, and turned it on herself, ramming it straight through the front of her throat.

As she dropped to the floor, I ran to her side—trying to stem the flow of blood with my fingers. "Let the police in and call an ambulance!" I screamed.

Charlie moved fast, and moments later, Detectives Campbell and Karlson were beside me—taking control. But it was too late.

Miriam bled out in minutes.

Stone dead.

CHAPTER 46

Charlie and I huddled together in shock.

One minute she'd been sitting there, calm as you like, the next she'd almost decapitated herself.

I'd turned to Charlie initially to comfort him, but he ended up comforting me instead.

"I can't believe it," I whispered. "Where was the knife?"

"I haven't a clue. Inside her jacket, maybe. She must've had it the entire time. She'd planned this from the start, the crazy bitch."

"No. You're wrong. She'd planned far worse. Thank God you'd had the foresight to send those details otherwise we'd both be dead."

DI Karlson had taken control, ushering us into the living room while they made the relevant phone calls and organised everything.

"We can't let the press know she's Charlie's sister—it'll be carnage," I said to him when he popped his head around the door to check on us.

Only Wayne and I know at this stage. But I don't know how long I can keep a lid on it. We could apply to the courts for a gagging order. That will only prevent the identity of people involved in the case being mentioned, but it might help for now at least."

"Thanks. That would be good," I said, squeezing Charlie's hand.

"Did you receive the statement and evidence I sent through to the police station last night?" Charlie asked.

"Not yet. But it's probably being processed."

"That saved our life," I said. "Miriam confessed that she came here with the sole intention of killing us in our sleep, and, if it wasn't for the email, she would've."

"I recorded it all on her iPod," Charlie said.

"Really? Oh, my God, I could kiss you. I didn't even think to do anything like that."

Charlie smiled sadly then turned back to the detective. "Has anybody picked up Cecil yet?"

"Somebody's heading over there now. We'll keep you informed. Do you have anywhere you can go for a couple of days? This is a crime scene until we gather all the evidence."

"I could ask Phil next door," I said, looking at Charlie.

He nodded. "Do you think he'd mind? Otherwise we could go to a hotel—now you know I've got a few bob tucked away for a rainy day." He winked at me.

The reference to his money made my stomach contract. I'd never known anyone with so much money, but he was so laid back nobody would ever guess he was loaded.

"I'll go and ask Phil first. I won't be long."

Phil was standing at his front door when I arrived. "What on earth's happened?" he asked.

"Long story. Listen, we're going to need somewhere to stay for a day or two. I don't suppose…?"

"Of course. Come on in. Where's Charlie?"

"He's next door. I'll go and get him and pack a couple of bags. We won't be long." I knew we needed to give him an explanation but that would have to wait. I didn't know where to begin, and I was too exhausted to go through it all again. Not yet, anyway.

When I got back, Charlie was upstairs with the detective printing off his statement.

"We'll need to take full statements from both of you, but this will do for now."

"You need to find Laura. I have a feeling she might be in Barraclough Bog, a patch of wasteland on the outskirts of Manchester, but I can't be certain," Charlie said.

"What makes you think that?"

"Cecil lives close to it, and the morning after Laura vanished, Cecil sent a photo to Miriam showing a picture of a rock. It was random. And he just said *Baraclough Bog* in the message."

"Don't worry. We'll look into it, and we will need to take your sister's computer too."

"You might be best off with her laptop—there's possibly more on there. Her emails and social media accounts sync from that."

"We'll definitely take that then, if you don't mind?"

Charlie nodded. "Whatever you need, mate. I just want to find Laura now and lay her to rest." His voice cracked and he burst into tears.

I wrapped my arms around him "Do you really think they killed her? It's strange she didn't admit it considering what she intended to do."

"I know she did. Laura vanished after she'd told them where to stick her money," he said between sobs.

"It's okay, let it all out. You'll feel better."

The detective nodded at me and headed back downstairs.

"Why didn't you tell me what you'd discovered last night? I knew there was something wrong, but I thought it was because of Alexis and her fancy man."

He shrugged. "I wasn't sure if she'd come. That's why I emailed the details knowing, if she did come, she'd try to manipulate me like she's done all my life. Hence the reason for asking you to stay today. I'm not bothered about Alexis. I'm pleased for her."

"How are you feeling now? That was bad enough for me—I don't have a clue how you must be feeling."

"Sad. I don't know why she lied, but I know Laura wouldn't have just left me. I hate what they must've put her through, but I'm glad she hadn't just taken off."

"That's understandable," I said.

"It's always been there, at the back of my mind, wondering what happened. Would she ever turn up? Now I know she won't. She's dead, which is just so sad—such a waste. The fact Miriam was the one who killed her blows my mind. I honestly didn't think she was capable of that."

"What about the confession about killing your parents too? Did you believe her?"

"Who knows? There'll be no way to prove it after all these years, I guess. So, what did Phil say?"

"He's expecting us. Go pack a bag."

CHAPTER 47

We decided to go the back way through the hedge to Phil's place.

Charlie had noticed the press were out in the street. I hadn't, but then I'm not used to spotting them like he is.

"I didn't ask if Thomas was invited," I said, scratching the little dog's ear.

"If not, we'll just take off again," Charlie said. "We have Miriam's car now." The mention of his sister's name caused an invisible shroud of sadness to settle around him. "Did you tell Phil what's happened?"

I shook my head. "Not yet, but we'll need to tell him something. We can trust him—we know that much already."

Charlie inhaled deeply as I tapped on the back door.

"Hey, guys, come on in." Phil opened the door wide.

"We have Thomas too, is that alright?"

"Of course, it is. Although I can't guarantee Kate will give him back afterwards." He laughed. "Right, I've put you in the spare room. It's a little prettier than mine," he said to me. "And, Charlie, you can have my room."

"But where will *you* sleep?" I asked.

"I often sleep on the sofa anyway, but the kids are at their grandparents' this weekend so there are plenty of options, don't worry."

"Okay, but I don't mind sleeping on the sofa."

"I wouldn't hear of it. Come on, let's take your bags upstairs and get you settled in, then you can tell me what's been happening."

Charlie paled at the mere thought of it.

I patted his forearm to reassure him I'd got this.

"Do you mind if I have a lie down?" Charlie asked once he'd been shown to his room. "It's been an exhausting few hours."

"Just make yourself at home, mate. You don't need to ask."

Charlie nodded and looked as though he was about to cry again.

I hugged him. "Do you need any medication to help you sleep?"

He paused, clearly considering it, then he shook his head. "I'll be fine. I just need to rest, and I'll be a box of birds."

I seriously doubted it. After what he'd been through, I suspected it would take more than a little rest to get him right. "Okay." I glanced at my watch surprised so much had happened today already, and it wasn't even lunch-time!

Back in the kitchen, Phil made a pot of tea and pulled out a packet of biscuits from the cupboard.

I hadn't eaten a thing since last night's dinner, but my stomach balked at the thought of food. "Not for me, thanks."

"So? Put me out of my misery. Is it something to do with Nigel?"

I shook my head. "No." And as I began to tell him tears filled my eyes, then ran down my face and off my chin.

Phil kept quiet while I told him everything apart for the occasional gasp that is.

"Jesus Christ!" he shouted and jumped to his feet when I described what Miriam had done to herself. "Poor Charlie. Poor you! Are you okay?"

"Shocked, of course. But I'm worried about Charlie. I didn't want to tell you yesterday while we were worrying about Alexis, but he'd contemplated suicide. I found him in the garage with a knife. Bizarrely, the same knife Miriam used on herself today."

"How awful. You should've told me. No wonder you wanted to go back there. And it was all a waste of time anyway—worrying about that bloody woman."

"How did that go in the end? Did you make up?"

"Well, she only went and asked Kate to be her bridesmaid. She was so excited I didn't have the heart to say she couldn't. And, to be honest with you, I'd convinced myself she was dead and was praying for her to walk in the door with some convoluted explanation, never really expecting she would. So, it was a best-case scenario, really. But she did make me angry when she breezed in as though she hadn't a care in the world."

"I know! I thought you were going to blow a gasket." I grinned.

"I very nearly did."

"Shall I walk with you to pick Kate up?" I asked a while later.

Phil shook his head. "The kids' grandparents are picking them up and taking them for the weekend. Which reminds me, I'd better get their stuff sorted, they'll be here soon."

"Can I help?"

"Not really, but thanks. You could make another drink if you like. Do you think Charlie's okay?"

"I'll go and check on him, but yeah, although it's terrible what's happened to him, I think he must be relieved. I mean, his tumour can possibly be treated, if it's not too late that is. And he now knows he had nothing to do with Laura's disappearance. So, although shit, at least he has answers—not to mention the chance of a future, which is more than he had yesterday."

"Yeah, I suppose you're right. I can't imagine how the poor bloke must be feeling though. It's a lot to take in."

"I know." I trudged upstairs and knocked on Charlie's bedroom door.

He coughed and cleared his throat. "Come in."

Pushing the door open, I found him sitting up in the bed, his eyes red-rimmed and his face blotchy. "Are you okay?"

"I feel like shit. How about you?"

"Numb. I can't believe all that happened in one morning. And here we are, just a few hours later, sipping tea and exchanging small talk. Mind blowing really."

"What's happening in the street?"

"I haven't looked. Do you want me to check?"

Phil's bedroom was at the back of the house, so I bobbed across the landing into Kate's room and peered from the window. Just like when Erin had been found, the street was chocablock with cars and vans except there hadn't been reporters then, probably because the house hadn't been connected to anything apart from being used as an access point. Now, there was a group of reporters and cameramen standing in a huddle beside Nigel's driveway.

"Seems we won't be going anywhere for a while—at least *you* won't unless you wear a disguise."

He nodded. "Story of my life."

"Do you regret it? Fame?"

He shrugged. "It's all I've known for years, but, had I known it would cost me everything then yes, I do. I'd much rather have the love of a good woman and a family than a bank account full of money I never get the chance to spend—money every other bugger wants to get their greedy paws on."

"Well, I don't. Although, I must admit I'm glad Alexis didn't get wind of your fortune as I reckon things would've definitely turned out differently."

"You're the only person I've got left. And you're only here because it's your job."

"Wrong!" I shoved at his arm suddenly annoyed. "I'm here because I want to be. And if you don't need me as a nurse, I'd just go back to work. But I'd still be your friend. I'd still care about you."

He smiled sadly. "Sorry. I'm being horrible, and I didn't mean it. But it's difficult to know who you can trust and who's out for what they can get."

"Phil and I are your friends. He's worried about you just as I am. And, for your information, he doesn't need your money. He got a huge insurance payout from his wife that he hasn't touched, so you can forget that. I'm not rich by any means, but I've never been motivated by money—so long as I have enough to feed and clothe myself, I'm happy. So put that out of your mind this instant. Now, come downstairs and have a cup of tea or coffee. I've told Phil everything, so you needn't go into any details with him or anyone if you don't want to."

"Thanks, Lizzi. I was lucky to find you. I love the way you won't allow me to wallow in my own self-pity."

"Get your backside off that bed then." I flounced from the room and headed down the stairs.

Someone knocked at the door when I was halfway down.

"It's okay," Phil said, rushing from the kitchen. "It's just the in-laws." He opened the door and welcomed a couple who appeared to be in their early sixties.

"What on earth's happening out there?" the woman, who looked like an older version of Alexis, said.

I wanted to turn and head back upstairs, not ready to talk to strangers about it.

"A man across the street has been arrested for something. Val, Eric, meet Lizzi, my neighbour. She and Charlie are staying here for a few days."

Nicely done, I thought as I shook hands with his guests.

"Got time for a cuppa?" Phil asked, heading into the kitchen.

"Do we?" Eric said, looking at his watch. "You should know." He guffawed making us all crack up laughing.

"Maybe a quick one," Phil said, filling the kettle. "So, what did you think of Kadri?"

"He seems like a gent," Val said. "Genuine and kind. I hope he can tame that daughter of ours." She raised her eyebrows at me. "Do you know Alexis?"

I nodded. "She's definitely a handful."

Phil placed four cups onto the table and took a seat. "So, what do you have planned for the weekend?"

"I'm not sure," Eric said. "I was thinking of bowling, but I didn't want a rerun of last time."

"Why? What happened last time?" Phil asked, his forehead furrowed.

Val dug Eric in the ribs. "Oh, nothing."

"Hey! I saw that. Come on, tell me what happened?" Phil asked, suddenly serious.

"It's nothing, really. Eric planned a night out at the cinema, but Ben refused to come," Val explained. "He said the movie was for kids and stomped off. We couldn't find him for ages."

"Bloody hell! Why didn't you tell me? He's out of order treating you like that."

"It's fine," Eric cut in. "Val took Catherine in to see the movie, and I kept calling him. He answered his phone eventually—he'd gone to Kevin's. We let him stay there until the next morning. When I picked him up, he was fine and he did apologise, but I don't want to make the same mistake again. I'd rather he chooses what we do."

"I'm fuming." Phil shook his head. "I know Ben's been through a lot, but he can't be getting away with doing things like this."

"Please don't say anything," Val said.

I felt for Phil. Just a couple of nights ago I'd asked him the same, and I now realised it was unfair of me. How could the poor guy be expected to parent successfully if we were all making these demands of him? I wanted to say something, speak up for him, but it really wasn't my place.

"Whose phone is that?" Phil asked, looking at me.

I suddenly heard it. Jumping to my feet, I located my handbag beside the back door and found my phone. It had stopped ringing by then. The number on the screen was one I didn't recognise, but it began to ring again.

"Hello?"

"Hi, Lizzi. It's Wayne."

"Oh, hi. Sorry I didn't recognise the number."

"I'm calling from the station. I just wanted to check on you after this morning. Are you and Charlie okay?"

"Hang on a sec." I glanced back into the room and smiled—all eyes were on me. Then I ducked across the hall into the living room, closing the door behind me. "Sorry, where was I? Oh, yeah. Charlie's not said much. He's been asleep since we arrived next door, but, apart from being incredibly sad, he seems okay. Did you get anywhere with Cecil?"

"Yes. He was picked up at the airport attempting to board a plane to America. Apparently, that's where the couple intended to go once they pulled everything off, but I didn't tell you that. The fact I'm just a trainee detective means I'm back to door knocking and tea making—yay! Such fun."

"My lips are sealed. Any more about Nigel?"

He sighed loudly. "Again, I shouldn't tell you this, but I'm sure it will be all over the news by teatime. He's been charged with murdering his wife."

I gasped. "I knew it. Didn't I tell you he was a wrong 'un? Who'd have thought it? Two killers in one tiny street. Well, three really, if you include Erin."

"That's just it. He's being investigated for that too."

"For killing Erin?" I squealed. "I bet he did it. I told Detective Karlson at the time."

"We're just trying to find some link between them. We have several things that match, but nothing concrete to go on. Anyway, I've said far more than I should. Are you coming in to make a statement sometime soon?"

"Yes. We were thinking tomorrow. But I'm worried about Charlie being seen. I think Miriam did a good job of keeping their relationship secret, but I'm sure if you discover she did actually kill Laura, they will make the connection to Charlie. We may have to go away for a few days till things calm down."

"Good idea. Thanks for everything. Your phone calls have given me a bit of kudos with my superiors. I can't thank you enough."

"My pleasure. But, to be honest, you're the only one who gave us the time of day when we thought Alexis was missing, so it's well deserved, I'd say."

"I appreciate it anyway. I'll let you get off, take care."

I held the phone to my chest for a few minutes, trying to process what he'd told me. Nigel had killed his poor wife—but Erin? Although I'd thought it possible, it still came as a shock. Maybe I would've been the next on his list. I shuddered at the thought.

Hearing Phil showing his guests out, I waited until they'd gone before returning to the kitchen.

"Any news?" he asked.

"They've arrested Cecil. He was leaving for the States, apparently."

"Thank God someone will be held accountable. It pisses me off Miriam took the cowards' way out."

"Me too."

No sooner had I returned to my seat than my phone rang again. Work flashed across the screen. "It's the hospital," I whispered before accepting the call. "Hello?"

"Elizabeth. It's Imran Singh. I just heard the news."

"Terrible, isn't it? It's not going to look great for the hospital when it gets out, I'm afraid."

"I had nothing to do with this. You do know that, I hope."

I paused, thinking about my answer. "I know. But where does that leave poor Charlie? He still has a tumour that may well be too big to remove by now."

"I know. I've tried to call him but the number I have is going straight to voicemail. Is he with you?"

"He's resting right now."

"Can you bring him in? All the tests will need to be redone as soon as possible if we're going to have any chance of putting this right."

"I'll see what Charlie says but, just out of interest, are you doing this to save your own bacon? To save the donations Charlie generously gives you? Or for Charlie's wellbeing? And be honest."

He went quiet for a few seconds. "Can I say all three? Ultimately I want to help Charlie—Mr Maidley. I'm still in shock over Cecil's appalling actions—but I really do need to fire-fight here. We'll all be tarred with the same brush as him if we're not careful. Damage limitation."

"Fair enough. I'll be in touch. We've got to see the police tomorrow, and maybe we'll come over straight after that."

"Anytime. As soon as you can. Let me know when, and I'll rearrange everything—make this as pain free for Charlie as possible."

CHAPTER 48

As Wayne had predicted, it was all over the evening news about Nigel killing his wife, and, tagged onto the end of the report, was a mention of a woman in the same street who'd taken her own life. So, for now at least, Charlie was okay.

By the next morning, the street was back to normal although we still hadn't had the all clear to return to the house.

"Thanks for letting us stay," Charlie said to Phil as we prepared to leave.

"Anytime. I'm just sorry Ben didn't get to meet you. He's football mad."

"We'll be back in a day or two—bring him over then."

"So, you're coming back here to stay?" Phil asked, his eyes searching my face, hopefully.

I looked at Charlie for the answer.

He shrugged. "It's as good a place to stay as any. My apartment in the city is only small, and, I must admit, I've got used to this place now."

"And you?" Phil asked me.

"I'll still need a nurse," Charlie continued. "Even if they can operate, I'll need help until I recover. But, worst-case scenario, I'll need—"

"Don't talk like that," I snapped. "They're going to fix you, you'll see."

He smiled sadly. "I hope so."

"That's settled then. When we get back, I'll make us all a slap-up meal and you can bring Ben over to meet Charlie then. It can be a thank you for looking after Thomas."

"Sounds good." Phil nodded, and picked Thomas up and held him like a baby. The silly dog just lay there, enjoying the attention.

I laughed and scratched the top of his head. "I know it's hard, but try not to miss us, especially with all the cuddles you'll get from a certain little girl, won't you?" I joked, rolling my eyes.

"Don't worry. I'm sure he won't," Phil laughed.

"Right, I'll go and get the car. Are you ready, Charlie?"

He nodded.

I slipped out of the back door and through the hedge. It felt strange to climb into Miriam's car after everything that had happened since she'd parked it up the early hours of yesterday morning. The key ring had a bunch of keys attached to it as well as the automatic key fob. Inside, a pair of beige driving shoes were in the passenger side foot well, a tin of sherbet lemons sat on the dash and a pair of sunglasses were hooked over the visor. Not many personal effects but enough to make my stomach lurch.

I stashed everything away out of sight, the shoes under the seat and the rest in the glove box—there was no point upsetting Charlie any more than he was already.

I drove out onto the street and into Phil's driveway where I tooted the horn. Charlie and Phil appeared carrying a bag each.

I jumped out and opened the boot relieved to find it empty. The police must've removed Miriam's bag if she'd left it in there.

We said our goodbyes and got on the road.

"Do you know the way to the police station?" I asked Charlie, suddenly realizing that, apart from going to the cinema that one night, I hadn't been into town. In fact, I hadn't been anywhere since then except for the school gates and the supermarket which is why I probably felt so jittery.

"I do. Would you like me to drive?"

I shook my head. "No, unless you want to, that is."

"I don't mind. It might help take my mind off things."

"Okay. How about you drive us to the hospital once we've finished at the police station?"

He nodded, a flash of something behind his eyes.

"Are you okay?"

"I think so."

"Are you worried about the hospital?"

"It's never nice having people prodding and poking at you."

"Can I ask why you didn't go private in the first place?"

"I've supported Grace Hospital since I first started out in professional football, so I never even thought about going anywhere else to be honest. They got me in right away, and never gave me any reason to doubt them—till now."

"You know the rest of the hospital staff can't be blamed for Cecil's actions, don't you?"

"Of course, I do."

"But if you don't feel comfortable going back there, you can make an appointment somewhere else."

"No, it's okay. I'd feel the same wherever I went now, I suppose. Turn left at the end of the road."

I indicated and pulled into the left lane before continuing. "I'll be with you from now on. And woe betide anyone who doesn't treat you by the book, or they'll have me to answer to."

He smiled. "That's good for me—not so good for them."

"After the hospital, we can go to my house if you don't mind? I need to check it's okay and pack a few more things—even grab my old jalopy of a car seeing as I don't need to be stuck indoors all the time anymore."

"Yeah, that's fine. I wouldn't mind doing the same if that's okay. I didn't even lock my apartment up unless Miriam did. There could be living creatures in the fridge by now."

"Eww!" I shuddered. "Bagsy not to be the one checking that."

"Don't worry. I'll just need you on standby in case I need CPR."

"Done." I laughed.

Five minutes later we pulled into the car park of the police station. DI Karlson was waiting for us when we arrived at the reception desk, as we didn't want anyone to recognise Charlie who was wearing a large black coat with a hood. Once we had been taken through to the back, they split us up to give our statements. DI Karlson took Charlie's and DC Jones took mine.

"I've applied for a gagging order," Karlson said, when we'd all met up again afterwards.

"Oh, good," I said. "We saw Nigel Mason on the news last night, and thankfully they only tagged Miriam's death on the end of it."

"Yeah, I noticed that too," Karlson said. "But these things do have a habit of being leaked, so don't be surprised if you wake up one morning to a street filled with paparazzi. But if we get the gagging order, at least that will prevent them being able to report it."

"I'd appreciate that," Charlie said. "But it's bound to get out eventually, I know that."

"Yes, it will, especially if we find Laura."

Charlie winced. "Are you any closer to finding her?"

"Yes. I think we are. Cecil has clammed up, but we accessed his and your sister's phone records, and on the night Laura went missing we noticed some strange activity on them both."

"What kind of activity?"

"I'm sorry, but I can't tell you any more at this stage. I'll contact you as soon as we find anything. I promise."

Charlie rubbed his eyes looking suddenly exhausted.

"Come on. Let's get you to the hospital," I said, worrying it was all going to prove too much for him.

As we walked to the exit, I turned to Karlson. "Is Nigel still being investigated for Erin's murder?"

"Who told you that?"

Shit! I'd forgotten Wayne had told me in confidence. "Just someone in the street last night mentioned it." I hoped he didn't press me, or I'd be up shit creek without a paddle.

"It's still early days yet, but we're not ruling anyone out at this stage."

"Fair enough," I said, able to breathe again. Me and my bloody big mouth. I couldn't wait to get out of there.

Afterwards, we headed to the Grace Hospital in Manchester. Once we were on the road, I called ahead and told them when to expect us. They assured me they were ready and waiting for Charlie.

When we arrived, Charlie put on the coat again, pulling the hood up—which was okay while we were outside, but threatened to suffocate him once we stepped inside the building with its stifling central heating.

As promised, we were met at reception and whisked away into a side room before anybody had the chance to recognise him.

The next few hours were exhausting for me—never mind Charlie. After all the tests, Mr Singh ushered us into his office and, almost in tears, apologised to Charlie for everything. "We will rush all the results through and be in touch with you over the next few days," he said. I was impressed considering it was the weekend.

We stopped at a pub for something to eat afterwards and then picked up a few groceries from the supermarket before heading to my humble home in Gorton.

"Not quite what you're used to," I said, as I turned off the main road. The cul-de-sac I lived on was the nicest street in the middle of quite a rough area, but it was home to me and all I'd been able to afford after Sean and I divorced. "I'll take my car out of the garage and park it on the road instead of this," I said. I pulled over on the street beside my minuscule driveway worried Miriam's flash car would be stolen or stripped of all its parts by the morning if not.

"What about your car?"

"Wait till you see it." I laughed.

As it did every time, my scruffy, old pale-blue car started up on the fifth try. The clanging and the ticking of the engine often reminded me of Chitty-Chitty-Bang-Bang, except it was in worse physical shape.

"Bloody hell! Why do you want to take that home with us?" He laughed when I got back in the car and drove it into the garage.

It felt nice for him to call Miriam's house home. I did feel as though I'd outgrown my little place now. Whatever happened down the track, I made the decision there and then to sell up. "Because it's all I've got!" I also laughed. "We're not all moneybags, you know."

"No, I didn't mean that. I meant why don't you just have this car."

"Because it's yours."

"I have my own car. A top of the range Astin Martin, so you may as well just keep this one."

"I couldn't possibly." I had no qualms about driving around in a dead woman's car, considering what the nasty cow had done to Charlie and Laura, not to mention what she had planned to do to me. "It wouldn't be right, and legally I'm not allowed to accept gifts over a certain value from a patient."

"But I'm not gifting it to my nurse. I'm gifting it to my friend."

"They wouldn't see it as that."

"Well, at least you can use it—call it a business deal—a company car. Once I no longer need a nurse, we can relook at it then."

"Are you sure?"

"Really. It's the least I can do for you after everything."

"I don't need rewarding for that. I only did what any nurse

worth their salt would've done."

"I don't believe that for one minute. I think what you did took a lot of guts, and I really appreciate it."

"Okay. I'll accept the car, thanks. But that's it now—no more gratitude payments. Deal?"

"Okay, deal."

I felt a little self-conscious taking Charlie into my modest home after he'd laughed at the state of my car, but I needn't have worried.

"This is cosy," he said, plonking his bag down in the living room.

"A little smaller than you're used to, no doubt, but I like it."

"It's no smaller than my place."

"Really? I thought you'd live in a mansion considering what you bought for Miriam."

The mention of her name caused him to wince ever so slightly.

"Sorry," I said.

"It's okay. I just needed a bachelor pad for myself. Although, when I was with Laura, we did look at a few houses—much too grown up for me, I thought at the time."

"Grown up?" I laughed.

"Yeah. I know I'm almost forty, but I've never considered myself grown up—not really. But Laura made me feel ready to take that step, to leave my selfish, party boy ways behind."

I patted his arm supportively then picked up the grocery bags from my feet and carried them into the kitchen. "You must've really loved her."

"I did. How about you?"

"What about me?"

"Is this where you lived with your husband?"

"God, no. I actually *had* a grown-up house." I grinned. "Four bedrooms, a huge bay window, white picket fence—the works."

"Sounds idyllic, what happened?"

I closed my eyes, my back to him, but he obviously sensed my reluctance to talk.

"I'm sorry."

I sighed. "No, it's fine. Let's make a cuppa, and I'll tell you all about it."

"You don't have to. I shouldn't have pried."

"Well, I know everything there is to know about you—warts and all. I feel it's only fair I let you know my story. Then, once it's out in the open, let's try to put it all behind us, both of us. What do you think?"

"We can have a good go."

I put the groceries away and made us both a drink. Then we curled up, side by side on the sofa, and I told him everything I'd told Phil just a few nights ago. It seemed easier the second time around.

Afterwards, we ordered a pizza to be delivered and settled down to a quiet night in front of the TV. We were both exhausted.

By ten pm we were ready for bed. I let Charlie have my room, and I got in the spare single bed.

The next morning, we packed up, and, after returning my jalopy to the garage, we headed over to Charlie's apartment at Salford Quays. He had been telling the truth—his apartment wasn't much bigger than my place, but it was certainly much flashier. We travelled up to the third floor in the lift and from the plushly carpeted landing, the wider than usual front door opened up into a sleek and ultra-modern living area that had stunning views overlooking the city. White walls, flooring and furniture was offset by a huge black rug, a black leather double sofa suite, and huge black and white artwork on each of the walls. The only colour was the odd splash of orange here and there. It was lovely.

"Oh, my God! It's beautiful. We should've come straight here yesterday instead of slumming it at my place."

"Don't be silly, I loved your house."

"Liar." I laughed. "Convincing performance, but, after seeing this I don't believe one word out of your mouth."

"I'm not lying. Your place is welcoming and cosy."

I nodded. That was true, and this apartment could never be called cosy, I'd be scared to do anything in it for fear of messing it up.

He flung open one of the doors off the living area. "This is your room for the night," he said.

"Do you have a cleaner?" I asked, still sizing up the place.

"Yeah, just once a week, and she only does the basics."

"How the other half live, eh?"

"Shut up!" He laughed. "Oh, well, time to brave the fridge."

I got a call from DI Karlson that evening as we strolled through the streets of Manchester on the way to Charlie's favourite restaurant.

"We've finished at the house. Just thought you'd want to know."

"Thanks for that. What do we do now? Is it a mess?"

"I've arranged for the trauma clean-up team to go around first thing in the morning as per your instruction. But it isn't too bad."

"Okay, thanks. We're in the city but will probably come back on Monday."

"Great. Enjoy the rest of your weekend."

I ended the call and glanced at Charlie. "Did you hear that?"

"Yeah. Hopefully we'll hear from the hospital by then too, and then we can plan around where we go from here."

"Did you sort out your phone?"

He shook his head. "Not yet. But I did find it and put it on charge. I probably have millions of missed calls and messages—it's been pretty nice not being tied to a phone, to be honest."

"I get that, but just for now, while you've got the hospital contacting you, you'll need to keep it on."

His eyes suddenly clouded. "Don't worry, I will."

"Are you nervous?"

"A little. It's strange. I'd resigned myself to the fact I was going to die, and now... well, I'm scared of praying for a good outcome. I still have a little hope not knowing. But what if it's too late? What if there's nothing they can do for me? I'll have to go through that entire thing again."

"Hey! Don't talk like that. Of course, they can do something for you. It's slow growing, you said."

"But what does that really mean? It's still growing all the time. Although not fast growing like a weed, it's still growing—wrapping itself around my brain."

"Well, whatever the results are, they can't be worse than what you were told before, can they?"

"I guess not."

"We'll know one way or another in a day or two and, whatever the outcome, we're in this together."

"Thanks, Lizzi. I needed to hear that. I love the fact we're mates—nothing else—no complications. You're like the sister I should've had."

I smiled, pleased he felt the same about me. "And you're the brother I never had. We're lucky to have each other. Now, come on, I'm starving."

We spent the whole of Sunday in our PJs in front of the TV watching episode after episode of Real Housewives of Cheshire. Neither of us had wanted anything too intense or sinister, and this seemed a good choice—in fact, strangely enough, we both really enjoyed it. We ate mountains of junk food and called out for Chinese for dinner—bliss.

On Monday morning, we packed up the two cars and I followed his flash yellow Aston Martin back to Kenby in Miriam's Audi.

On the outskirts of the village, I called Phil. "How's that little dog doing?" I asked when he picked up.

"He's fine—not missed you at all. Kate's got him dressed in a purple tutu."

I barked out a laugh. "That's animal cruelty."

"So, sue me. What you up to?"

"I'm almost home. I was going to ask if you want to bring the kids to dinner later, to say thanks for looking after Thomas, and to let Ben meet Charlie."

"Yeah. That sound great. What shall I bring?"

"Just yourselves. I'll make kid friendly food. Don't worry."

"Can't wait. Oh, and Lizzi?"

"Yeah?"

"I'm glad you're coming back. I've missed you."

My heart missed a beat. "You too," I said, hurriedly hanging up, feeling on cloud nine.

I tooted the horn as Charlie turned off the main road, heading to the house, while I continued on to the supermarket. It felt strange to be going back to Miriam's house after everything, but we'd discussed it yesterday. We decided we needed to continue as though Friday hadn't happened. My only concern was the blood stain on the wooden floor. If they hadn't managed to remove it, it would be a continual reminder, but Charlie could afford to have the flooring removed and replaced.

I stocked up on lots of goodies and bought the ingredients for home-made burgers, potato wedges and coleslaw, and decided on apple crumble and ice cream for dessert. I was determined to get Ben onside, if at all possible.

I sensed something had happened when I pulled onto the driveway and noticed the front door wide open. Charlie was pacing the hallway wringing his hands together.

"What is it? What happened?" I ran to his side.

"I had the call."

"From the hospital?"

He nodded.

"And?" Shit, I'd only been apart from him an hour at the most, and he was suddenly a total basket case.

"I didn't answer."

"Fuck! Charlie! Call them back."

"I can't. I'd rather not know."

"Don't be so stupid. We *need* to know. If they're going to operate, they'll have to book you in ASAP. Do you want me to ring?"

"Would you?"

"Of course. Give me your phone."

I returned the call but it went unanswered. After leaving a message, I hung up noticing Charlie, hovering outside the kitchen doorway, holding the grocery bags from the car. "Come on in. There was no answer." I glanced at the floorboards beside the dining table relieved there was no obvious stain.

"I take it you spoke to Phil?" He nodded at the bags.

"Yeah, they'll be here just before five o'clock."

"And we *can* trust this Ben, can't we?"

"I hope so. He's football-mad, apparently. Phil's secretly hoping you'll be a positive influence for him. He's not been coping very well since his mum died."

"I can identify with that—poor guy."

"Exactly."

The phone began vibrating behind me on the table.

"Oh, shit!" Charlie froze.

"It's okay. Calm down." I nodded, reaching for the phone. "Hello?"

"Can I speak to Charles Maidley please?"

"Is that you, Doctor Fris?"

"That's right."

"It's Lizzi, I met you on Saturday at the hospital. The thing is, Charlie's right here, but he's scared of speaking to you."

"Well, if it helps, I have good news."

I gasped and turned to Charlie. "He has good news. Do you want to speak to him?"

"Put it on loudspeaker, maybe," he said, looking as though he might throw up.

I did as he asked. "Okay, doctor. You're on loudspeaker."

"Are you there, Mr Maidley?"

"Yeah, I'm here."

"Like I just told Lizzi, I have good news for you."

Charlie gasped a few times; I thought he might hyperventilate. "Okay."

"How are you fixed if we admit you on Thursday evening, ready for surgery first thing on Friday?"

"This Friday?"

"Yes. Is that a problem?"

"No, I don't think so. That should be fine." He looked at me for confirmation.

I nodded rapidly feeling tears of relief filling my eyes. I was so pleased it wasn't too late.

"So, what's the prognosis?" Charlie asked.

"I'm confident I can remove the mass fairly easily."

"All of it?"

"I'm hoping to. Although large, I don't think it will prove too difficult. But the sooner we get you in the better."

"Oh, wow!" He shook his head as though in disbelief.

"How have your symptoms been? Any seizures?"

"No. Nothing. I've been a bit tired, and my eyes have been acting up, but other than that I feel quite good at the minute."

"That's good. Okay then, we'll expect you by around six o'clock on Thursday night." The phone went dead.

"I told you, didn't I? Oh, my God, I'm so chuffed for you," I said.

Tears filled his eyes, and he was too choked to talk. He just nodded and hugged me, holding on tight.

I could feel his entire body trembling.

CHAPTER 49

Bang on time, Charlie, Kate and Ben stepped through the hedge and tapped on the back door.

I could tell from Ben's crossed arm stance and stony face that he was there against his will.

"Hi everyone." I bent down to pick up Thomas who was running on the spot excitedly. "See? You did miss me, didn't you? You little rascal."

"No, he didn't!" Kate squealed.

"He didn't?"

"Nope. And we've not brought his bed back. Maybe he'll come back to my house one last night?" she asked, her hands together as if in prayer.

I ruffled her curls. "It's not up to me. Ask your dad."

"I already did. He said I had to ask you."

"Okay, we'll see. Let's go through to the living room. Charlie's waiting for you."

In the living room, Kate jumped onto the sofa. "Hi, Charlie," she said, pumping her fist off his.

"Hey, sweetheart. How are you?"

"Good."

I glanced at Ben. His face was a picture, and he was nudging his father repeatedly. "Ben, meet Charlie. I believe you're a big fan of his?"

And just like that, Ben's demeanour changed from grumpy, grisly teen to a chatty and pleasant young man.

"Fancy a drink?" I asked Phil.

Phil nodded and followed me back to the kitchen.

"I hope you're hungry," I said to Kate, who trudged in after us. "I've made some huge burgers."

"Yum! I'm starving," she said.

"Good. Maybe you can help me set the table."

Dinner was a complete success. Ben had settled down as we'd hoped and was talking Charlie's socks down. They'd arranged to spend an hour together in the back garden after school the next day so Charlie could give him some pointers with the ball.

After dinner, Kate stayed at the dining table drawing, while Charlie and Ben went back through to the living room.

I loaded the dishwasher and Phil made a pot of coffee. Just as we were settling down beside Kate, someone knocked at the front door.

I was surprised to see DI Karlson and Wayne on the doorstep.

"Oh, hi," I said, confused.

"Hello, Lizzi," Karlson said. "Can we come in for a second?"

I nodded, and stepped aside, allowing them to enter.

"Kate? Why don't you take Thomas through to the living room for a few minutes," I said, as we walked into the kitchen.

Kate eyed the intruders and then her dad who nodded. She picked Thomas up and stomped through to Charlie.

"What can we do for you?" I asked, aware the last time we'd been in that room together was when Miriam's life was ebbing away.

"Wayne has told me you may have CCTV footage from the night Erin went missing."

"Oh, I guess so. I'll ask Charlie if he'll check it out. Hang on."

I followed Kate to the living room. "Sorry to interrupt you, guys, but the police are here and want access to Miriam's computer again. I think they're after evidence against Nigel."

"The password is Maidley70. Do you want to do the honours?" he said.

"If you're sure. Can you keep an eye on Kate?"

"Of course. We can play go fish again."

Kate jumped on the spot. "Yay!"

"But you have to let me win."

I left them negotiating the terms of the card game with much hilarity. Back in the kitchen, I beckoned for the detectives to follow. "You come too, Phil," I said before heading up the stairs.

I opened up the computer and entered the password then clicked on the camera icon on the screen like I'd seen Charlie do just last week. "I don't know what to do from here," I said, giving up the chair to Wayne.

He had no problem locating the night in question. He fast-forwarded through the footage going from dusk to darkness in minutes. Sudden movement caused Wayne to stop and rewind the film.

I gasped as I watched Erin, wearing the same white cotton mini dress I'd found her in, walk down Phil's driveway and let herself in his back door.

"What the hell?" Phil said, clearly shocked.

I looked from the screen to him and back at the screen totally lost for words.

Wayne began forwarding the film in double time.

We watched the next few minutes in total shock. Barely a word was exchanged.

Heading back downstairs, I said, "Give us a minute. Kate's in there and we don't want to freak her out." I looked at Phil and held his hand before pasting a smile on my face and entering the room.

Kate and Charlie were sprawled out in the middle of the floor surrounded by cards. "Kate, sweetheart, come with me, please," Phil said softly.

"But we're playing go fish, Daddy, and I'm winning."

"Would you take Thomas into the kitchen and give him one of the spare burgers from the fridge," I said.

She looked from her dad to me before picking Thomas up and heading out the door.

Charlie looked up, clearly confused, the smile freezing on his face when he saw Karlson and Wayne in the doorway. "What's going on?"

Phil walked over to Ben. "Come on, son, we've gotta go."

Clearly puzzled, Ben got to his feet.

DI Karlson stepped into the room. "Ben Mathews, I'm arresting you for the murder of Erin Lieber."

EPILOGUE

"What time are you leaving?" Charlie asked as I emerged from my bedroom.

"In half an hour. Are you sure you're feeling okay?"

He nodded, stroking his newly shaved head. "I'm fine. Don't worry about me."

"Please don't turn up at the school without your hat on. You look like Frankenstein's monster with all those stitches, and you'll frighten the little kids."

"Good job I'm not feeling self-conscious about my looks."

I grinned. "Sorry, you know what I meant. It is a little horrific for kids to see."

"Kate doesn't mind it. In fact, she thinks it's awesome. But don't worry. I'll wear my cap when I pick her up—now get going, will you? You look nice, by the way."

I glanced down at my grey woollen trouser suit. "Thanks. Now, can I trust you to take your medication on time?"

"Yes," he huffed.

"And make sure Thomas has a wee every couple of hours?"

"I will! Bloody hell, Lizzi. I have been left alone before you know?"

"Not since having brain surgery, you haven't."

"That was three weeks ago. I'm practically back to normal now."

"I'm glad to hear it."

A car horn sounded outside.

"Okay, I'm off. I'll call you later."

"Say hi to Ben for me. Maybe I'll be able to visit him myself next time."

"I'm sure he'd like that. We just need them to agree to move him closer—wish us luck."

I picked up my handbag, and Charlie walked me to the door. I felt torn between caring for Charlie after his operation and accompanying Phil to the hearing about Ben. He hadn't needed a trial as he'd confessed everything right away to the detectives. In fact, he was relieved to finally get it off his chest, by the sounds of it. He told them about how, the night he'd argued with his grandparents, he'd stormed home, startled to find a woman sprawled out seductively on his father's bed.

They'd argued at first, and he'd chased her and confronted her outside underneath the camera. In the scuffle she banged her head on the wall then she screamed at him and threatened to tell the police.

The next minute, in a blind rage, he chased her down to the creek and strangled her.

The fact he was a minor still coping with the death of his mother played in his favour. He was sentenced to serve four years in a specialist secure unit, where he would be able to continue his education and receive psychiatric treatment with the aim that he would be rehabilitated and eventually released. Now the only thing left to arrange was to get him moved closer to home.

Charlie waved at Phil as Lizzi climbed in the car. He'd really grown to like Phil over the past few weeks and realised his first impressions of him had been totally wrong. He was pleased the couple's relationship seemed to be developing nicely—although early days, Charlie could tell they cared for each other deeply.

He watched as the car disappeared around the corner.

No sooner had he got back inside than someone knocked on the door.

"What did you forget?" he said, as he flung the door open expecting Lizzi to be standing there. But instead, Alexis smiled back.

"Hello, Charlie. Long time, no see."

"Alexis," he replied, curtly. "If you're looking for Phil, he and Lizzi have just left for the day."

"I know—Phil told me when I called for an update on Ben yesterday. I'm here to see you."

"You'd better come in then." He took a step back and allowed her to enter. Feeling suddenly self-conscious about his head, especially after what Lizzi said about him looking like Frankenstein's monster. "Hang on a minute, I'll be right back."

He hurried to his bedroom and pulled on his hat before checking his reflection in the mirror. Not perfect, but he would have to do.

"So, what can I do for you, Alexis?"

"I wanted to apologise for running out on you like I did. Kadri turning up like that completely threw me. I just got caught up in the whole romantic thing."

"Surely you didn't come all this way to apologise to me. I'm not bothered—we had dinner—once. End of."

"It felt like more than that to me, Charlie. We had a connection, and I know you felt it. But I just wanted to give the baby's daddy a chance to make it up to us."

"And how did that work out? I'm guessing not very well otherwise you wouldn't be here."

"He lasted a week before he started drinking and gambling again. I don't want my baby growing up in that environment."

Charlie pondered on her words. Since Laura's body had been found buried face down in a bog, he had been plastered all over the news. Had it filtered through to Turkey? Possibly. He doubted Phil would've told her who he was as he'd warned him about her in the first place. Maybe she was genuine. It was difficult to trust anyone anymore.

"So, are you home for good?"

"If Phil will let me stay."

"Didn't you mention you were coming back when you spoke to him yesterday?"

"No. He sounded stressed. I wanted him to get today over and done with before I bombard him with my troubles."

"Fancy a coffee?" he asked.

"Do you have any herbal tea? I'm trying to avoid having too much caffeine—I have the baby to consider now."

"I'll check. I never drink that stuff, but Miriam might've bought some." He rummaged in the food cupboard and pulled out a box. "Raspberry tea okay?"

"Lovely, thanks. So, I take it you had your operation?"

He nodded.

"That's good. Are you cured now?"

He poured boiling water onto the teabag. "I hope so. Let's just say the future certainly seems brighter than it did."

"I'm so pleased for you. Will you move back to the city?"

He placed the cup in front of her on the table. "I don't think so. I'm quite enjoying living here."

"With your sister? How will that work out?"

Charlie's ears pricked up. So, if she hadn't heard about Miriam, she probably hadn't heard about him. That knowledge made him feel a little better. Not that he'd keep it from her indefinitely, but certainly for a little while. He'd see if anything developed with her thinking he didn't have two pennies to rub together. "Miriam's out of the country, and I don't expect her back."

"Oh, nice. And she doesn't mind you staying here? Or do you think she'll sell?"

"I can stay."

The morning flew by, and they talked non-stop about everything and anything. Their conversation was easy—effortless. He really liked her but wouldn't allow himself to fall so easily this time.

"I need to let Thomas out. It's a wonder he's not cross-eyed by now. Then do you fancy a sandwich?"

"Love one." She smiled at him. Her beautiful blue eyes shone, and he felt quite giddy.

Alexis watched as Charlie bent and picked up the little dog. She'd been right to come back here—Charlie was the full package. He was handsome, caring, loyal—but most of all, mega-bloody-rich.

She reached in her bag for her phone and located Kadri's number.

I'm in. Mr Moneybags has fallen
for it hook, line and sinker. Ka-ching!

ACKNOWLEDGMENTS

As always, I need to mention Paul, my long suffering husband. Your support means the world to me.

To my wonderful critique partners Susan, Marco, Jay, Sandra Marika & Serena—you're the best.

To Mel and all my friends and fellow authors—thanks so much for letting me bend your ear.

The wonderful ARC group – you're awesome.

To all the team at Junction Publishing - you are amazing!

And finally. To my wonderful family, especially Joshua, David, AJ, and Marley, my lovely grandsons, who give me immense joy. I am truly blessed.

ABOUT THE AUTHOR

 My name's Netta Newbound. I write thrillers in many different styles — some grittier than others. The Cold Case Files have a slightly lighter tone. I also write a series set in London, which features one of my favourite characters, Detective Adam Stanley. My standalone books, The Watcher, Maggie, My Sister's Daughter and An Impossible Dilemma, are not for the faint hearted, and it seems you either love them or hate them—I'd love to know what you think.

If you would like to be informed when my new books are released, visit my website: www.nettanewbound.com and sign up for the newsletter.

This is a PRIVATE list and I promise you I will only send emails when a new book is released or a book goes on sale.

If you would like to get in touch, you can contact me via Facebook or Twitter. I'd love to hear from you and try to respond to everyone.

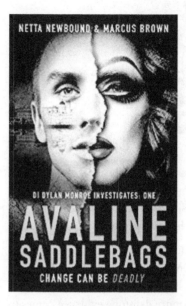

Following the brutal murders of Jade Kelly and Gina Elliot, newly promoted DI Dylan Monroe is assigned to work the case, alongside DS Layla Monahan.

As the body count rapidly rises—each slaying more savage than the last—it soon becomes clear the butchered and mutilated victims have one thing in common—they are all male to female transsexuals.

With time against them, Dylan is forced to go undercover in the only place that provides a link to the victims—Dorothy's, a well-known drag and cabaret bar in the heart of Liverpool.

Avaline Saddlebags is a gripping, often amusing, psychological thriller with an astonishing twist that will take your breath away... change can be DEADLY!

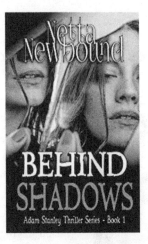

Amanda Flynn's life is falling apart. Her spineless cheating husband has taken her beloved children. Her paedophile father, who went to prison vowing revenge, has been abruptly released. And now someone in the shadows is watching her every move.

When one by one her father and his cohorts turn up dead, Amanda finds herself at the centre of several murder investigations—with no alibi and a diagnosis of Multiple Personality Disorder. Abandoned, scared and fighting to clear her name as more and more damning evidence comes to light, Amanda begins to doubt her own sanity.

Could she really be a brutal killer?

A gripping psychological thriller not to be missed...

An Edge of your Seat Psychological Thriller Novel

For Melissa May, happily married to Gavin for the best part of thirty years, life couldn't get much better. Her world is ripped apart when she discovers Gavin is HIV positive. The shock of his duplicity and irresponsible behaviour re-awakens a psychiatric condition Melissa has battled since childhood. Fuelled by rage and a heightened sense of right and wrong, Melissa takes matters into her own hands.

Homicide detective Adam Stanley is investigating what appear to be several random murders. When evidence comes to light, linking the victims, the case seems cut and dried and an arrest is made. However, despite all the damning evidence, including a detailed confession, Adam is certain the killer is still out there. Now all he has to do is prove it.

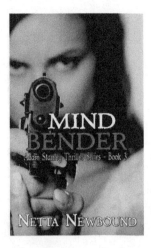

An Edge of your Seat Psychological Thriller Novel

Detective Inspector Adam Stanley returns to face his most challenging case yet. Someone is randomly killing ordinary Pinevale citizens. Each time DI Stanley gets close to the killer, the killer turns up dead—the next victim in someone's crazy game.

Meanwhile, his girlfriend's brother, Andrew, currently on remand for murder, escapes and kidnaps his own 11-year-old daughter. However, tragedy strikes, leaving the girl in grave danger.

Suffering a potentially fatal blow himself, how can DI Stanley possibly save anyone?

A Compelling Psychological Thriller Novel.

In this fast-moving suspense novel, Detective Adam Stanley searches for Miles Muldoon, a hardworking, career-minded businessman, and Pinevale's latest serial killer.

Evidence puts Muldoon at each scene giving the police a prima facie case against him.

But as the body count rises, and their suspect begins taunting them, this seemingly simple case develops into something far more personal when Muldoon turns his attention to Adam and his family.

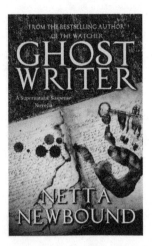

Ghost Writer is a 24,000 word novella.

Bestselling thriller author Natalie Cooper has a crippling case of writer's block. With her deadline looming, she finds the only way she can write is by ditching her laptop and reverting back to pen and paper. But the story which flows from the pen is not just another work of fiction.

Unbeknown to her, a gang of powerful and deadly criminals will stop at nothing to prevent the book being written.

Will Natalie manage to finish the story and expose the truth before it's too late? Or could the only final chapter she faces be her own?

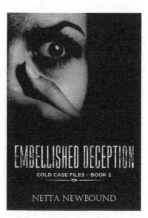

A Gripping and Incredibly Moving Psychological Suspense Novel

When Geraldine MacIntyre's marriage falls apart, she returns to her childhood home expecting her mother to welcome her with open arms. Instead, she finds all is not as it should be with her parents.

James Dunn, a successful private investigator and crime writer, is also back in his hometown, to help solve a recent spate of vicious rapes. He is thrilled to discover his ex-classmate, and love of his life, Geraldine, is back, minus the hubby, and sets out to get the girl. However, he isn't the only interested bachelor in the quaint, country village. Has he left it too late?

Embellished Deception is a thrilling, heart-wrenching and thought provoking story of love, loss and deceit.

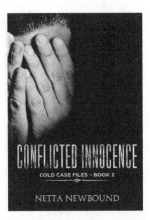

CONFLICTED INNOCENCE
COLD CASE FILES - BOOK 2
NETTA NEWBOUND

An Edge of your Seat Psychological Thriller Novel

Geraldine and baby Grace arrive in Nottingham to begin their new life with author James Dunn.

Lee Barnes, James' best friend and neighbour, is awaiting the imminent release of his wife, Lydia, who has served six years for infanticide. But he's not as prepared as he thought. In a last ditch effort to make things as perfect as possible his already troubled life takes a nose dive.

Geraldine and James combine their wits to investigate several historical, unsolved murders for James' latest book. James is impressed by her keen eye and instincts. However, because of her inability to keep her mouth shut, Geri, once again, finds herself the target of a crazed and vengeful killer.

A Gripping Psychological Suspense Novel.

Geri and James return in their most explosive adventure to date.

When next door neighbour, Lydia, gives birth to her second healthy baby boy, James and Geri pray their friend can finally be happy and at peace. But, little do they know Lydia's troubles are far from over.

Meanwhile, Geri is researching several historic, unsolved murders for James' new book. She discovers one of the prime suspects now resides in Spring Pines Retirement Village, the scene of not one, but two recent killings.

Although the police reject the theory, Geri is convinced the cold case they're researching is linked to the recent murders. But how? Will she regret delving so deeply into the past?

THE BEST-SELLING SERIAL KILLER THRILLER THAT EVERYONE IS TALKING ABOUT

Life couldn't get much better for Hannah. She accepts her dream job in Manchester, and easily makes friends with her new neighbours.

When she becomes romantically involved with her boss, she can't believe her luck. But things are about to take a grisly turn.

As her colleagues and neighbours are killed off one by one, Hannah's idyllic life starts to fall apart. But when her mother becomes the next victim, the connection to Hannah is all too real.

Who is watching her every move?

Will the police discover the real killer in time?

Hannah is about to learn that appearances can be deceptive.

Netta
Newbound

AN IMPOSSIBLE
DILEMMA

Victoria and Jonathan Lyons seem to have everything—a perfect marriage, a beautiful daughter, Emily, and a successful business. Until they discover Emily, aged five, has a rare and fatal illness.

Medical trials show that a temporary fix would be to transplant a hormone from a living donor. However in the trials the donors die within twenty four hours. Victoria and Jonathan are forced to accept that their daughter is going to die.

In an unfortunate twist of fate Jonathan is suddenly killed in a farming accident and Victoria turns to her sick father-in-law, Frank, for help. Then a series of events present Victoria and Frank with a situation that, although illegal, could save Emily.

Will they take their one chance and should they?

An Edge of your Seat Psychological Thriller Novella

All her life twenty-two-year-old Ruby Fitzroy's annoyingly over protective mother has believed the worst will befall one of her two daughters. Sick and tired of living in fear, Ruby arranges a date without her mother's knowledge.

On first impressions, charming and sensitive Cody Strong seems perfect. When they visit his home overlooking the Welsh coast, she meets his delightful father Steve and brother Kyle. But it isn't long before she discovers all is not as it seems.

After a shocking turn of events, Ruby's world is blown apart. Terrified and desperate, she prepares to face her darkest hour yet.

Will she ever escape this nightmare?

Made in United States
North Haven, CT
22 August 2023

40605123R00168